MEN, COUNTRIES AND GOD

The Diary of an Iranian Woman

HOMA ZAKLAKI

To Maman, Baba and our brothers, M. Hassan and
M. Ali, for their unconditional love

And

To our kids, who keep us sane

"Need is not always a consequence of lack, a by-product of poverty. There are needs which are products of completion; what is beautiful is in search of native eyes that cherish it, what is abundant is in need of someone in need so that it can give; strength is in need of another strength in order to challenge it...and the heart that has words longs for a Mokhatab...."

Dr Ali SHARIATI

DREAM ONE

Utter darkness surrounds me. From far away in the distance comes a faint sound, a chanting. I turn around and walk towards the cry. My eyes fall upon a door. I open it a little wider and poke my head inside. A group of white-veiled women are sitting huddled shoulder to shoulder.

I am in Tehran.

An elderly woman catches sight of me and murmurs something, a whisper that sweeps through the crowd, "Homa's granddaughter is here."

A current of joy runs through the women. Nine of them rise to their feet and rush towards me, taking turns to hug and kiss me. I let them lead me to the centre of the room. A stir and rustle pass through the group: "Homa's granddaughter."

More women leave their seats and gather around me. "May Allah bless you, may you be happy," they say. "You have her eyes." Each one hugs me, planting three kisses on my cheeks.

"May Allah bless you, may you be happy."

These words echo, high and wavering, in the room. Suddenly, sun dazzles my eyes. We are standing in the courtyard of a mosque. At this moment, the women hush each other and step to the side. A figure approaches me, radiant and solemn, in a sweeping maroon robe with a green scarf loosely covering her grey hair, clutching something in her left hand.

"This is for you. It's a gift from your grandmother," she says. "It was entrusted to us shortly before her departure twenty years ago."

With her eyes she leads my gaze towards her palm. I feel dizzy.

"May Allah bless you, may you be happy."

LONDON

Monday, February 21, 2005

Everything we have always desired is unbelievably close. The enchanted Aladdin lamp is right here, just an arm's length away; you only need to reach for it and it would be yours - a hell of a lot of courage is needed.

The empty suitcase rests against the wall of the bedroom while my shirts, skirts and trousers, jumbled on the bed, grumble about the uncertainty of their fate; so does the pile of letters and junk mail that has assembled in front of the door to welcome me.

"Expelled from there, deterred from here," I recite aloud a Farsi proverb, finishing off with a lopsided smile as a sort of exclamation; at this point, the silence in my flat becomes suddenly loud - much louder than I remember from the time before my trip.

It is not only the silence that speaks in this particular tone, cold and unconcerned, but also the smell of neglect that has taken possession of the rooms in my absence. The empty fridge completes the air of lofty indifference.

How ironic to be sitting in the opulent half of the world without even a piece of bread in my home, whereas in its other half, wherever I went, 'have you eaten yet?' preceded every greeting.

Before retiring to bed I flirted with the idea of doing some grocery shopping at Sainsbury's, but a brief glance through the window reinforced my resolution to stay here, with my face in my journal and my back resting against this comfy heap of pillows, until the sky becomes more welcoming.

Even though London's sky can be as moody and eccentric as the taste buds of a pregnant woman, I can see that those grumpy clouds mean business; they won't dissolve without an outpouring of rain.

Without doubt, London and its sky pick up where I left them three weeks ago, and yet it seems that all around me has changed. The minute I stepped out of Woodside Park tube station - no, even before that, at Heathrow - it was as if I had just woken up and was seeing everything for the very first time. This strange feeling even pervaded my phone call with Omid an hour ago.

"*Gherty*, when did you get back?" *Gherty,* meaning foxy, is one of Omid's many nicknames for me. It is unusual for him to retain the details of my life. Not that I've ever minded. Surprisingly, this time, not only had he remembered my return date, but also he was curious to know how I had liked Bangladesh.

"I loved it. It truly surpassed my expectations."

I forget his response. It was a teasing one, I think, or something along the lines of 'good for you, sis' - some *Omidy* remark. I skipped my trip and asked about his new job. He raced from one topic to another until we came to his back pain.

"This bloody loading and unloading of suitcases is breaking my back. I mean, I don't complain, you know. Vienna airport is not Heathrow. Okay, tell me about Bangladesh."

"Yeah, it was er…"

"I am very proud of you. I couldn't do that. It pisses me off when I see those hungry African kids. Listen to Aljazeera. These bloody governments are corrupt. You think this tingling in my leg is nothing?"

"You have tingling? That might be…"

"The pills the hospital gave, I mean, these bloody tablets, I don't like them, bloody pills," he said. "Okay, *gherty*, you had a good time? Good. Do you think, I mean, would I? If I lose my legs, I mean, who cares!" He laughed again.

"No, you won't lose your legs. Trust me."

"Of course, I trust you. I let you go now. You must be tired. I love ya, *gherty*. Remember you got a little brother who loves ya very much."

"I love you too, *dash*." *Dash*, or bro, is my nickname for him.

As soon as he hung up I was proven right with my weather forecast; torrential rain is rattling the windows and hammering on the roof. The storm feels comforting. A dry and grey sky is gloomy in the daylight, whereas the arrival of rain lends the same scenery a touch of romantic melancholy: the light turns dim and the air is no longer depressing but expectant. The same is true of my previously reserved flat, which, on the pretext of the downpour outside, has become a friendly and cosy shelter.

I lean over to the pile of clothes and fish out the maroon silk shawl to wrap around my neck. I bought it at a street corner from a scrawny woman in a frayed white *shalwar kameez*. She looked like the kind of an old woman one would like to have around; one of those who can play with kids, listen patiently to youth and console the grown-ups. I can still see her plunging those rugged hands into the colourful collection of scarves around her, in search of the most fitting answer to my request for 'your warmest shawl'. I stood with my arms folded across my chest for what seemed like ages until she suddenly lifted her wrinkled face, opened my self-embrace and pressed a red bundle into my hands.

"For you," she said, with a twinkle of triumph in her hazy eyes. I had to restrain myself from bursting into laughter at her resemblance to a toothless witch, poking her head from a fairy tale book and handing me an enchanted Aladdin's lamp.

Thinking back, that was the day I met Belal.

The raindrops are now beating down at my window. I draw in the warm scent of the shawl to fill my lungs with the promise that is woven into its fabric: the promise of something different, something better, maybe even some magic.

Wednesday, February 23, 2005

"Solmaz!" Hearing my name called out in that distinctively familiar voice was the peak of my first day back at work. I was in the queue in the canteen, mentally running through my morning cases, anxious that I might have overlooked something significant, when his hands clasped my shoulders from behind.

"*Diruz dust, emruz ashna* - yesterday friends, today strangers," he teased, in a volume that is never at its fullest in public. "How come you're not answering my calls?"

"When did you ring, *dash*?" I squeezed him tight and long.

"Last night."

"Sorry, I crashed out early."

There is something very familiar about Peyman; he never fails to brighten my day. Even our first meeting many years ago felt like a *re*-meeting; we never had a period of strangeness, just a continuation of a relationship without the memory of its beginning.

"Why did you have to come jet-lagged to a busy Wednesday clinic? You didn't plan it well, Solmaz *joon*." Calling me *joon* - dear - is the only sign of affection he ever displays in public - this and hugs.

"You don't look well rested yourself." I said this not only for his sunken cheeks but also his slumped posture, not to mention the dark circles adding an extra rim to his John Lennon glasses. "What about investing nine quid in yourself?"

His hazelnut-tinted eyes stared at me quizzically.

"Haircut and wash for only nine pounds down the road, huh?" I said. I love his curly black hair. Whenever it grows long, he looks like a baffled scientist.

"You are only getting sweeter with the years," he said, a smile forming on his skinny face. "By the way, belated happy birthday. Come and sit down. Let this humble servant get you a warm meal. And then you can tell me about Bangladesh."

13

I pointed to the long list of tasks in my hand and shook my head. "It has to wait. I'm in over my head..." but before I could complete my sentence, his 'spoiler' went off. He looked down at his bleep, tucked into the pocket of his green scrubs.

"Theatre! I gotta run." Peyman squeezed my arm quickly, and off he went.

"I'll ring you after work," I shouted after him, a promise I was not able to keep. By the time I got back to the ward I was swamped with work. My new junior doctor, having been all by herself the entire morning, resembled one of Dali's surrealist pictures: bewildered, and scattered all over the place. The poor girl! I had to let her go home early. On her exhausted face I could recognise a reflection of my own first internships in Vienna: pockets stuffed with books, notebooks and stethoscope, feeling excited and inadequate, all at once. In time, we all grow into that white coat, but I suspect the sense of inadequacy never leaves us for good. We simply learn to live with it; it's part of the doctor package. My only regret is that the everyday life of a doctor has hardly anything in common with the magic pull of those heroic TV doctors of my childhood, who enticed me into studying medicine. There are a few exceptions, of course. Of those the most filmic and bizarre happened to me during my recent three weeks in Bangladesh, with caesarean sections being the most surreal of all. I would perform them in a large theatre hall with swathes of operating beds separated by curtains, with lights going on and off and the supervising surgeon's attention being drawn more to my biography than the scalpel in my untrained hands, so close to the baby's head and the mother's bladder. Very soon, the Hindu surgeon thought he had the gist of my story and came up with a one-liner to introduce me and amuse his colleagues: "That is Dr Solmaz, born in Tehran, studied in Vienna, lives in London and volunteers in Dhaka."

In Belal's view, that white-bearded doctor had taken a

fatherly fancy to me. Had Belal not said that at the beginning of our encounter, when our relationship was still formal, I would have bought into his interpretation of that doctor's trust in my surgical skills.

No doubt, there was some filmic quality to my work in Bangladesh, but more so my meeting with Belal. That would be an entirely different story.

Thursday, March 3, 2005

Strange as it is, these are the very first words I wrote about Belal in my diary: *My thirtieth birthday. And I spent it with a married man. He stayed with me instead of going home to his wife and children. Unease and guilt came over me.*

It's three o'clock in the morning, and I am leafing through the old entries in my journal because of a dream. It was one of those dreams that sneak across the borders of the two worlds, feeling real for quite some time after waking up so that lucidity becomes an act of forceful recollection. You open your eyes to your everyday - the bedroom, the city noise, the time on your mobile - but you don't recognise anything, don't know how the hour, the place and the sound relate to you.

My heart was racing and I was gasping for quite some time after waking; I sat upright in bed, turned on the bedside light, and had actively to remind myself that I was in London. The dream itself was very brief. In it I realised suddenly that I had left Bangladesh without saying goodbye to Belal, a realisation that sent me into a state of panic as if I had committed a fatal act - ridiculous! Not only did Belal and I have a chance to say goodbye in Dhaka; more importantly, a missed farewell to someone neither close nor dead does not amount to anything disastrous in real life.

I remember that the first time we met I thought him

ordinary, the second time arrogant, and on my birthday, the night before my return, a sexist. But jump forward in time to my last day in Dhaka and we had transformed into friends.

It all started with me telling Rekha's mother of my wish to spend my birthday in a hotel in Dhaka. Being an overly dutiful and protective hostess, she was not at all pleased with my decision. That is why she chose her son's best friend as my 'guardian' in Dhaka; my accommodation had to be in the vicinity of his office, she insisted. And so Belal was introduced to me, at a function in the hospital, without leaving any lasting impression; he was slim built and his features were like any other Asian man: a fleshy nose and full lips. To be frank, I couldn't have picked him out in a crowd. Fortunately, I did not need to. Later that day Belal's driver came to show me to his car. Since he was going to be my chaperon for a few days, I made sure to scan him more carefully as we approached; he was in a dark blue suit, leaning with his back against the car and tapping one foot impatiently. He dropped the cigarette in his hand and stubbed it out as soon as he noticed me.

"Hello again." I gave him a smile. "Thank you for the ride."

"No problem." He turned to his driver. His eyebrows were drawn in, creating deep lines on his forehead. They exchanged a few words in Bengali while I seated myself in the front, then the driver took the back seat and Belal drove off. We maneuvered through the mayhem of cars, rickshaws and pedestrians, beneath an orange sun tinged with red as it shone down through the smoky Bangladeshi sky. I leaned back on my seat, listening to the shrill orchestra of honks and watching the vast green fields pass by, until eventually they sunk into the pitch-dark night. I was not in the mood for conversation. Neither was Belal. His indifference hurt my ego and made me curious in equal measure. By now I was used to full-on attention from Bangladeshis both in and out of Rekha's mother's house; everyone sought my company and bent over backwards to please me. Belal instead seemed even less interested in me than I was in him. As if his silence was not irritating enough, he also had one Bengali song on repeat - a patriotic one, as I could tell from the numerous repetitions of '*mera Bangla*' in the lyric. Since the ride was going to stretch over three hours on those jam-packed Friday roads, I decided to attempt some small talk.

"Have you ever met Rekha?"

"Yes."

"She is actually the mastermind behind my visit to Bangladesh."

"Is she?"

I turned my gaze to him. He, however, stared ahead at the dimly lit road.

"Yes." I suddenly felt the need to embellish my story. "The initial plan was a two-week trip to a hospital in Azad Kashmir. One of my Kashmiri colleagues had suggested it." I remember thinking that by now he would be admiring the adventurous streak in me. "When I asked her about the safety of the place, she simply said, 'If you die, you will have died in heaven on earth.' I told her, 'Fair enough, but my parents might not appreciate it much.'" I looked at him again and smiled. Nothing, not the slightest twinge on those thick lips. I had the fleeting impulse to shout, 'Come on, man, that was funny.' I didn't.

"Anyway, my annual leave was drawing closer and I jumped on Rekha's suggestion to visit the charity hospital where her mum works." I babbled on, trying to spice it up a bit more. "I always wanted to work in a developing country. It was on my to-do list. You know, things you do before you turn thirty. I keep one of those." One fancied that at least the number thirty would intrigue him, but no, he was not going to budge. I would have to try harder.

"Are you married?" I asked.

"Yes."

"Did you have an arranged marriage?"

"Yes."

"Oh! Arranged marriages can work out as much as love marriages can fail." I did not really believe this, but thought it the right thing to say. Still, it didn't prod him out of his reserve.

"This is one hell of a traffic jam."

"Yes. This is Bangladesh."

I gave up. His silence finally stamped out the conversation like one of his cigarettes. For the rest of the ride I joined him in silent awkwardness.

Awkward also was our final goodbye. One minute Belal and I were sitting opposite each other in his office, chatting and exchanging stories about our families, and the next minute he looked at his watch and stood up to leave.

"We'll stay in touch." His voice had changed; it seemed nervous. Then he pulled out a paper from his pocket and slipped it onto the desk. It was a business card.

"My driver has already put your suitcase in the car. You can go downstairs in about half an hour."

I looked up at him stunned. "Are you, er, do you have some change for me?" I had plenty of change myself.

"*Ha.*" The coins he retrieved from his wallet clinked as they dropped on the desk next to the card. "Have a safe flight." He reached out for a handshake; his hand was cold and the touch light. "*Khoda hafez,*" he whispered, without looking at me.

I stayed behind on my chair in the empty room, staring confused at the closed door with watery eyes and a pang of grief in my heart. I couldn't make sense of myself. We had known each other for only five days and for four of them I hadn't even liked him, so why on earth this sadness, I asked myself.

By the end of my trip Belal had become sufficiently distinct to me from all other Bangladeshi men, to say the least. In all fairness to him, his conduct remained proper at all times. For instance, he did apologise for that hasty goodbye in Dhaka by sending me an email as soon as I got back to the UK. *I am sorry,*

I don't know what came over me. Keep in touch please, it read. My dream does somehow resemble the silly sentiments of my last night in Bangladesh. ...Oh, my God. It is getting on for 4 a.m. Enough time travelling. I am on-call tonight.

Friday, March 11, 2005

It was pouring as I trudged out of the tube station. I pulled out my umbrella, fighting to keep hold of it as the wind tried to snatch it from my hand. A brief stop at the Turkish restaurant downstairs became the last struggle of the day before I finally made it home, slumped on the couch and wolfed down the chicken *iskander* takeaway. The next thing I remember was being jolted awake by the ringing of the phone - I had nodded off. It took me a fraction of a second to spot it next to the remote control and empty take-out boxes.

"Solmaz *joon*, *salam*. Are you well?" It was Maman from Iran. "Have you heard from Omid? I can't find him."

I reassured her about Omid.

"I know you don't like hearing this," she began with a cautionary note, "but I recently had a *nan gerdui* and it got stuck in my throat when I remembered that you love walnut cookies..."

As a child, whenever I heard this I imagined a piece of *koobideh* kebab, spinach *bourani* or *loobia* rice being lodged in Maman's throat, making her choke. Now I was past those literal readings.

"Once Omid and you have had some, I feel better. A mother likes doing these things for her children..."

This is how I have always known Maman: communicating her affection by feeding us. Then she passed the phone to Khaleh Laleh, who was visiting them. I had to make a real effort to remember the names of my cousins and various other relatives, and politely asked how each of them was doing. Sometimes it takes a genius to remember who is alive and who dead. Now and then Omid and I catch ourselves coming across a name and arguing about whether he or she is still with us. Honestly, when you don't have any contact with them it doesn't make much difference whether they are in or out of the game.

It must be fifteen years now since I last went to Iran. There was no need to go back, really; Baba and Maman were in Vienna with us. Besides, the novelty and excitement of our visits there were waning for our relatives, in the same way they were growing tired of the Milka chocolates we brought as souvenirs from Vienna. Each visit chipped away at our illusions and the sweet memories from the past; each time there were fewer people to pick us up at the airport, just as there were fewer tears at farewells. We all went about our own lives and seemed to have less and less in common as the years went on, so that soon the most natural thing was to spend our summers in Vienna. That is not entirely true though; Baba never ceased to go back regularly to Tehran, either to buy and sell flats or just to visit his family and travel to his childhood village in Azerbaijan.

Maman, on the other hand, had to be prompted to accompany Baba to Iran after many years to finalise the sale of our house. Being in Iran is more of a hassle for a woman than a man: it starts with the expectation of taking gifts, then all the restrictions on the street as to how to dress and behave; there are also the myriad questions our relatives pelt her with, about Omid and me - questions she hates. Like the one Khaleh asked me today, "Solmaz *joon*, why don't you get married?"

This is a reasonable query, I reckon, but the problem is that it is not addressed to the right source. What the heck do I know? It takes two to tango. I can't marry myself. But then again, she did not expect an answer.

"Solitude is only for Allah. It is a sin not to get married,"

Khaleh went on, stressing the importance of marriage and children for a woman.

"It is never too late to get married," I broke in. "I can always do as Naneh did."

"Oh, *khoda nakoneh* - God forbid." I could picture Khaleh biting the side of her hand twice before saying that.

The fact that Naneh, my grandmother, had remarried in her sixties didn't strike me as anything unusual as a six-year-old child. Only as a grown woman did I realise what a stir her decision had caused in the whole family - a realisation which only deepened my admiration for all her other acts of strength and courage. She was the one sustaining her five daughters following the death of my grandfather shortly after Maman was born. Naneh used to knit finely stitched socks and sell them in the bazaar or give Quran lessons to make ends meet, and then when Maman, her youngest child, married at the age of sixteen, Naneh found herself a husband. It must have been a shock for many people to suddenly find that little, pious old widow, whose veil made public only one eye, remarrying in the last season of her life. Naneh, however, as I can tell from stories Maman has related to me over the years, was not a woman to lose any sleep over people's perception of her.

One evening especially had etched itself in Maman's memory. Naneh had just finished her prayer when Maman, not being able to restrain her distress, disclosed that friends and relatives were badmouthing her. Naneh did not react at first. She simply continued folding her white *chador* in neat layers, kissing the prayer stone and placing it next to her beads on the *chador*. Then, as she wrapped them all in her prayer mat, she apparently said in her characteristically gentle and unhurried voice, "People like to talk. If not about me, then they'd find something else to gossip about. Don't take it to heart." She comforted Maman. "People even talked behind Prophet Mohammad's back, peace be upon him." Usually, she would leave it at that, but Maman remembers how once Naneh spelled it out, "Not that I married for sex. I am old. I need a man to help me on my pilgrimages to Karbala. When I am alone, they carelessly toss around my luggage in the bus."

It has just occurred to me that my maternal line mirrors somehow Iran's ambiguous character. I say that because alternate generations flipped between religiosity and secularism, a trend that would suggest I belonged to the religious group.

I was a pious child in Iran, the favourite of adults and the foe of my peers. It was on board an Iran Air plane that Maman urged me, then eleven, to take off my scarf before we landed in Vienna. I felt naked and ashamed. As a child I was more of Naneh Homa than Maman, who took after her grandmother.

My great-grandmother is said to have been a gracious and elegant woman, wearing frock coats and fur hats. Her daughter, Naneh Homa, on the other hand, chose the veil at a time when it was banned under Reza Shah. Only at nights could she leave home, sneaking from rooftop to rooftop to *hammam* for her weekly bath. Next came Maman who, unlike her older sisters, paraded about in miniskirts and danced the cha-cha until she caught the attention of Baba, a man fifteen years her senior. After having snubbed promising proposals from educated and wealthy men in order to complete her high school, Baba's scrawny appearance alongside his tireless persistence persuaded her.

"Out of sympathy I married him," Maman said - a point she was always keen to underscore to women admiring her beauty in parties in Tehran, to new friends on walks in Vienna, or to Baba's friends who complimented him on his perfect wife.

Probably the only trait Maman and Naneh Homa had in common was their voice. When we were children, Naneh would visit us weekly, bringing me *pofak namaki* - cheesy puffs - and playing with me while Maman was washing, cleaning and cooking.

"You work all the time. Lay aside what you are doing. Come and sing me something," Naneh would request. If we were lucky, Maman would sit with us and chant Naneh's - and now my - favourite Azari song.

"...In the street I have sprinkled water
There shall be no dust when my lover comes."

Maman's eyes would shimmer with tears; she would swing her hands and body and continue in a voice as intensely sad as the dusk:

"He shall come and go in such a way
That there shall be no clash between us...
In the samovar I have put fire
In the saucer I have placed a sugar cube..."

Monday, March 14, 2005

These days, when I leave the hospital, a glimpse of the last daylight accompanies me to the tube station; winter is nearing its end.

Peyman and I sat for a coffee in the canteen after work, but even today it was impossible for us to engage in any sort of satisfying conversation. It has been so long since we last sat down for a proper chat; it was before their trip to Turkey - well over three months now. Only a year ago this would have been unthinkable; no day would pass without each of us knowing every plan, thought and shifting mood of the other inside out, while nowadays our talks have something of a fast-food character to them: in-passing and non-nourishing. Today was no exception.

"Have you now checked off 'working in a developing country' from your five-year plan?"

"No. Absolutely not. That was only a three-week taster. I'm working on the real thing," I said. "You still remember my five year plans?"

"I used to think I was the only unplanned item on your weekly to-do lists."

"A woman…"

"A woman with a life is a woman with a plan. Don't worry you've hammered your words into me."

I could see a tinge of tension in his eyes. He seemed restless, shifting in his seat and checking his watch time and again.

"It is a man's world. A smart woman needs meticulous planning, doesn't she?"

"And I was never a good enough planner for you."

"What?"

He didn't answer. He glued his eyes on the blank-faced Asian girl who was clearing the tables; his gaze followed the clinking of cups and plates, the empty cans and bags of crisps from the tables onto her tray. Then he peered out of the window.

"He's killing himself, stupid guy!" Peyman's gaze was frozen on the cigarette smoke rings rising from the hand of a patient who, with his other hand, held a drip holder with a catheter attached to it. "Shirin has been a bundle of nerves since we've come back from Istanbul." Peyman took off his badge from around his neck and placed it on the table. "Seeing her parents has made her more homesick."

It was his second visit to Istanbul in little more than a year. Turkey has turned into a lifesaver for Iranians: no questions asked, no visa required. They allow Iranians from around the globe to come in and reunite - practically a sanctuary for refugees like Peyman. It was in Istanbul that he officially proposed to Shirin, his online fiancée, who, accompanied by her older brother, had come to meet him in person.

"How did you like your in-laws? What are they like?"

"Well, they're alright - simple people." He scratched his neck. There was clearly something more on his mind. I wanted to ask what was really troubling him, but before I could, he rose up from his chair.

"I gotta go. Shirin's waiting for me. She's not strong and independent like you."

"Huh? What is with you today?"

"Your friend is here." He pointed to the door. Rekha was approaching us.

"Don't leave on my account, sweetie." She gave Peyman a peck. Rekha's heavy perfume and usual cheerfulness lifted the mood.

"Sorry, I must get going. I've to dash to Edgware Road to run some errands for Shirin."

"If that doesn't settle the question of 'who is the boss here'? We need to buy you a pair of trousers, sweetie."

"I leave you girls to it." Peyman didn't acknowledge her teasing even with a smile.

"Everything alright here?" Rekha asked.

"We'll catch up another time, okay?" He threw me a quick glance and left.

"Solmaz, honey, you look fab. Bangladesh seems to have done you heaps of good." Rekha first squeezed me tightly in her arms, then pushed me away and scanned me from head to toe, giving an approving nod. I rolled my eyes in disbelief. She couldn't, in all honesty, have been so enthralled by my jeans and sweater. I looked like a tramp next to her snazzy elegance.

"My family looked after you well?" She hitched up her skirt, revealing more of her shapely legs, and sat down.

"Oh, yeah. They were very friendly. And your house is so huge and beautiful. Remind me again, why did you leave Bangladesh?"

"Sweetheart, you say that after having met my mum?" She flipped back her long black hair, and a few strands tumbled over her red blouse. With the top buttons undone, she was showing quite a lot of cleavage. "They loved you, honey."

After three years I still can't make Rekha out. She appears always to be in the same mood, always warm and perky, always willing to impart a compliment or two and bring a smile to my face. When we first met, I found it refreshing that she resembled a glamorous fashion model rather than a boring doctor in a hospital. Her true calling must have been fashion, not medicine. Likewise, I used to think that, other than her wish to find a man, Rekha didn't have any ambitions whatsoever. "Striving for achievement is only for those who are hungry for love," she frequently points out. That her intelligence and sophistication exceeded her glamour is something I came to know only later. Yet, she only talks about Vogue and men.

Occasionally, when we are speaking on the phone, there is a long pause so that I check whether the line has gone dead. Silence, I know now, is another of her characteristics. Very often, when I would expect some emotion or opinion, she merely goes quiet. It's not a silence that signifies indifference or rage, not the silence you use to punish someone or protest, like Baba often does. Neither is it the silence that avoids confrontation, like that of Maman. Nor does it seem to convey consensus or wisdom. Her silence certainly does not speak volumes. It is rather a bland silence, like the dull taste of dry rice; a silence that dampens excitement, like someone who takes a needle and sticks it into your soaring red balloon.

This time around, I invoked that notorious silence by announcing that I had signed up for three years' voluntary work with International Medical Charity, IMC.

"On a whim?" Rekha said. "When?"

"Last night. It wasn't out of the blue. You know I've been pondering about it for quite a while now. It's always been on my to-do list, so I decided no more waiting."

Rekha just looked at me. A long silence, a long awkward pause, then she asked for the time, eyed my wrist and smiled. It was my watch. It still follows Bangladeshi time - I can't bring myself to change it to London time.

"Sweetie, you've met someone there, haven't you?"

"No. Where? Whom? I was working all the time. It's simply a reminder of my good time there, nothing else."

"So I gather. Hmm, fabulous. I'm glad you liked it. And what did you say you did on your birthday?"

"Nothing. I spent it alone in a hotel room. You know, reflecting and so on."

Our little chit-chat faltered after that, and eventually ended in a dead flat line.

Tuesday, March 15, 2005

Yesterday was the kind of socialising that leaves one feeling lonelier than before. Later, in the tube, that sense of emptiness was only intensified. For a moment or two, I felt poised in space, looking at us passengers from above; a cluster of disenchanted, frustrated and weary shadows - spirits trapped in the hangover of adulthood. In the West there is not much time for being. We are in a constant terror: terror of loneliness, the ticking of time and above all of loss, but also anxious to become or have this or that. In Bangladesh I sensed no need to become, to have. I could just be. *'Here we don't wait for anything but a bus,'* Shariati would say, and there a miracle feels immediate; one is waiting for a miracle.

Why did I keep the whole story back from Rekha? I didn't have any reason to hide Belal, but that kind of stuff spreads fast and wide. I don't want her mum or her brother to read the wrong things into it. Rekha was already making too much of the Bangladeshi time on my watch. She gave me the same mischievous smile I saw on Belal's face on my birthday night, when I asked him, 'Would you like to come up for coffee?' That offer had slipped past my better judgement. I remember how I was taken aback myself by that strange woman talking for me, especially because that was when I still thought Belal a chauvinist.

My birthday began with me being chauffeured by Belal's driver to a one-day intense shopping spree in Dhaka. When he dropped me at his office, Belal coaxed me into dinner. He took me to a fancy restaurant, high over Dhaka; a tranquil place with elegant round tables and large windows, and a bird's eye view of the city. While Belal muttered the names of some dishes to the waiter, I remember my eyes running over the walls decorated with rural scenes and thinking to myself, 'Wow, for once in my life somebody else is taking charge and mapping out an evening for me. I like that.'

"Anything you don't eat?" Belal asked.

"I eat just about everything provided I get *gulab jammun* for dessert."

It was me who kept the conversation flowing, uttering my impressions of Bangladesh, my thoughts on social inequalities and women's status, constantly drawing parallels between Bangladesh and Iran. I talked without ceasing. It was only when I leaned over to reach for the bottle of water at Belal's end of the table that I suddenly became aware of his gaze. All along he had been listening with eyes fixed on me and a half-smile on his face.

"But what do I know?" I snapped out of my musings. "You don't talk much?"

"I get bored at the sound of my own voice." His demeanour didn't alter. Belal pointed to the orange-brown ring on my left middle finger. "Is it an *aqiq*?"

Astonished to hear the same word we have in Farsi for the seal-stone agate, I explained that it was from Naneh Homa. She had brought it home from one of her many pilgrimages to Karbala.

"I wear it as a reminder to stay a good girl."

"Who says you need a reminder?"

28

If it was not for his serious tone and matter-of-fact face, I would have thought his remark humorous or sarcastic. Instead, I blushed. He was not looking at me, but motioning to the waiter to bring the tray with the selection of cakes and pastries. I checked my watch. It was already past ten.

"Doesn't your family wonder where you are at this time?"

"I always go home late. I don't need to answer to anyone."

His reply sent a shiver up my spine, and my thoughts travelled back to Tehran. I have an enduring memory of one night when I was about eight years old. I remember getting out of bed to pour myself a glass of milk, and seeing Maman sitting on the sofa and absent-mindedly fiddling with the knitting on her lap. She was still up, worrying once again about Baba's whereabouts that late at night. Her brown eyes were filled with loneliness and grief. There and then I vowed I'd never marry and have children. I also devised a plan to make it come about: if I didn't learn how to do housework, stayed far away from the kitchen and earned my own money, I wouldn't end up like her - waiting for a man.

The image of my mother played on my mind and made me irritable. I seized the napkin from my lap, folded it neatly and laid it next to my empty plate.

"You should go home. Your wife must be waiting for you." I straightened my back and leaned forward, ready to go.

"Don't worry. Let's celebrate your birthday."

At the time I didn't understand, but I do now. I was swayed by his insistence as much as the confidence in his voice. He had a skill I had never come across before, the skill of paying attention. It was the intensity of the attention, perfectly measured and timed, like a long leash that sets you free to explore who you are but always draws you back before you stray too far.

He lit a match and planted it in the middle of one of the three *gulab jammuns*. I quickly blew out the makeshift candle and threw it away. I grabbed the fork, poked it into my *gulab jammun* and whirled the soft brown balls in the syrup.

"When I was a child," I lowered my head, "my father used to come home very late, like you."

At that instant I sensed the brush of his fingers on my face. He took a stray strand of my hair that hung perilously close to my bowl and tucked it away behind my ear.

"Let's go." I pulled back and got up.

The waiter packed the cakes for a takeaway, and we drove in silence back to the hotel. And then, when he pulled up to the entrance, the memorable 'would you like to come up for coffee?' popped out of my mouth.

"Let me park the car."

A momentary lapse of judgment, and Belal was with me alone in a hotel room. I turned on the TV, handed the remote control to him and went to call the room service.

"What will you have?"

"Espresso, please." Belal started switching channels.

Soon, with a tray of two espressos before us on the round table, I plonked myself down on the chair opposite his, feet drawn up beneath me. He left the TV on a channel that was playing a Bengali movie. Then, as if our night has not had enough unexpected twists and turns, he somehow managed to work the topic of polygamy and extramarital relationships into our banal conversation.

"How common is it in Iran? Don't you Shi'as have the temporary marriage?"

"Look, for a start that certainly is not what Islam says." My feminist buttons pressed, I set off on a lengthy lecture. "Those primitive bastards exploit Islam to their own ends." My voice rose, and the angrier I got, the faster I preached. Belal, however, stayed calm and quiet from start to finish. All I got in response to my fiery polemic was a poker face.

"Hmm. The differences between sexes are God-given," he said.

"It is late. You should go."

"You want me to go? *Accha* - okay." Belal stood up. "Sleep tight."

"Thank you for the dinner."

"My pleasure." There was a twinkle in his dark brown eyes, framed by long, thick lashes - longer than mine. It suddenly dawned on me what I had seen in those eyes all evening: a mixture of amusement and disappointment.

In a way it is hard to describe. Nothing that happened that evening made the slightest sense, even to me. There was a part of me that hated him and a part that could not let go.

The events of that evening in Dhaka feel unreal now that I am in London. And irrelevant. What matters today is that he is the only person happy to hear my news. I texted earlier to inform him of my application for the voluntary work.

What about Bangladesh? he replied.

Bangladesh...what?

The voluntary job! You should visit us. Come to Bangladesh.

I was moved. I explained I had put in an application for India. *It's out of my hands.*

Try, he texted back.

Monday, March 21, 2005

Two incidents, one trivial and the other less so, overshadowed my day to a disproportionate extent.

The first one happened this morning when I was roaming Accident and Emergency in search of the surgeon to hand over a patient with abdominal pain who had turned out to have appendicitis and not a ruptured ovarian cyst. I bumped into a group of nurses, two women and a man, looking at some baby pictures. I joined them in an outpouring of 'ooh', 'aah', and 'sooo cute'.

"Do you have any children?" the man asked me in a Nigerian accent.

"No. And I don't want any either," I said without thinking.

"You are selfish." He fixed his big black eyes on mine.

"How so?"

"You are a doctor, you live in Europe and you earn good money. You can give a child good education, a good life, but you don't want one. This is selfish."

At that exact moment the surgeon should have turned up or my bleep should have gone off, but I was instead left to my own devices. The best I could come up with was something to the effect that there were already plenty of children and I would rather use my education to help them than producing more, and some other regurgitated rationale.

The second incident was my annual call to Amu Hamid to wish him happy Nowruz for our new year.

"Solmaz *joon*, how's life? You doing okay at work? You should become a gynaecologist," Amu Hamid suggested. "How much do you put aside every month? You should seriously think about investing in a flat here in Tehran. Many Iranians living abroad do it…"

Amu Hamid - unlike Baba - takes a real interest in my life, but today I was tired and wished we could have the kind of chats Baba and I have: the weather in London, bronchitis and arthritis.

The only way out was to change the topic.

"Have Baba and Maman told you I was in Bangladesh?"

"Solmaz, why do you keep doing that, girl? Why do you take all these decisions without consulting us first?"

For a fraction of a second I was perplexed. What did he mean? Which decision? I have always made my own decisions. From the age of thirteen I would go to the doctors on my own for my migraine. Maman used to come along at first, but then I was constantly interpreting the doctor's words for her so it was easier if I went by myself. I was the one taking my parents to their appointments, be it to the doctors, banks or embassies. They never attended a parents' meeting at my school, they couldn't and didn't need to. I was a good student. Instead I would go to parents' meetings for Omid, especially if a teacher asked to speak to a family member about his inexplicable absences.

Migration leads to a host of changes, not to mention the blurring of parent-child roles. Whereas under normal circumstances parents are supposed to introduce the child to the unknown world, migration means that it is the child, equipped with the new language, who effectively becomes the bridge between the parents and the new world.

"Spending money on a trip to Bangladesh, and all alone?" Amu's voice brought me back to the present. He sounded disappointed. "I understand you are educated and grown-up and know much more than us, but we have experience. Experience is not bought in the bazaar, it comes with years." He carried on talking about drawing on other people's life experiences to avoid repeating their mistakes.

"With all due respect, Amu, I haven't sold any shares of my life to others."

There was silence at the other end, and I imagine some headshaking. Amu didn't comment, and within minutes we said our goodbyes.

Shortly afterward, Maman called and said Amu had taken offence at my utterance. Apparently, he had rationalised my words as a language barrier. Surely I could not have meant those words. "Her Farsi is failing her," he had reasoned - and Maman had agreed, reinstating the peace.

"Maman, I knew what I was saying and actually meant it."

I didn't tell Maman that I somehow took pleasure in the fact that Amu was upset. It meant that he had at least heard me. Part of me felt all grown-up. It was almost as if I was compensating for Maman's silence by standing up to Amu.

I have this rigid image of Amu in my head that makes me just as guilty as him of confining today's person to yesterday's memories. It is as if a picture has outgrown its frame, but we choose to stay loyal to the frame rather than to the picture itself. I am stuck on that black and white picture of him and Baba in the mahogany frame that looked at me from the mantelpiece of our living room in Vienna. They were in their thirties, Amu standing next to Baba with his left hand resting on the shoulder of his older brother; both looking proud - thrust-out chest, slim built body with bony cheeks and salt and pepper hair. Their features, elegant and sophisticated, their pose reminiscent of those handsome models in Armani or Boss ads, seemed to have been designed for a life of art and glamour - if only fate had played along. Whereas now the deep furrows etched on their faces narrate a whole different story: one of two young boys moving from a village in Azerbaijan to Tehran, working and sleeping in factories until they made it.

"We grew up on our own. It shouldn't be this way for our kids." Amu insisted on this more than Baba.

For as long as I can remember, two traits have defined Amu's complex character: melancholia and arrogance. His melancholy sprang partly from his nature and partly from grief over his unfair lot in life, and his arrogance was the result of overcoming that same lot. These, coupled with his knowledge of worldly affairs, have made him an authority figure in our family. It was him, not Baba or Maman, who asked me in my early twenties what I intended to do with regards to marriage and family life. Up to that time, I used to think that Amu Hamid perceived me as many others did: an idealist, a moralist, a *non*-woman. To this day, my married cousins in Iran assume I remain single because I don't know what true love is.

They are mistaken. Even as a child I used to harbour my own fantasies of the perfect man. I dimly recall my first image of him from when I was ten or so. He had to be in jeans and a leather jacket, like James Dean in the videos we watched. I certainly couldn't get my head around why my older cousins wore suits when going to a girl's house to woo, and I so wished I could have helped by telling them how unhip and dull it made them look. Later on, in my teen years, I hankered for a passionate, gloomy, but rebellious man like the intellectual Dr Ali Shariati, the Iranian Che Guevara - the peaceful version, using words as weapon.

"Solmaz seems melancholic. Don't let her read Shariati. So many of our youth were made suicidal by his views." Maman's friends worried that Shariati was not a good influence on me. How could he be, when his political and intellectual controversy has outlived him? A man, jailed, exiled, and then murdered at forty-two, a misfit before and after the revolution, can't be the best role model. It was pointless to explain to Maman's friend, the anti-depressant Shariati was for me - my roadmap in a foreign land, my anchor in the confusions of puberty. He kept me safe and he kept me sane. Above all, he was the teacher my parents couldn't be.

God, humanity and love - these are the tasks we are entrusted with. A man after my own heart; it was love at first words. Our partnership started off with a tango. I remember how I would pore over his allegedly 'Marxist-Islamic' books from the 60s and 70s on social justice, the 'true' Islam and the 'true' Muslim, put them away in anger and call him 'westernised', but then go back to him again for direction. As my doubts about Islam grew, he turned into a mediator between Islam and me.

Be that as it may, Islam eventually lost its validity for me, and so did its God. On 28 August 1994 I had an official meeting with God, "This isn't working anymore. I need to understand You, but I don't. I'll go find You and once I do, I'll come back. Wait for me."

I left the God that brought us together. I never left Shariati. Now we waltz. The tension that delivered the passion has transformed into a tranquil dance. He was the first man in my life, and the second could not have been more different. No, it is not entirely true. I suspect he just added to my expectations. His kindness, adoration and unconditional love - the kind that doesn't care about shaved or unshaved legs - set the bar higher for the one I'll fall for in future.

Sunday, April 10, 2005

It is 5 a.m. I can't sleep.

Yesterday was not exactly a *blissful* day. Peyman and Rekha came over as planned to study for our advanced resuscitation course. The first thing I heard when they both stepped in was a loud 'let's get cracking' from Peyman. Then he apologised that Shirin was waiting down in Cafe Republic, hence the rush. So we got cracking, but half an hour into our discussion we were interrupted by the buzzing of Peyman's mobile. It was Shirin. I suggested I spoke to her and asked her to come up, but he shook his head. He tensed up in his chair and typed a reply. Recently, I've come to notice a slight hump on his back that he didn't have when I first met him.

Peyman read the first scenario aloud for me, while Rekha played the role of an unconscious woman with vomit in her mouth. I knelt beside her on the floor and started to talk us through what I'd do.

"I suck the vomit."

Payman burst out laughing.

"No sweetie," Rekha lifted her head off the floor. "Suction! You *suction* the vomit." She winked at me and rested her head back on the floor.

Within minutes another round of buzzing intruded. Tension clouded Peyman's face.

"So, a fifty-year-old patient with known abdominal

36

aneurysm complains of severe abdominal pain. He is shouting for help. What do you do?" Rekha went on while Peyman hurriedly keyed in replies.

"I check his airways and breathing."

"*You do?*" Rekha said.

"Yes! ABC - airways, breathing, circulation."

"Oh, bless you. Sweetie, he is shouting. What do you guess that means? It means his airways are clear."

I was thrown off by Peyman. I know him well enough to sense when his arm pain recurs. Whenever he is sad or angry, he becomes subdued and clutches his right arm in an attempt to ease the pain; one of the many souvenirs from his teenage time in the prisons of Tehran. How cruel to be locked away for two years for handing out anti-regime fliers. Peyman was lucky though. His cousin was executed for the same offence.

"What about *you?*" Rekha asked yesterday while Peyman was fiddling with his mobile. "Listen up. It would do you a world of good if you'd make an effort to meet new people. Expand your circle. Sweetie, there are many Iranians in London, mingle with your own people."

"Own people?"

"Yes, own people. Trust me. Look at Peyman and Shirin: Well, as the proverb goes, *Birds of a feather flock together...*"

Her voice trailed off. All I could hear was my own thought, 'He is drifting away from me.'

That said, it should be mentioned in his favour that it was me who encouraged, almost pushed, Peyman to register at an Iranian online dating site. As a young doctor in London, he was spoilt for choice; girls in as well as outside Iran responded to his ad. Then again, I didn't expect him to be so at home in this 'one-size-fits-all' model of the traditional family life. He is the man, the husband, the breadwinner, and Shirin is the woman, the wife, the caretaker of the domestic sphere.

Saturday, May 7, 2005

A flawless painting, all the dots and lines in the right place and at the right angle, the colours merging into each other without a smudge or blotch; as impeccable a picture as you could get, yet somehow dull and lacklustre. That was the reflection Fardin evoked when he extended his hand to greet me.

"It has been ages since I saw him, but he hasn't changed a bit," Rekha said when I joined her at the cafe. "Still handsome and charming." A smile formed on her lips as if she was recalling a pleasant memory. Fardin's name has repeatedly cropped up in our conversations since I've known her.

"How do I look?" Rekha asked.

"You haven't changed a bit either, and look as gorgeous as always."

"That is sweet. I'm actually glad I bumped into him. You'll finally get to meet him. He's such a gentleman, honestly, he is. He's the most sophisticated guy I've ever come across." She reached out and put her hand on my arm. "And, his cooking skills are on a par with a celebrity chef. Whenever we were on call together, he'd bring us home-made food. What's that Persian thing, something with aubergine? Ah, so yummy."

I wondered whether she was infatuated with Fardin.

"Don't be silly. He's everything a woman would wish for, but not a Bangladeshi, nor a Hindu. My parents would never consent." Rekha glanced at the door and then turned back. "On the other hand, he'd be just right for you, darling." She based that presumption on the following arguments: Fardin was Iranian, a promising physician, divorced and ready to settle down now - 'an all-around grounded man,' she called him.

"I am not even sure I am interested in grounded men." I tried not to hurt her feelings. "Wouldn't you rather have an exciting, passionate guy, huh?" I pleaded as if Rekha was the genie who could grant my wishes.

"The interesting ones are usually not monogamous." She waved at someone over my head.

Fardin bent forward and planted a peck on Rekha's cheek. His Iranian hooked nose and black hair eclipsed her still beaming face.

"You must be Solmaz." He turned to squeeze my hand - a firm, determined handshake. "I hope you don't mind me tagging along."

"Not at all."

He fetched a chair and squashed himself in-between us. I would have guessed him older than his twenty-eight years. With the goatee and a hint of belly under his khaki blazer, he could easily haved passed as a professor.

"What movie are you ladies watching?" His American accent struck me. Like many Iranians, he must have picked it up from Hollywood movies. Whenever I meet a foreigner speaking good English, I become painfully aware of my own pronounced accent.

"*Guess Who,*" Rekha replied.

"I must have seen a write-up about it somewhere. Isn't it a remake of Guess Who's Coming to Dinner? It is the comedy version of a classic. It won't be easy to outshine the original." There was an air of confidence in his tone.

"So, have you two known each other for long?" I broke my silence.

"Yes." Fardin gave Rekha's arm a gentle squeeze. "Rekha is a very dear friend."

"You gotta watch this one; he's a charmer as well as an excellent doctor. You Iranians are really intelligent."

"I wouldn't generalise," I protested.

"Why not?" Rekha said. "I know we shouldn't, but I like generalisations. They make life so much simpler, for one, and when you get to the bottom of most generalisations, there's always some truth in them, for another."

"Otherwise, there wouldn't be any patterns, right?" Fardin seconded Rekha's view and turned to me. "Solmaz, I hear you grew up in Vienna. What brought you to England?"

Opting not to disclose my bunch of complicated reasons, I said I was here for the UK's excellent reputation in medical training.

"When was the last time you were in Iran?"

I paused to calculate. Fardin's eyes widened when he heard it has been fifteen years.

"My parents were with us, you know, there really was no reason to go back," I said.

"Sure," he replied with a nod of his head. "But it's changed a lot since then."

I didn't ask in what way.

"Do you follow the happenings there?" he asked.

"Not really."

"Then you must have been one of those expats who mingle with Europeans a lot. Those are the folk who get out of touch with Iran."

I smiled in response.

"But surely you didn't miss our boys' performance in the last World Cup in 2002," he said. "I flipped out when Iran didn't qualify..."

This was the kind of small talk I dread most. I dread it when people reminisce about their favourite music, a certain children's programme or that historic moment in their past, a moment they share with a whole nation. When they do this, I tend to smile to cover up the fact that I don't have a clue what they are talking about - and even if I know it intellectually, I just can't relate to their sentiments, despite my earnest efforts. I don't know the gothic or punk culture and the Bauhaus music that the long-haired anaesthetist feels nostalgic about. Even less do I follow the nurses when they talk about their children's favourite character in Teletubbies. In his testament, Shariati

40

advises his son to travel to Europe, but not until he has seen Iran - because otherwise, Shariati's reasoning goes, he would go and come back 'blind'.

I haven't travelled Iran. My feet were in the shoes of a child when I last trod the Iranian soil. And now, after nearly twenty years of having the Western soil beneath me, I still am a stranger. You can call me blind, for I don't seem to find my way around here. Streets, sounds, scents and images don't conjure up any flashbacks of my sweet childhood, no memories of innocence or joy. The long and short of it is that when someone like me keeps changing countries, she becomes a hoarder - a hoarder of disjointed stories. They are baby stories that never evolve into a complete and coherent tale. How could they? I can hardly make sense of them myself.

Stories hanker for listeners. They come to being when you pour words into the cup of a listener - but which listener is interested in fragments, in an unfinished, incomplete work? Everywhere I have been, everywhere I have lived, I have stayed longer than a mere visitor but never long enough to become a native. I feel a hypocrite no matter what. When I speak as a native, I feel a liar. When I speak as a visitor, again I feel a liar. I am more than a visitor and less than a native: I am a foreigner. And believe me there are so many flavours to us foreigners. We vary, not only depending on the soil of origin and how ripe or raw we are at time of harvest - immigration - but also the way we are processed and blended with additives - integration.

Fardin must have noticed the embarrassment on my face, because he switched the conversation to something lighter. "What did you do for Nowruz?"

The flush left my cheeks as I proceeded to tell him about the phone calls to Iran and the care package sent by Maman.

As we left for the movie, Fardin rested his hand on my back, urging Rekha and me to go ahead, and just before the exit he came up to open the door for us. At the box office he

41

insisted on paying for the tickets; an offer that I accepted after Rekha poked my arm.

It wasn't too bad an evening. When Fardin first strutted into the cafe, his expensive designer clothes, coupled with Rekha's smitten remarks about him, gave off an arrogant vibe. Surprisingly, as the evening went on, I felt a lot more at ease with him. What is more, I didn't make a fool of myself. I always fear I might be seen as one of those people Shariati likens to '*Coke poured into a glass*': bubbling up at first, and flat once the fizz has settled.

"He took to you right away, honey. When you were in the bathroom, he said we should go and visit him in his flat, that we could go swimming in his building and he would cook for us," Rekha claimed later in the tube.

"I can't."

"Why not?"

"You know I don't wear a swimsuit in public."

"Poor dear, you say you are not religious, but you have the shyness of a pious woman. If I had your figure, I wouldn't hide it in a Mao style outfit," she said. "Darling, you need to loosen up."

Friday, May 27, 2005

Tomorrow Shirin is leaving for Iran. She will be gone for three months. I just called to wish her a safe journey.

"Solmaz *joon*, I'm the one travelling, I should have called you."

She used the formal 'you' in Farsi. Why was she addressing me formally when we have always been informal? Why the sudden change? It never occurred to me to wait for Shirin's phone call. Adhering to formalities and customs has never been a strength of mine - they are cold and empty.

"Friends don't stand on ceremony," I said.

We exchanged more small talk about her flight schedule and the weather in Tehran, then she abruptly said goodbye and hung up. I sat there baffled, listening to the dead tone of the phone still pressed against my ear.

From the day Shirin came to London, I have applied all my wit and flair to court her friendship - flowers, jokes, compliments, invitations to restaurants, and phone calls whenever Peyman was on call and she alone - all in vain. It is not as though she didn't know about me before their marriage. As a matter of fact, Peyman was obsessed with telling all the girls he chatted with on the dating site about me, to the extent that I suspected he was deliberately doing it to gauge their reactions. Shirin, he said, was very cool about me. "She must be an interesting woman. I am looking forward to meeting her," had been her response.

Shirin, with her blonde highlighted hair in puffy strands and heavily-lined lips and eyes, was not what I envisaged as the right match for Peyman. But each to his own.

A few weeks ago, there was a glimmer of hope when Shirin's call woke me up early on a Sunday morning. I saw her ringing me at such an ungodly hour as a mark of our closeness - an excitement that dissipated when she proceeded to a fairly detailed description of her vaginal discharge. Talking about the genitals of the women in my immediate social circle lies beyond my medical comfort zone. I can be a doctor to them concerning anything except their genitals. My unease grew as I listened to Shirin's account of the colour, intensity and quantity of her discharge; nevertheless, I suppressed my disgust and went along with it. I diagnosed thrush. Yet, it didn't stop there. She told me that a gynaecologist in Tehran had warned her the problem might occur once she became sexually active.

Superb. Picturing Peyman having sex with Shirin has absolutely made us bosom friends.

"Such a bitch," Rekha snapped when hearing this story. "She's added insult to injury."

"I don't know. Maybe she was genuinely worried and needed a girly chit-chat." Not that I believed my own words.

Sunday, June 5, 2005

I have picked up a summer cold and feel out of sorts.

First, I called Maman for sympathy. "It is very simple. Pour some water into the pot, add two of those soup sachets I sent you, a handful of *zereshk* - barberries - and parsley. If you don't have any soup noodles you can use rice. But make sure to use fresh lemon juice. It makes it taste better and is full of Vitamin C."

But my fridge was empty and my body too limp.

My fingers scrolled down the contacts on my mobile: Accountant, Bahram the builder, Fardin, Maman, Omid, Peyman, Rekha. With Peyman being on night shift and Rekha preparing for her membership exam, there was no one to call. Then the phone rang. It was Fardin; my hoarse voice immediately gave away my affliction.

"Come over. I'll throw you something together that'll work wonders."

A look around me at the pile of books on the desk and the bundle of used tissues on the bedside table and there was no doubt as what to do. At a snail's pace, I put on my old jeans and a comfy sweater and dragged myself out.

The crisp air infused me with some energy, and it stayed with me on the stuffy Circle Line till Kensington High Street. From there it took me only five minutes of walking to Fardin's place. He received me in the hallway. The first thing that leapt out at me when the lift door opened was the Boss logo on his shirt - no, the second, after the smile that shifted the straight lines of his goatee. When he drew closer to peck me on the cheek - I had warned him of my germs - I noticed his brown shoes with yellow stripes; they perfectly matched his brown jeans and yellow shirt. That explains his allure to the fashion-savvy Rekha.

The smell of fresh herbs, cooked rice and some hearty soup grew as we proceeded to the kitchen. A pair of pink gloves screamed at me from the sink above the shiny silver cabinets.

"Please tell me you don't wash up with those camp gloves on, do you?"

He laughed. "You have an inquisitive eye."

He put on the kettle. Next he took two pieces of toast and a garlic clove. I watched him rub on garlic, spread some butter and sprinkle salt on the toast.

"Have some bruschetta with your tea." He placed one piece on a tissue and handed it to me. "Doctor's orders."

Fardin turned to attend to the rice, and I sauntered, teacup in hand, into the living room, a spacious place with a dinner table at one end and two dark brown leather sofas facing the TV and a marbled mantelpiece at the other. The only decoration was ivory curtains, a heavy Persian carpet, and a canvas print of an airport poised above the sofa - all very upscale and exquisite.

"You've got yourself a lovely place here."

"It's fine for now."

"What do you mean 'fine for now'? It's perfect."

"Well, this flat could be anywhere, in New York or even in Tehran. It's not an English house, but it's right for now."

A king-size bed occupied most of his bedroom. The second room was made into a study with a desk and a small bookshelf. I let my eyes wander over the books. A lonely edition of the *Divan-I-Hafiz* in Farsi stood out among the many medical books and the encyclopaedia of world history. I nosed through his collection of DVDs, *Casablanca*, *Taxi Driver*, *Scent of a Woman*,

45

Godfather, Mrs Robinson, Everything You Always Wanted to Know About Sex and also some Iranian titles: *At Five in The Afternoon, Kandahar, Taste of Cherry,* and so forth. Hard to say whether they reflected his taste or that of a film critic from some newspaper.

By the time I had finished my exploration and returned to the living room, a lavish dinner was set on the glass table with a single candle burning slowly on the side.

"Wine?" he offered.

"I don't drink alcohol."

"Not at all?"

"I never used to and don't see the point of starting now," I said. "So, are you studying for your exams?" I gestured to the heap of the books in the corner of the room.

"Yes, and also doing a joint research project with the American Heart Foundation."

"Hats off. I'm really impressed. How did you get into that?"

"Hard work and determination."

"Ah. That's your formula for success?"

"Not only this. Any form of success boils down to setting a goal, focusing and persisting - not giving up when the going gets tough. Where other people might give up, I plan, map out the steps ahead and plug away."

"So, no taking risks?"

"I do take risks, calculated risks. I work within the rules though, I don't invert them."

I was stunned by his fierceness.

"What's that grimace?" He must have noticed my raised eyebrows. "Did I intimidate you?"

"Nope. Not at all."

"You're still friends with your ex. How's that going down?" Fardin segued to a new topic.

"Fine, just like this delicious soup," I said with a grin.

"You've a dimple when you smile. That's cute."

"What about yourself?" The moment seemed opportune to

satisfy my curiosity and draw out some information about his divorce.

"I neither think nor talk about it. When something is over, it becomes irrelevant to me, and I leave it in the past where it belongs."

Hearing him say that, I had a strong sense that he could easily break a woman's heart.

After dinner, Fardin put *Breakfast at Tiffany's* into the DVD player and went to the kitchen to brew some more tea.

"Tell me," he shouted from the kitchen. "How was it growing up in Vienna? It must have been thrilling to be surrounded by so much history and culture. Vienna Opera House, the waltz, Mozart, er…"

"Yeah, mountains, the blue Danube, Sigmund Freud."

"And Sacher Torte."

"Yeah, Sacher Torte is not really my cup of tea. You've been there?"

"Of course, last year on a conference. Do you go back often?"

"Not very often, you know, I don't get much time." It was not wise to tarnish his regard for Austria and, in effect, its former resident. He didn't need to know that if it wasn't for my family, I would never set foot there again, that my stomach churns each time the plane touches down in Vienna and that all I associate with that country is rejection.

"My favourite thing about Vienna is its pastries. In my opinion, they are unrivalled. Oh, and I do miss the bread and the cosy cafes." I huddled by the sofa, stretched out on the Persian carpet and wrapped my big shawl around me.

As soon as Fardin returned, he dimmed the light and joined me on the floor before pressing the 'on' button.

As Holly - Audrey Hepburn - scrunched her nose and snubbed Paul - George Peppard -, Fardin, his body nestled against mine, put one arm around my shoulder and began to stroke my hair. 'What is this guy up to?' My left brain protested. 'Who cares? He feels warm. It is nice,' my reptilian brain hushed. His touch hypnotised my senses until the Cat, Holly and Paul embraced and kissed under the pouring rain.

With 'The End', my mind reclaimed control. I pulled myself out of his arms and sat cross-legged opposite him.

"Fardin, what was that?" I asked, in the same tone a teacher might speak to a child who has misbehaved - calm but firm.

"Excuse me?"

"I mean you playing with my hair. What were you doing?"

"Whoa, what is that supposed to mean?" He jumped to his feet and sat on the sofa. "Hey, hit the brakes." The initial shock in his voice gave way to anger. His face hardened. "You're reading way too much into it. I didn't expect *you*, an educated girl brought up in the West to have these old-fashioned ways of thinking. Even the girls back home would have known that I was simply being friendly."

"I don't care what other girls do or think, whether in Iran or Europe. For all I know cuddling a girl and playing with her hair at the second encounter implies other not-so-friend-like intentions."

"And how did you figure that?" Fardin crossed his arms over his chest and frowned. "You know, after this irrational reaction of yours, you could be as well lying here utterly naked and it wouldn't turn me on."

"Likewise."

"Hey lady, I was just being friendly." He got up to switch on the lights. That was my invitation to leave.

"I'm sorry if I misjudged the situation," I said before we ended the night with a cold goodbye and a limp handshake - but chances are I was right. Even naked I would not turn him on - I can't believe he told me that. No, I was right. As so often with men, they become angry when shamed.

Who am I kidding? That serves me right. I brought this on myself. I mean it did seem like a good idea at first, but let's say from now on I won't make a decision when ill. Men simply don't get friendship with women, and I clearly don't get it that men don't get it.

Tuesday, June 28, 2005

"Do you like it here?"

I was filling in a patient's drug chart when one of the midwives shone the bright neon light at me. It was not the first time this question was put to me, and neither will it be the last. A couple of years ago, at the job interview, my consultant too was curious about it, prompting me to reply with an enthusiastic "I love it!"

And of course I did.

Cruising the streets of London, being asked for directions by people oblivious to my dark hair and deaf to my accent; watching a huge crowd of Muslims congregating in Trafalgar Square, overtly bearing their Arabic banners and trumpeting their beliefs; drug reps picking halal restaurants when organising free meals for doctors - cosmopolitan London struck me as a friendly fairy godmother after years of step-motherly treatment in Austria. What a relief!

I had come very far from the days of 'How many wives does your dad have?', 'Do you have a camel in your house in Tehran?' in my school years or 'If you can't see this fracture on the XR, you'd better go back to your cashier job in Aldi', as a medical student in Vienna. Not only that; I was no longer the proxy of Islam. An eleven-year-old finds it rather overwhelming when suddenly being questioned about anything and everything she grew up taking for granted. I mean, only a year before I was just a pupil wearing a decent uniform and a head scarf at a school in Tehran, knitting pullovers for Iranian soldiers in the war with Iraq, and, like my other classmates, struggling with maths, learning to read the Quran, being anxious to memorise the names of all the kings and dynasties, the events around the constitutional revolution, the clergies' conflict with the Shah, and so on. Then all of a sudden I found myself surrounded by girls pulling at the dark hair on my forearms - up until then I didn't know they were there - raving about their new boyfriends and the jealousy of the ex, boasting about their alcohol consumption and how 'plastered' they had been over the weekend, while biting on their *Semmel* with *Leberkaese* during lunch hours.

I was embarrassed about my accent, eating rice with a spoon, and the aloneness in those long breaks, so I would bury myself in one of Shariati's books or the notebook of a pupil whose handwriting I could decipher, in order to copy the lesson from the last class and look up the new words in my German-Farsi dictionary. As if this pressure was not enough, during the lessons I was in the spotlight, my classmates' gazes turning to me when the topic in the class happened to be Persian-Roman wars, the crusades, the Palestine-Israel conflict, or virginity and why men were at liberty to marry up to four women in Islam. Suddenly this visibility, this otherness, this aloneness; suddenly the necessity to be vigilant when I simply wished to *be*, to form an opinion when I would rather experiment and explore at my leisure. Suddenly you are called, against your own will, to grow up. Being different necessitates a sudden spurt of growth, and puts an end to your carelessness, to the comfort of disguise in familiarity.

"How long are you going to stay here?" The midwife kept going.

I resisted the impulse to tell her that I didn't have anywhere else to go, that London was as good a home as I would ever get, and instead said, "Don't know."

Her question haunted me for hours on end. Irrespective of how innocent or well-intentioned a question like this is, it prods you out of your amnesia. You tend, during a busy day immersed in routines and practicalities of work, to forget 'who' you are, or at least the 'who' you are being perceived as. I am just a doctor like any other, doing doctor stuff. But the question sets you on a vicious cycle of doubt. It spurs a sense of insecurity, and with that a series of other 'whats' and 'whys' of life. After all, this is not your home, and - hideous as it sounds - if your presence is not a necessity, then maybe *you* are not a necessity. Your very existence in the world comes under scrutiny. With roots in nothing solid, I could as well float and dissipate.

This never-ending otherness, always being the other to someone else's 'I': as a woman and as a foreigner you are always the other to some strong autonomous presence that rules your little existence, tolerates your co-existence under this or that condition, but never fully permits your presence.

I feel the *aqiq* on my finger, and Belal's words come to mind, 'Who says you need a reminder?' - I do.

I wish I could dip my oars into the waters of time and row back to my childhood with Naneh: a world rich in possibilities and promises, but more than anything a safe haven - home, the place where you don't need to explain anything, where you simply are. I would lie again on the roof of Naneh's house on a warm summery night, stargazing, or I might choose a cold winter night, my legs beneath the *korsi* - a low heated table - and a woollen blanket draped over its top to keep in the warmth, listening to one of her Persian tales, one of those that end in: *Dastaneh ma be sar resid, kalagheh be choneh naresid* - 'Our story is done, still the crow hasn't reached home yet.'

Sunday, July 17, 2005

This morning, I gave in to my yearning to go to the woods: Hampstead Heath - that is as much of a wilderness as I can get here in North London.

It was my first time there. When I got off the tube at East Finchley, I went to the lone taxi driver and asked the way.

A short walk uphill, I strolled through the entrance of the park, choosing the paths as they came along: one time turning left, another time right, once up, once down. And it turned out to be just perfect, despite - or perhaps because of - my ignorance of the way ahead. It was as though one was delving into the depths of a lover or digging deep into one's own subconscious: bountiful, exhilarating and often breathtaking, a sensual experience to the core. I stroked the bricks of a wall, its red shades brightly glistening under the rising sun's warmth. My fingers brushed the rough earth and the leaves, some smooth, some ragged, and I perched on the immense lap of a tree. It was close to lovemaking; sincere, real and complete - so complete that the tree and I didn't find it necessary to exchange names or phone numbers.

Re-entering civilisation, I moved aside furniture in my living room and threw a one-woman party. Dancing, or rather bouncing, swinging my arms and kicking my legs, to Barry White's *Just the Way You Are*. I listened to music from the 60s and 70s while reading the British Medical Journal, and then I slipped in some more hopping and whirling to Gloria Gaynor's *I Will Survive* before flopping at my desk to email to Bangladesh:

"Where are all the kings and princes?
If they knew of the joys in the lands of our aloneness
They would raise their swords in order to conquer it."

I opted for Shariati's words to relate my Sunday to Belal.

By then I was in the right mood for Maman's Sunday call. Maman's calls can be ordered into two categories, the first being, 'I was worried about you' and the second, 'Do you think I have cancer?' Today I had a serving of both.

"When I turn my head, I go funny, it's as if I'm spinning. I'm afraid it might be a brain tumour." She paused. "Do you think it's cancer?"

Maman thinks cancer is the only disease that kills. That is why all her ills translate into it, and my reassurances don't usually provide relief for longer than a phone call.

"Have you spoken to Omid lately?" she asked.

"Yes, I have."

"I couldn't sleep last night. I was worried sick about him. I dreamt about Omid. I didn't want to say anything to you and make you worry too. Your Baba wanted to ring him, I said, 'Please don't. You won't find him and then I worry.' Do you think he's smoking hash again? Solmaz, I have only you. You're stronger than a man. Speak to him, tell him Maman is not well, tell him I've chest pain." Maman believes that as long as she was in Vienna keeping Omid under her surveillance, everything was safe. Since she found weed hidden in one of Omid's socks a couple of months ago, she worries he might be back on drugs.

"It still sends a shiver down my spine when I remember that incident." She means that night five years ago when we found Omid smashed and dopey at Karlsplatz tube station. I don't blame her. She is not alone in this horror.

"See, Maman. We are past the days of long hours in the bathroom, the red eyes, and the money that went missing; therefore, I think he's alright. Besides, I asked him, and he denies it. I choose to believe him."

"*Insha'Allah* - God willing. It's all in God's hands. Let's see what happens."

"Nothing will happen if we don't do anything. Nothing will change if we don't take control, but as I said he's okay."

"I pray to God you're right. Parents may be able to provide a good dwelling for their children, but not a good destiny. Say

Solmaz, do I need to see a doctor for my funny head?" And so it went on...

The talk with Maman called for an antidote. I took my mobile and texted. *I am good, thanks for asking.*

"You're funny." Fardin rang right away.

"Yep, I am."

"You were rude."

"Yep. Guilty as charged. I was not in a good shape that day. Sorry."

"To expect a beautiful girl to be funny and polite all the same is pushing it a bit, I suppose."

"Ah, this is the charm Rekha warned me about," I said.

And all was good again. We agreed to meet up soon.

Saturday, August 13, 2005

"Mine is with friend a sacred oath
For as long as I have a soul
Her devotee and temple both
As my own soul, I extol."

Peyman has inscribed Hafiz's poem on the card he gave me - a sort of response to my latest flare-up of 'I worry I might lose you'. It was his idea to have a pizza night. Peyman and I guzzled like two starved dogs, but once our stomachs were full we resembled two wild horses set loose, galloping into the past, racing for memories. He said he was missing Maman's cooking. Her *ghormeh sabzi* -herb stew - was his favourite.

"Do you remember that one time I made *ghormeh sabzi* for you?" I tested his memory.

"You mean how you bought it for me?"

"I could have gotten away with it if you hadn't spotted the takeaway boxes."

It was 1996. Peyman had failed his pathology exam when

he had suddenly gone blank during the oral. The professor had cocked his index finger and put it to Peyman's head.

"Would it help your memory if someone were holding a gun to your head?" he had asked. That remark hadn't amused Peyman at all. The whole incident had stirred up a series of flashbacks of his ordeals in Iran. 'The wasted generation' is what he and his friends in Vienna used to call themselves. Most of them were just like him, political refugees who felt their revolution had been hijacked by Mullahs and that they had been cheated of their future and their country.

'You give a penny to a Mullah, you won't ever get it back. How do you want then to reclaim a country from his hands?' We used to laugh at this post-revolutionary joke based on a Mullah's actual speech.

I was too young to be directly affected by the revolution, but for those Peyman's age the consequences were great. I remember how heartrending I found the story of his attempt to smuggle himself through Turkey and Greece in the baggage hold of a bus, the many times he had been caught and spent time in Greek prisons or was sent back to Turkey. He doesn't revisit that chapter of his life much. Neither does he often talk about the fatal car accident of his parents shortly after his arrival in Austria. Were it not for him, I wouldn't have possessed even the little political education I have now.

"Politics doesn't know any mother and father," Baba used to come out with this famous proverb to bicker with Peyman. He delighted in having a gentle son-in-law who would sit for hours, lending a pair of patient and interested ears to his rambling on Iranian politics. Most of their discussions were a repetitive mumbo jumbo. Occasionally Baba objected to a point just for the sake of livening up the conversation, and Peyman never tired of playing along. Peyman was more a son to my parents than a husband to me, probably because he needed a family more than a wife. On our first anniversary, he invited

Maman and Baba to join us at a romantic restaurant I had picked and proceeded advising Baba on his health issues and listening to Maman's gossip.

I still recall their devastated faces when, after three years of marriage, I announced our divorce. Maman literally begged me to stay with him.

"Life would become impossible to live, Solmaz, if everyone reasoned and weighed up things the way you do. You drill down through everything," she cried. "He is an orphan. Stay with him."

That Peyman and I could be the best of friends and still decide to part ways passed their comprehension. To Maman and Baba, as to many other Iranians - and for that matter non-Iranians - the only legitimate reasons for divorce are wife-beating, drugs or financial issues. The fact that we fought every other day, didn't laugh at the same jokes and seemed to speak entirely different languages though communicating in Farsi, didn't amount to much. It did to me. All those unhappy couples, my parents, uncles and aunts I have seen marooned in a cancerous marriage; all those who age together, but can't stand one another; all those who are lonely in their togetherness; I knew we would become like them. I let go of a husband in order to keep a friend.

Why doesn't anyone tell you that in marriage you get disappointed in yourself far more than in your partner?

Still, when I look to the past, I marvel at our innocence - an innocence that was not only determined, but also confident that we could make it work despite our differences.

In my early days as a doctor in the UK, we often wrote down 'exhaustion' as a cause of death on death certificates for very elderly people who gradually faded away. Similarly, our love affair died of exhaustion.

Nowadays, when I ask Peyman whether he is happy with Shirin, he says loudly, "VERY happy!" And I smile. A simple yes would have done it. I wish he could decode my smile.

Thursday, September 8, 2005

It's 7 a.m. - that means twenty-four hours on my feet without any sleep.

My gloved hands firmly pressing on the woman's abdomen; Edwin pulling out a mass; cord clamped, then cut; baby boy handed over to the paediatrician; suctioning blood; scooping uterus, placenta removed; swiftly stitching layer by layer and closing off the skin. Perfect.

"It's always a pleasure to be on-call with you," he said, and he looked at me, the tiniest hint of a smile on his lips, his gaze holding mine until I averted my eyes.

Edwin, the gorgeous Nigerian registrar - he is a gifted obstetrician and the darling of all the nurses and midwives. He doesn't have Belal's dreamy eyes, but he looks at me in the same bold way Belal did. I like the frankness and brazenness in his gaze. I don't understand why he displays his attraction that openly. Yesterday in the multi-disciplinary meeting, there were about twenty of us facing the screen for the Power Point presentation while bolting down our sandwiches when Edwin crept up on me from behind and planted a kiss on my cheek. After the meeting on my way out of the hall, one of the consultants turned to me and said mockingly, "It seems you've made good friends here."

Edwin is a married man; his flirtatious actions add to his charming and enigmatic aura, bolstering his charisma, whereas people would only think the worst of me. For instance, today, just before heading to the changing room, he shouted after me, "Hey, Dr Solmaz, I'll see you in doctors' mess for breakfast."

Tempting - but it wasn't meant to be. A message from Omid on my mobile took care of that: he wanted me to ring him back immediately. I obliged. Words gushed out of him. He rambled about how much he loved me, how sorry he was, all was well, nothing to worry about, and so on and so forth. As he raced from one irrelevancy to the next, I was struggling to tease out of him the reason for his urgent message. I finally butted in. He has lost his job.

"That chap at work had it in for me. The bastard kept picking on me and got me fired." There was no strength in me to question the story he was weaving about yet another layoff. I let him air his anger. He sounded nervous and embarrassed.

"It's okay. We'll figure out something," I said, in an attempt to console him.

His voice changed. It was not agitated anymore, but subdued. He needed money to pay the bills before Maman and Baba return to Vienna this Saturday. I promised to send him money after my shift.

"I'll pay ya back soon, sis. Don't tell Maman and Baba. I got an interview for a receptionist post at a student hostel soon."

He has pinned all his hopes on this one interview, which would mean a physically less demanding post than his previous jobs. As a dropout with no particular training, his job prospects have been so far in construction, removal companies and petrol stations.

"I'm at work now. I'll call you back tonight."

Our phone call ended in much the same way it started, with a whirl of 'thanks *gherty'* and 'love ya, big sis', a ritual that serves to conceal his shame and remorse, just like his talkativeness and self-deprecating laughter. For someone who has for most of his life depended on others for everything, it's surprising that he has never become accustomed to it. Helplessness and dependency remain unnatural to him. Yet, they have taken their toll on his body. He has shrunk over the years. He used to be much taller than me; tall and strongly-built. Nowadays, he works out on a regular basis and has managed to build up muscles again, but he seems physically broken, like someone who has battled a long illness and failed to regain his previous physique. I didn't know drugs could bring about such irreparable damage. The realisation hit me two years ago, when I ran to Vienna after, in retrospect, his last relapse. He was on a hospital bed, his eyes old and hollow, his cheeks sunken and his head bald, so frail and skinny that the veins on his abdomen were visible. His broken jaw was in wires, allowing his mouth to open only wide enough for cigarettes and a straw for fluids. He had been beaten up.

That night it hit me. I realised that my baby brother from the years in Tehran was gone; that night I grieved the loss of the Omid I knew.

Still, a picture of him from a distant past endures in my memories. 1984 re-emerges, with Iraqi planes cruising the skies over Tehran; our house immersed in darkness. As soon as the air raid sirens went off we rushed to the basement, which had turned into our second home, fully equipped with candles, snacks, drinks and blankets. Maman lit the candles. The droning of the bombers and the ear-splitting noise of the explosions somewhere in the city still reached us there. Maman was muttering some prayers in Arabic while Baba, smoking one cigarette after another, had his ears glued to his radio, waiting for the all-clear signal. Omid was calm. He was not afraid. Why should he have been? He had Naneh's amulet around his neck, protecting him from any ill whatsoever. Naneh had scribbled *ayatul korsi* - Quranic verses - on a piece of paper and put it in a small pouch, making a special talisman for him.

I clearly see Omid squatting on the floor, the tip of his tongue running over his lips, entirely focused on the sketch he was drawing. His thick black hair cast a shadow on his cheeky face and handsome innocence. Even at the age of five, Omid could easily draw pictures of anyone he met. My favourites were his caricature drawings of Baba and Amu Hamid. Baba tolerated his 'hobby', but never approved of it. Once, in anger, he took Omid's drawing book and ripped out all of his paintings.

"Artists eventually end up penniless and addicts," he yelled. Omid didn't shed a single tear. In fact, I have never seen him cry.

The twenty-four hour on-call is taking its toll. There is a spinning wheel in my head - Maman, Omid, Edwin, Peyman, Belal, it spins... Maman, Omid, Belal, my head goes on spinning, Belal, Belal... During the caesarean section, I caught my thoughts constantly travelling out to him. What was really behind that serene coolness, those brown eyes, that bold smile? Nothing? Belal and his world - they both promise somewhere that is not here, that is not my past. By their otherness, just for the merit of their otherness, they make me dream of another life, another future.

Friday, September 30, 2005

Tonight I dragged Fardin to my favourite night spot in Angel - the 'Round Midnight Blues and Jazz Bar'. It was packed as expected. A couple was about to leave and waved us to their table.

"Ah, we are lucky. Come on," I said, and we slipped into their empty seats.

"Where is your handbag?" Fardin looked concerned. He must have thought of loss or theft.

"I don't have one." Pointing to the pockets of my jacket, I demonstrated that it was large enough for my purse, mobile, and even some tissues.

"I see. It is only ladylike to carry a bag."

"Is that a violation of rules? Have I now fallen into discredit?" I joked.

"Ready to order?" Fardin was clearly infuriated, but held back. That propelled me into a 'dare-you' mood.

"Let me show you a trick I learned from my granny." I

grabbed his handkerchief, turned and twisted it until I had made a mouse, then holding it between my palms I ordered, "Jump, jump, little mouse," and sure enough, the mouse leapt forward.

"Impressed?"

"Very much." His tone was cold.

At least the waitress who was now standing at our table giggled.

"We'll have the specials tonight," he said.

Overcome by an urge to tease him even more, when no one was watching I stuck a straw into each of my nostrils and gave him a huge grin. For a fraction of a second Fardin gaped at me, but then he forced his face into a quick smile, acknowledging my joke before snatching the straws from my hands.

After dinner, we reconciled by engaging in a more amicable social activity: talking about sex. Sex seems to be a big theme in his life; he owns up to having a casual sex-partnership, conveniently with one of his nurses. He also boasted about his conquests in Iran and prided himself on mastering all sorts of tricks to seduce every woman he set his eyes on. By his own admission, among them were married and older women, as well as the so-called decent Muslim girls in hijab. This piece of news did not come as a shock to me. It is merely a confirmation of what I already know, namely that many Iranian women opt for operations before their marriage to restore their virginity. Rekha once shared with me a well-kept secret among Hindu girls: a bride merely needs to get the groom drunk, and he won't notice that she's not a virgin on the wedding night. I guess it is only the West that is fooled by the black hijab or colourful saris.

"How many women would you reckon you've slept with?"

"I don't keep score."

"Is my name on your list too?" It was only the next logical question to ask.

He fixed my gaze with a twisted smile and waved at the waitress, "The bill, please!"

"Ah, not giving too much away too soon?"

"Absolutely."

"I wouldn't hold my breath."

"Not for the world."

That closed the conversation.

He has trouble written all over him. The old me wouldn't have gone anywhere near him, but this one does. I am experimenting, reinventing new ways of being Solmaz, one who is not so damn serious; one who is capable of letting her hair down and having fun.

Wednesday, October 19, 2005

After four long days of silence, I had an email from Belal in my inbox today.

Sorry, I couldn't email you earlier. Firstly, I was busy; secondly, I was busy, and thirdly, I was busy. Please forgive me...

Some businessmen from the Netherlands were the reason for his busyness. *When I had to give a lift to the daughter of one of them I remembered you. It appears to be my fate to chauffeur beautiful women,* his email read. *I don't even know why I'm telling you this.*

Good question - why? I didn't like the comparison at all. He went on asking about my application to International Medical Charity. I haven't let on yet that I've requested IMC to swap my preferred place of work to Dhaka. I keep it a surprise. No news from them yet.

Waiting, waiting, and waiting some more.

Meanwhile Fardin seems to be a good distraction. Last night he demonstrated his culinary skills once more by making a delicious tortellini, but for a change he left the dinner plates on the table afterwards, dimmed the lights and came to lie on the couch with me wrapped in his arms. Diana Krall's vocals and vanilla-scented candles, together with his fingers endlessly twiddling with a lock of my hair and letting it fall again, lulled my senses. We didn't speak. I am not sure where his mind was. I know, however, what crossed my mind when I lifted my head from his chest and looked at his thin lips, 'I am thirty and I've never kissed any other man but Peyman. I wonder how his kisses feel.'

The thought created a ripple of excitement in my body. Why not? Who says it is wrong? It is just a kiss. A wave of compulsion broke over me. Then another thought struck me. Why should I wait for his move? Why should he be in charge? There was no reason for him to be holding all the cards in this game.

Without further ado, I drew my lips closer to his. He jerked back, his brown pupils dilated. I made another attempt. Fardin cocked his head away from me.

"Okay, if you don't want to." I pulled back. Just at that moment he grabbed the back of my neck with both hands and drew me to his lips. We kissed.

"How was it?" Fardin asked.

"Not bad," I said. "It's better, though, when you're in love."

Fardin's face didn't change at my response. Not having the slightest interest in figuring him out, I revelled in my own answer and the detached tone with which I had delivered it. I have played him at his own game.

Tuesday, October 25, 2005

Getting an outside call in the hospital can portend many things: a new admission, a GP bombarding you with queries, a community midwife in need of advice or a radiographer or lab technician who is geared up to find a flaw in your request - none of them pleasant. But not today. It was Fardin's voice on the phone - very much unlike him to bleep me at work.

"I got my results," he said with a sigh. "I failed."

He was talking about the second part of his membership exam. Officially, any doctor's future career as a consultant hinges on getting college membership, and unofficially, it seals one's respect and esteem in the medical community.

"I've never failed at anything before. How am I supposed to tell my parents?"

This was a serious setback to him. Uncertain of what to say, I suggested he came to my place. He is on-call tonight, so we deferred our meeting until Saturday.

How distant our two worlds are! Fardin's father is a consultant in one of Tehran's prestigious hospitals. His people are schooled and accomplished, whereas I am the only college graduate amidst a large middle class family who are either illiterate or have a secondary education at most. Just imagine the contrast between his family of doctors and academics and mine. On my last summer holiday in Iran, age fifteen or so, I presented a drawing of mine to a group of aunts and uncles. The picture depicted a lonely wanderer standing at a crossroad, in front of her paths of dark and light. When I explained it to them, the women stared at me and the men laughed. One uncle said, "You read too much, Solmaz. See, I have good eyes at this old age because I've never read."

Fardin doesn't know anything about my family. He doesn't know about Omid's past or Baba's history of gambling. Baba was not shrewd enough for the emotional and mental challenges of a foreign country; he didn't bargain on being a helpless foreigner, depending on other people for his voice. Luckily, there were other Iranians like him, men who suddenly felt redundant and superfluous, spending their days hooked on BBC Persian while gulping down strong tea and smoking hash - until they were introduced to a new remedy: Casino.

Vienna's Casinos embraced this bunch of migrants, handing them the chips without demanding any linguistic skills. Omid and I would watch Baba and Maman sprucing up; Maman touching up the make-up she always puts on first thing in the morning, slipping into black skirts and elegant blouses, the matching shoes and handbags a must, just like the small scarf and long jacket she wears - the first to conceal the lines on her neck, the latter to hide her wide hips. Baba would be clean-shaven and in a suit and tie, their perfumes filling the living room, where Baba would puff on one last cigarette before they headed to the casino, often returning after midnight.

"It makes me forget myself for a few hours," was Maman's excuse. A few hours of oblivion that came at a very high cost. As the years rolled on, money started to dwindle, which meant that Baba moved back and forth between Austria and Iran, spending less and less time in Vienna.

Fardin doesn't know any of this. And it shall stay that way for now.

Sunday, October 30, 2005

Today I acted cool - just like a man.

Fardin spent the night here at my flat. We ate, cuddled up, watched a movie and kissed. This time I did enjoy it. I like the firm grip of his hands at the nape of my neck. He wants me, but there is no overt force, only sheer intent, implicit in what he wants - a truly seasoned kisser.

"Is that where you are planning to put me up tonight?" he pointed to the sofa in the living room.

"No. We share the bed. You on the right side and me on the left."

Snuggling down in bed, we had a tete-a-tete about our ideal partners. He declared in a rather self-evident tone that she had to be a virgin.

Was that guy for real? It was the last thing I wanted to hear from a guy lying next to me. I looked at him in disbelief.

"Why is her chastity at the top of your list? I propped myself up on my elbow. "Humour me."

"I don't want another man to have touched my wife."

Whoa! I was boiling inside that he didn't even make a pretence for the sake of our delicate context. I let the night pass peacefully. He had just failed his exam. Rolling away from him to the furthest edge of the bed, I turned my back to him and said good night.

I closed my eyes, only to see inside my head the smirking face of a distant cousin from my childhood. Maman and I had stopped off at Baba's and Amu's factory in central Tehran, and he had come to the office to have tea with us. Pointing at two new girls in the office at the sewing machine, Maman had suggested that he took one of them as his bride. He had jumped on her comment with an 'oh, just watch' as though he had been waiting for his chance to open the eyes of all those naive and ignorant folks, the ones like Maman. He called over one of the girls and requested she sat next to him. Then while talking he put his hand on her lap, without any objection from her. After she left, he turned to Maman with a grin.

"They are loose, these girls."

'Don't run fast, girl', 'Girls shouldn't cycle', 'Solmaz, my mummy says girls shouldn't jump' - the rationale behind all those don'ts eluded the sports enthusiast in me. I was a child of eight or nine at that time. 'It's not good for you' was the only response to my constant 'why?'. Somehow, someday I figured out, as children often instinctively do, that those measures were in protection of my precious hymen.

Those memories were only intensified by Fardin's deep breathing. Unperturbed by our earlier discussion, he had fallen asleep.

This morning over breakfast he revealed that it was the very first time for him to have spent a night in the same bed as a woman without having sex with her.

"I don't just kiss and cuddle a girl for weeks on end without anything else. It is regressive."

I was unsure whether I should take offence. Did he mean I was 'regressive'?

On his way to work he threw a cursory glance at the old chairs crammed onto my balcony.

"Next time I come, I'll tidy up that mess for you."

As soon as Fardin was gone, our breakfast plates still on the table, Edwin rang the doorbell. I remembered he wanted to pop in to collect our audit notes. I ushered him in while I searched for the notes.

"See, that is how I like you. Not the talking and philosophising you sometimes do, but these ones here."

I turned around to see him gesture to the three pictures on the wall, my favourite snapshots from my voluntary work in Bangladesh.

"One afternoon with you in bed," he proposed matter-of-factly.

"I am flattered, but no." I was really flattered. I have never had that attractive a man making advances.

"It'd be utterly innocent. We'd be naked without having sex."

I shook my head no.

"I find you intriguing."

"You are married," I jogged his memory.

"Do you know what 'intriguing' means?"

I knew.

"Don't get me wrong. I love my wife. She is the one for me." He took my hand and placed a kiss on it. "Good things come to those who wait," he added on his way out.

One man out and the other in.

I could have been the female clone of Tony Curtis in *Boeing, Boeing,* where he is a womaniser, juggling three beautiful stewardesses at once. I suppose the only difference is that I didn't have sex with either of these men. Had I slept with them, I'd, in all probability, feel a slut as opposed to a smart player having fun in life.

I wish I could have just sex with no strings attached. I can't. I would feel exposed and judged unless love was involved. And yet, it was the hottest twenty-four hours in my life. My flat is nothing less than a volcano. If there was a prize for chastity and another one for stupidity, I would snatch both just like that.

Later, lying in the lavender-scented bath, I realised how alone I feel when it comes to sex. When was I ever taught anything about sex? What do I know about it? What I know are just the hushes and giggles of Maman and my aunts. What I remember is how my body was shamed into a secret life. Many months into my first periods, I was still washing off blood from my pants instead of wearing a pad. I remember wrapping a large scarf tightly around my chest to stop it from bursting into breasts, believing if I persevered I would outwit nature - as if by defeating the messengers I could dispel the curse of the feminine. But my body had a mind of its own.

On the other hand, my cousin's breasts received an altogether different treatment from me. My cousin Nasrin was just six months older than me, but somehow all her body parts seemed to be growing exponentially while I was still running around in the body of a nine-year-old girl. One day when we were having a bath together - we often did at that age - she encouraged me and my younger cousin to touch her breasts. They felt small, firm and smooth under my hands. I was petrified at the sudden rush of heat through my body. Another similar experience that has stuck with me occurred in my German language class at the age of eleven in Vienna. Masood, not much older than me, leaned over my shoulder to point to a page in my book. My whole body heated up, and my face went as red as chilli pepper.

No, I didn't outwit nature.

I am hungry for love. My body aches for the tender caresses of a man's hands, my lips thirst for his, my breasts yearn for his kisses. I desire that split second, that moment I feel the warmth of another skin about to touch mine; that moment our lips are apart, yet close enough to inhale the breath exhaled by the other. And I long for the liberation that follows, finally the weight of another body on mine, the kiss, and the penetration.

But my heart protests - my heart wants the heart of a lover. My body is a rebellious teenager and my heart a hopeless romantic. One wants to seize the moment and the other is on vigil.

Sunday, November 13, 2005

"I do not know what will become after my death.
I do not want to know what the potter will make from the dust of my body.
But I am so hopeful that he makes a whistle from my neck
In the hands of a mischievous child
With one steady blow after another,
His best and loudest.
The sleep of the dead is awakened,
And in this way I may break the quiet of my passing..."

These words of Shariati are pinned to the wall next to his picture over my desk. Lying on my bed, I find my eyes travelling to them. I feel inadequate. I don't make heads or tails of myself anymore. There is Fardin, who has sneaked his way into my life and become a permanent actor. Then there is Belal, whose emails instil warmth and quirkiness into my daily grind.

And me???

I often catch myself daydreaming about Belal, picturing

myself folded in his arms - then a sense of guilt engulfs me. He is a married man.

And Fardin - is he falling for me?

I should get up and do something useful. But what?

"Shame on you." Shariati's eyes peer into mine.

What do you expect from me? To save the world? I just don't know where to start. What on earth am I supposed to do?

Earlier I drew the curtains open and peeked out of the window, then immediately pulled them closed. A part of me wants to leap out of bed and venture into the world, but the other part only wants to cloister herself away.

This restlessness, this chaotic jumble of feelings, the onslaught of clashing thoughts and swinging moods resemble an ambush of meteors in the darkness of my soul. I strain my eyes to see what they are shining on; alas, before I can know anything, they die away, as shooting stars do, and I am left again, blundering around in the dark.

Some part of me has gone astray. There is a self far away, on a misty road, alone, waiting for me; my soul has, sometime, somewhere, stayed behind, and my body kept running to nowhere.

Wednesday, November 30, 2005

So, Dhaka it is.

I received a call at work today. A lady with an American accent was on the line.

"Hello. This is Janine from International Medical Charity."

My heart missed a beat at the mention of IMC. With bated breath, I listened. Janine proceeded to refer to my application and asked if I would be willing to start earlier than the date specified on the form. Another doctor had pulled out at the last minute and they required somebody to fill in for him in two months' time.

"As it happens to be in Dhaka, we were hoping you could step in."

I gasped.

"Would this be feasible for you?"

So, Dhaka it is.

For the first time in my life, I shed tears of joy. I don't remember when I was last that happy. I had an hour to go before I could leave the hospital. I carried on with my duties and let the news sink in, savouring it without letting anything spoil it, not even that ill-tempered patient who threatened to make a formal complaint because she had to wait 'ages' for her discharge letter.

Today nothing can upset me.

As soon as I handed over the patients and the on-call pager, I fished out my mobile and sent Belal a text message. I wanted him to be the first to hear my good news.

Before long my mobile droned: *Gulab jammun is on me.*

Saturday, December 17, 2005

No amount of work or study stretches far enough to offset the dull December evenings.

Not much is happening. With the deadline of her exams looming, Rekha has flung herself into studying, and I only get to see Peyman at the hospital canteen: brief meetings - our 'news-in-brief-at-six friendship'. Fardin has just come back from his twice yearly visits to Tehran. Judging from his overjoyed voice on the phone, he has had a good time. He has decided to buy a house in London, a place somewhere green, but not too far from the city.

The highlight of my days has become seeing Belal's name in my inbox, be it on my mobile or computer. I write to him of various things - the events in my life and my own observations

71

and analyses of them. He makes sure each of them gets a comment, mostly just a short remark but nevertheless kind and caring. Hardly ever does he say anything about himself. From what I read between the lines, he must be very busy. All the more reason for appreciating the fact that he frees up time to answer my emails.

Yesterday, I hit on an idea of how to learn more about him; I designed a survey about his likes and dislikes - how clever of me! This morning I received his monosyllabic reply.

What colour do you like most? *Azure blue.*

What book don't you get tired of reading? *Tagore's poems.*

What is your favourite animal? *Manimal.*

A man of few words. The longest answer was to the question: Your best virtue? *Patience. Good things come to those who wait* - The exact phrase Edwin had used when he came to my flat.

What would you take to a lonely island? *You.*

Thursday, December 22, 2005

Rekha bore resemblance to a runaway cast member from the set of 'Sex and the City', her full breasts almost popping out of her tight-fitting purple dress. Her outfit reminded me of Naneh Homa's words: 'It is the duty of a Muslim to care for her body, to respect and cherish it, otherwise our bodies will complain to Allah in the afterlife.' Imagine a cluster of breasts, feet, ears, floating in the air, yelling and recounting their tales of distress and abuse on earth!

I was in a light mood, mainly because everything went smoothly at the Bangladeshi embassy today. Having the whole day off, I was not the slightest bit disconcerted when I was asked for more documents and needed to go to print out the emails from IMC in support of my application. The flight is booked with Emirates. All under control. I was so happy that I could have kissed every single passenger in the tube. They were all beautiful.

Rekha's high heels clinked on the pavement as we ambled to the Café Valerie in Marylebone High Street to celebrate the completion of her exams. She had brought along a friend, an Indian girl around her age who, in contrast to Rekha, was modestly dressed. The first thing she said, when she heard that I was an Iranian, was, "Are you divorced?"

I asked whether Rekha had told her so.

"No. My brother-in-law used to date an Iranian girl." She said that he had seen her on and off for a year, but in the end he broke up with her. "He thought Iranian women were not wife material. Eventually they get divorced."

Later, she - her name escapes me - imparted her own love story with a Muslim guy. The outcome of their affair was only to be expected: they broke up as both sets of parents disapproved. The interesting part was when she looked at Rekha and me, adding, "You know what I mean," as a sort of affirmation of her decision. "What do your parents say about you being still in contact with your ex-husband?"

I recounted my condensed version of how Maman and Baba had problems with it at first, but Peyman and I got our own way as we just persevered longer than them. "You know what I mean?"

No, I could see on their faces that none of us knew what the other meant.

It was an awkward moment, but not the last one. Next Rekha made a splash by announcing that her family has started looking for a suitable match for her. That came as a surprise to me. Rekha has always seemed too modern in her outlook to follow traditions. Besides, I believed her to be a romantic girl. I don't know why I thought that. Maybe because she is always perky or maybe because of the *Asian Bride* magazines she keeps on her bedside table. She is such a paradox. When you speak with her, she possesses an enormous intellectual insight into the complexity of the human psyche - but when it comes to living her life, making her daily choices, she tucks them away. They are good for dinner table talks, but somehow they don't mesh into the fabric of her life.

Love is practical for me too. I have a self-invented test to weed out temporary passion from enduring love: make love, not protected by the darkness of night but exposed by the sun in the middle of a hot and bright day, and do it with open eyes. I'd have patented this if Elvis hadn't beaten me to it: *Too many moonlit kisses seem to fade in the warmth of the sun.*

Love is practical for me, but as it turns out not as practical as for Rekha.

"I can't get my head around why people have relationships with no future," she said, as the two of us walked back to Warren Street. "If you are a Hindu and he is a Muslim, why start something in the first place? That is a sure recipe for heartache."

When I reverted to her news about getting serious about marriage, she said, "It would make my parents very happy. Besides, I am twenty-eight years old, already a spinster by Bangladeshi standards." And she concluded with, "You know what I mean."

A wave of gratitude washed over me. I've always had plenty to criticise about Baba and Maman. I never credited them with liberalism. Marriage was never high on their agenda for me - education was, especially for Maman.

Baba never meddled in my life, never questioned me about my decisions. The most he did was demonstrate his disapproval of Peyman's visits to our house and our continued friendship after our divorce - not with harsh words, but in his own subtle way. I remember what happened whenever Peyman would enter the room and greet Baba. Without any hint that he was taking in the happenings around him, Baba would keep his gaze fixed on the TV screen until Peyman was literally standing in front of him, shouting a loud *salaam*. Then Baba would lift his eyes and put on a surprised face.

"Eh, *Agha*, you are here? When did you come in?"

He does respect me. I feel that. Not that Baba values women. He calls them 'womenfolk'. None of them is trustworthy, except his own mother. He has never been faithful to Maman. Somehow I despised both of them for it: Baba for the pain he caused Maman and Maman for her meekness, which she called a virtue. Khaleh Laleh always consoled Maman with the words, "A man is a good husband as long as he is not a wife-beater and brings money home."

'To men wrongdoings, to women forgiveness,' as a Persian saying goes.

I actually don't know Baba at all. I never understood why he asked people who were going to Tehran whether they could take stuff for him, even though he didn't have anything to send. "Let's see what they say," he said.

Or when we'd go to see his lung specialist in Vienna - I was his interpreter; Baba and Maman never learned much German - Baba, who had just smoked a cigarette outside the clinic, would say, "Tell him I have halved my cigarettes." In reply to my protest, he would answer, "Let's see what the doctor says."

Baba is a mystery to me. He is as much a mystery as Belal. You know what I mean?

Friday, December 23, 2005

Our afternoon started off on a promising note. Fardin picked me up at the library and, since the rain had set in, hailed a cab to Covent Garden.

"A tall latte, extra hot and wet in a paper cup, isn't it?"

Fardin sought my approval while placing himself before me at the counter in Starbucks. The warmth in his eyes prompted me to smile. When we sat down, he pulled out a book from his bag and placed it in front of me. He had brought me a diary with Shariati's quotes and pictures from Iran. I was touched, especially because at best he was indifferent towards Shariati.

His gallant gestures were enough to wipe the slate clean, I thought. He was also remarkably talkative. He found the idea of having his own place in London exhilarating.

At that time, I didn't foresee that I'd leave him at the end of the day wondering whether I'd be better off alone on my weekends. The first indication of it came when he was telling me of his house viewings. He was 'appalled' by the condition of some of the houses: messy, with peeling paint, mould, and holes in the walls.

"The Indians and their reeking curry spices." He shook his head in disbelief and disgust. "Do those people know what airing is?"

"Come on. Their food is tasty," was all I could utter in defence.

"Why don't you come along with me on my next viewing and see it for yourself. They are downright dirty."

Things only spiralled downwards thereafter.

Fardin had made a reservation at a French restaurant with live music. A female singer was on the stage - her voice charming, but slightly high for an intelligible conversation. To be heard, I had to raise my voice. I was in the middle of playing back my evening with Rekha and her friend when a lady from the neighbouring table shushed me silent. Fardin squirmed in his chair, turned to her and, with a bow of his head, apologised.

I felt embarrassed, not so much for having been chided than for the company who felt embarrassed because of me. When the singer took a break, Fardin, who had kept quiet so far, turned to me.

"I doubt it is wise to drop everything, hand in your notice midway through your training and pack up for Bangladesh. It will be difficult to get back onto a training scheme when you return after a three year break."

"It isn't a break. I'll be working."

"Still, career wise it is a setback," he said. "Rekha is right. You are a romantic. Look at you and me. Time is ticking away and we are both single, have no family, no house, no permanent posts, not settled - we are failures." Fardin leaned back on his chair and stared into space.

Failure? To my mind, he was admiring and respecting me for my choice... What a fool I have been.

Monday, January 9, 2006

In retrospect, I can identify a theme for my last couple of weeks: marriage and family.

Today, in the family planning clinic, Edwin and I reviewed a Pakistani woman with a coil and recurrent infections. She reported that her husband 'fooled around' and also had a second wife in Pakistan, hence the infections. She pointed out she didn't have any other choice: she had five children and also a couple of terminations in the past. A coil was the best option in her mind, for her husband wouldn't use condoms.

"He is a chef, and some nights when he comes home late and is really pissed. He wakes me up and wants sex. If I say no, he threatens to go to a prossie."

"Such a pig," I said later.

"I agree." I was glad Edwin felt the same. I was about to compliment him on that when he added, "A man should know where to draw the line. She doesn't need to know."

"Oh, that is the line?"

"And for God's sake use condoms," he continued.

Before I could say anything, the nurse came in with a Somali patient. Her complaint was pain during intercourse. "Especially when I am on top," she stressed. When she was gone, Edwin turned to me.

"Did you hear how emancipated she is?" A big smile spread across his face. "She goes on top."

"Whoa, what a consolation! Being or not being on top - is this really your definition of emancipation?"

"Solmaz, are you sexually frustrated?" His eyes were boring into me.

"Why are you making it about my sexual life? Is sexual freedom the sole conquest of feminism? Is this all Western feminists have to show for themselves? The only alternative they can propose to the 'poor' veiled Muslim woman?"

"Don't drag me into an argument. You are not veiled, Solmaz." Edwin shifted on his chair, drawing nearer. "And you need a man." His aftershave wafted into my nostrils. "All work and no play..."

At that very instant, I received a call from Fardin. Edwin slid back and hovered over the notes, scribbling while I answered my mobile. When I was done, he turned to me.

"I don't want to muck up a serious relationship for you."

I immediately corrected him: no, I was not dating.

"Then what are you and this chap to each other?"

What are Fardin and I?

Fardin is for me what casino was for my parents: distraction. Every time I feel I have made a breakthrough with him, every time I think we have come closer, or at least that I know where I stand with him and what I am dealing with, he proves me wrong. Like the casino, he makes me win but then claims back even more. So I end up going back, thinking that this time it will be The Time.

'Too bitter to swallow, too sweet to spit out,' that's Maman's perception of her children - Omid and me.

What are Fardin and I to each other?

When I dialled Peyman's number today, it was to bat around all these things with him. Shirin picked up. Peyman was out.

Should I open up to Shirin? She is a woman after all and will understand. I battled with myself. This could even be the ice-breaker I've been waiting for. I started telling her about Fardin and the hot and cold game our relationship has turned into.

"...a nice guy, always polite with good manners..." My words must have struck a chord with her as she butted in.

"Solmaz, it is really easy to catch a man."

What followed threw me completely: she imparted her wisdom on how a woman could optimise her chances.

"First, it is fundamental to establish which field you are playing in."

In her opinion, I've been behaving naïvely so far. Fardin is an intelligent and experienced man, so 'other variables underscore this relationship' - she sounded rather like a social scientist.

"Being an Iranian man, he is attuned to being looked after and being cared for," she set me straight. "He's not like a European man who can be easily won over by simple acts of kindness and pampering, by a good meal and a well set table..." She kept on jabbering, but I had stopped listening to her.

A ripple of fear was mounting inside me, dissolving my own issues. Instead I was anxious for Peyman. From the beginning, Peyman has been making allowances for Shirin, arguing that she is an Iranian woman brought up in Iran and thus accustomed to that culture and mentality. Today she did not sound like the helpless woman who is reliant on Peyman for everything under the sun.

Thursday, February 9, 2006

Either don't befriend a mahout or build a house the size of an elephant, reads the proverb Peyman just sent me. His text message is referring to our conversation last night. We were on-call together, and I was secretly hoping that it'd be quiet and we could say our goodbyes. Somewhere after midnight, we each finished our last rounds and sneaked into the doctors' mess. I made us coffee while he got us two Mars bars from the vending machine. The sink in the doctors' mess was stacked with dirty cups and plates. There was not a single clean mug in the cupboards either. I needed to dig deep into the sink and fish for mugs to wash for our coffee. Then I cleared away the heap of yesterday's newspapers from the large brown sofa so we could plonk ourselves down there, side by side.

"Can I pick your brain or are you too tired?" I asked.

"Fire away." Peyman's hazelnut eyes, now bloodshot, stared at me from behind his John Lennon glasses.

For the umpteenth time he listened to me harping on about my forthcoming trip and my misgivings that I don't have anything to fall back on if Bangladesh doesn't work out.

"I had to break into my savings. I mean, I was just starting to settle in in London and get a sense of security knowing that I had a placement in a teaching hospital. Am I being stupid? Am I a romantic?" I didn't tell him about Fardin's comment, to spare myself the embarrassment and Peyman the anger.

"I would formulate it differently. It is a matter of 'how many *tomans* - Iranian currency - are you with us?'"

"What?"

"Our team leader in Mujahedeen used to ask us that. In other words, 'How far will you go for us?' or 'How much are you ready to sacrifice for the cause?'"

Slogans and poems run in his blood; the latter because he is Iranian and the former, I suppose, is either a personal characteristic of his or a generational feature of those actively implicated in the 1979 revolution - there were many slogans flying around at that time. Old habits die hard.

"You are the romantic one," I said.

"So it appears." He took off his glasses to clean them. "You have had your vaccinations?"

"Yep."

"Are you sure you don't want me to drive you up to the storage?"

"No, Fardin is taking care of that. There is not much anyway, mainly books, then my bed sheets and blankets and some cutlery."

"What will you do with Fardin?"

"What do you mean? We are only friends."

"If you say so." He lay down on sofa and put his head on my lap. "You'll let me know whenever you need money or help with anything else. I can pitch in."

"I'll be fine. But maybe you could give my parents and Omid a ring now and then and check on them. Peyman, say, am I wasting my life?"

"Of course not." He closed his eyes and murmured, "Not as long as you know your 'why'. You can wander around the world if you know your centre. The whirling dervishes can do the whirling because they know the why and they know the where, their home, the centre."

Friday, February 10, 2006

What a day! Fardin and I had our first proper argument. One moment he was nothing but charm, and the next moment he couldn't stand the sight of me.

First thing in the morning, I rang Maman and Baba in Vienna.

"Don't forget the moth repellents. The silk shirt I bought you last year is very expensive; and that porcelain bowl is antique, wrap it in bubble paper." This was Maman's goodbye.

"You know best what is right for you, my daughter," was Baba's farewell. "Take care. By the way, make some enquiry into their fabrics. Maybe Amu and I can make some business there."

Omid's was, "Hi *gherty*, how are ya? Can't speak long, gotta go to work. I hope you'll be doing more than fine, big sis. Love ya and miss ya more."

After this rather bizarre goodbye with my family, Fardin came to move my boxes to the storage. He gave me perfume as a goodbye gift.

"It is advertised by Katherine Zeta Jones,' he said. "Her elegance reminds me of you."

All was still good in Leicester Square, where we stopped for a late breakfast, after which he smooth-talked me into shopping with him.

We edged our way through the crowd to Regent Street, where Fardin right away stormed into the Hugo Boss store. I hung around as he sized up each item carefully before moving on to the next one. Something important - God knows what - hinged on him picking the cream of the crop.

My mobile's buzzing was timely.

Hi. Just came out of a meeting to have a cigarette. You okay? Belal had texted.

Hey, long time no hear. How are you?

I thought you were busy with your new friend and wouldn't notice anyway.

I was trying to come up with a witty reply when Fardin called me over.

"What do you think of this one?"

Looking at him standing in front of the mirror, holding a blue shirt and scanning his reflection, was off-putting.

I do like men looking nice and elegant, but it should come effortlessly to them, like the magician who brings a rabbit out of his hat with a simple 'ta-da'. I don't remember Peyman caring so much about shopping, neither does Baba. And Omid, well, he can pull off anything.

On our way out of the shop, still puzzling about a reply to Belal, I heard Fardin mumbling, "These Arab dickheads." He jostled through a group of veiled women with Harrods shopping bags in their hands. Embarrassed, I smiled at one of them, who uttered a faint sorry for her bag's banging against my leg.

"What was that again?" I asked.

"Those illiterate morons gall me."

"You Iranians can be such racists."

"Pardon me?" Fardin came to a standstill. "*We Iranians*? Do you care to explain?"

"You are so damn aware of rights and wrongs, like in that French restaurant: you were concerned what others think - others meaning civilised Westerners. You think you are better than Arabs, Indians and any other dark-coloured *primitive* people. That is so typical of you Iranians, needing constantly to prove your equality - if not superiority - to the people in the West. In case you haven't noticed it yet: the West accepts and values only its own."

I could see the heat rising in Fardin's face. He seemed frozen to the spot, but I was in full swing.

"Admit it, it is an Iranian-specific complex, a mix of arrogance and shame. Arrogant and superior because of our past great civilisation, and inferior to the West because of our present failings. For Iranians, it's all about designer clothes, crystal chandeliers, delicate chinaware, eighteen carat gold…"

"You are the one with the inferiority complex," he struck back. "Do-gooders like you need miserable people because going to their rescue makes you feel good about yourselves.

What is more, you have utterly outmoded views. Revering Shariati? He is dead, and absolutely obsolete in today's Iran. He doesn't matter. We now have many other visionary intellectuals far more sophisticated and politically literate than he ever was. Take a good look at reality. The world has moved on and so has Iran, but you are stuck in a bubble of your own making. You are totally out of step with what is going on." Just when I thought it was over, he added, "You are just a *jujeh*. Only a *jujeh*!"

Jujeh. Green, wet behind the ears, like a young hen.

I was struck dumb.

This was pretty much the end of our day. The Sunday evening had barely started to display its full glory when, having had made mincemeat of one another, we sped wordlessly towards the tube station.

"I'd better go home," I said the minute we reached Piccadilly Circus, and I walked off. I was wishing for the shelter of the earlier rain, but instead it was clear. The English sky was swaying to an opposite rhythm from my mood.

Saturday, February 11, 2006

My plane is about to take off. I have a bad migraine.

With all my stuff gone into store boxes, my flat had assumed the appearance of a box too, lifeless and practical. I made sure the landlord's cutlery was returned to the cupboards, took one of his mugs for my last coffee - even that tasted cold and distant; then I locked the door and, as planned, left the key with the manager at the Turkish restaurant downstairs.

As I was stretching out in the passengers' lounge and looking out at the clusters of light on the runway, I came to a long overdue decision. I moved to a quiet corner by the toilets and switched on my mobile.

"I think we should cease contact," I said. I waited for his reaction. There was no sound so I continued with my reasoning, "I can't kiss a man in a casual way and spend time with him without eventually falling for him, and, truth be told, I don't want to fall for you. We are so different." I came to a halt, waiting, hoping, to hear his protest.

"Okay, if that's what you want," Fardin replied without hesitation. There was no regret or any other sentiment attached to those few words. It hurt.

No more playing with fire.

DREAM TWO

A cool breeze caresses my face. I stroll along a sandy beach, holding my head high, letting the warm sun revive my tired body. The sky is clear with subtle touches of vibrant colours, turquoise mixed with pastel green and red with pastel orange. Suddenly I catch sight of a shadow beneath my feet. What's blotting out the sun? I tip my head back to gaze at the sky. There is an eagle, a magnificent eagle soaring above me.

BANGLADESH

Sunday, 12 February, 2006

The smell of humidity and the heat at Dhaka airport - nothing short of a Turkish bath - hit me on the passenger stairway, splitting up every fibre of my body and re-joining it anew. The tension and heaviness of the last months lifted. I thawed. It was easy to find my way around the small airport, whose familiarity was still fresh from my first visit a year ago. As before, I saw only a handful of Westerners alongside mostly Bangladeshi men. In fact, as we were lining up to board in Dubai, I tried to figure out the ratio of Bangladeshi women to men. One to ten was my guess.

My bored eyes roamed over those men, clean-shaven and wearing jeans and shirts or dark suits, guest workers toiling in the Gulf, returning home with hands full of duty-free bags. The only thought the sight evoked in me was that they were probably simple men with hard lives, large responsibilities and petty hopes; fathers, brothers and sons whose duty-free bags were crammed with all sorts of duties. They needed, I imagined, to travel on from Dhaka to their respective villages. And there my imagination hit a dead end. I knew so little about their lives, and they seemed so irrelevant to my life, posing neither a threat nor a desire, that my curiosity was satisfied there and then. I, like the Westerners, waited at the end of the line while Bangladeshis hurried on before us into the plane. It struck me how comfortably they moved in that undifferentiated mass, whereas to be lost in a crowd has always unsettled me.

Thanks to Emirates Airline, the digits on my boarding card placed me next to a quiet Spanish man. Over the noise of slamming cupboards and screaming children, we engaged in forced small talk to prove our mutual politeness and respect - and from thereon kept to ourselves. I slept through a good part of the flight.

In no time I was standing in the foreign passport line at Dhaka airport and nodding goodbye to my Spanish companion, who had lined up in a shorter queue with the sign 'Crew, Foreign Investors and Diplomats'. As instructed by IMC, I walked up to the gate towards a piece of cardboard bearing the words 'Dr Solmaz London', held up by a middle-aged local man.

"Welcome," he smiled. "Welcome doctor," he shouted. "Welcome."

And I plunged for a second time into Dhaka.

The drive to the accommodation took a little over an hour. We drove past the railway station into a maze of narrow alleyways where small shops nestled between scrappy blocks of flats and heaps of brick and rubble. Tanvir - that was the driver's name - slowed down and came to a halt in front of a three-storey building. I ran my fingers through my tussled hair and fixed it into a tight knot before getting out of the van. We trudged on upstairs to the top floor, where a lean-faced man with long ginger locks strode up to us. He introduced himself as 'Andrew, your predecessor', and grabbed my suitcase from Tanvir.

"*Donabat*, Tanvir," Andrew thanked him. "See you tomorrow morning."

"*Khoda hafez*," Tanvir said, and put his right hand on his chest before marching downstairs again.

"Bring her here. I've set the table," a voice, deep and joyful, called out. I neatened my wrinkled white shirt and followed Andrew into the kitchen to meet Karl, the doctor I will be working with.

Only a few minutes in and Karl had already made a start on

relating to me every detail of our work. He talked about the organisation and its principles, the weekly meetings with other volunteers and the types of patients we encounter in the slums. Time and time again, he said something to the effect that our work offered 'humanitarian' and not 'developmental' aid. Honestly, I was then and am still too exhausted to grasp the difference between these two terms.

"*Ja*, officially we are not allowed to work in Bangladesh." Karl spoke with an unmistakable German accent. "Officially, we are only visiting this IMC organisation and are volunteers." A retired surgeon, he is bald and sturdy. "Some of these people are seeing a doctor for the very first time in their lives," he resumed.

I treated every word that hopped out from between his white teeth - they seem to be real, not dentures like Baba's - as a life-saving tip from one soldier to the other before a battle. His left hand was resting on the table next to the biscuits. I noticed a thin silver ring on his finger. Checking a man's wedding finger is something Rekha has instilled in me. I don't know how long he talked, but it seemed forever to me.

Luckily for me, Andrew finally shushed Karl. He didn't like it; I could see it in his thick eyebrows - those rushed and careless coats of dark ink almost touched each other. Even the hair in his nostrils fluttered a little.

"Solmaz," Andrew interjected. "There is only one thing you really need to know." At this remark, I raised my reserves to listen very carefully. "Especially when you feel frustrated, as you certainly will. Remember, you are not yet another stone scattered in a stony desert, but rather a stone stacking on top of all the previous ones to build a home." Andrew's voice became fatherly. "I have found this notion helpful."

I felt awkward with this display of sentimentality from a stranger, and a grown-up man at that. However, he emitted a genuine altruism that endeared him to me. A shame that he is heading back to the States tomorrow. Karl will be saddled with me for the next two months. I can speak German to him - how bizarre!

The sun is going down now. The muezzin's call to prayer is filling up the flat.

"*Ja, Mensch,* you need to get used to this daily *Geschrei,*" Karl grunts from his room, warning me of what he considers a 'shriek'. But hearing the melodious *azan* I get swept over by a sweet homely feeling. The *azan*, those Arabic verses always present in Iran, always in the background, summon infinite memories that translate into visceral sensations in me: a smile, a sigh, an ache and joy in the heart.

This familiar strangeness. Wherever I go, the strangeness is familiar to me and sometimes the familiar seems so strange. On the one hand, I feel inadequate because I don't fit in anywhere; on the other hand - much to my shame - I detect an inner pleasure in the belief that no place, no community and no person is good enough for me. Maybe it is typical for an outcast to shift between these extremes of inadequacy and narcissism.

Tuesday, February 14, 2006

My first food poisoning ever. Not unusual in a country like Bangladesh, and yet surprising since it's only my third day here. The constant visits to the toilet aren't as bad as the throwing up. The worst part is the retching.

Karl has been very good. "Don't worry," he grinned when he caught me between the toilet and my room. "It happens to the best of us. It didn't even spare a tough guy like me."

It couldn't have been later than five o'clock in the morning. The muezzin was singing again, calling the devotees to the morning prayer.

Soon, Karl was in my room with his medicine bag. He

pushed a pink Venflon into my left elbow. I followed his hands as they withdrew the needle, taped the plastic cannula to my skin and attached it to a long line leading to a saline bag. He took a syringe and injected it into the drip.

"And this is your antiemetic."

Karl saw to me again before heading off to work. "I'll check on you at lunchtime, between the two clinics." He unfolded the mosquito net around my bed.

I woke up to noises from the kitchen - the clunking of plates and the whooshing of running water in the sink. Our cook must have arrived, I reckoned. I met Nalak yesterday. He is probably in his late forties. Every morning, I am told, he comes to straighten up the place and cater for us, preparing meals and leaving before we return. He is a Buddhist, belonging to indigenous hill tribes from Chittagong - many of them come to work in Dhaka, Karl filled me in yesterday. This explains Nalak's Burmese appearance: slim, dark-skinned, with almond-shaped eyes and wide cheeks. There is a dignified manner about him, the way he walks with his head bowed and the way he is not wasteful with words.

He stuck his head in at the door earlier and mumbled a Bengali word. I raised my eyebrows and stretched my lips into a smile, the former saying, 'I don't get a word of what you say' and the latter, 'So, so sorry about it'. He strode out and came back with some dirty shirts on his arm. I shook my head. I don't have anything to wash yet. Soon he will be cleaning Andrew's empty room. It can't be that difficult to tend to our modest residence, which is no more than three small bedrooms, a shared bathroom and a kitchen with the basic utensils - no luxuries at all, not even a television. My room has a bed, a table, a wooden dresser. The only non-essential item is the picture on the wall: a village woman in her maroon sari crouches over her pots and pans. I watch the ants, flies and cockroaches dawdle over her world and in my room.

The spinning of the ceiling fan is hypnotic. I lean back on my pillow and let yesterday's memories trickle through me just like the saline dripping into my vein. Karl demanded I took the day off and rested well. I stayed back in the flat; despite my exhaustion, excitement ousted any tiny inclination to sleep. I rang Belal to give him the flat's phone number. He suggested I went up to his office and, since he wouldn't take no for an answer, I caved in.

Not too long after that, his driver came for me.

I might have been delirious from lack of sleep, but still the strangeness of the moment didn't escape me. It was surreal. I can't say what time of the day I got there. My body clock was too messed up. His driver showed me to an elevator to the fourth floor. I trailed after him past a medium-sized room with filing cabinets against one wall and men sitting at rows of desks to right and left. As I glanced at their faces, it crossed my mind that they could just as well be those who had got off the plane with me the day before. A small hallway led us to an open office door. Stale cigarette smoke was the first thing that came to greet me - or was it the chatter of CNN news?

There he was, in a grey suit behind a large desk, a cigarette in one hand and the phone in the other. Our eyes met. We both smiled.

"*Thik acha*," he rose, stubbed the cigarette in the ashtray on his desk, swapped the phone into the hand that had been holding it and stepped around the desk. "*Ha, ha. Khoda hafez.*" He put the receiver down and extended his hand towards me. "Welcome to Bangladesh," he said, in the tone with which a host greets a guest in his house.

Belal pulled a chair for me in front of his desk, and went back to his swivel chair behind it. He kept his poker face but, looking more carefully, I could see a fixed smile in the corner of his mouth.

"I expected your call yesterday." Before I could reply, he

added, "I understand. You must have been washed-out after the flight."

While I answered his questions about the flight and my job schedule, a scrawny boy served us two black coffees. Balal said something, and the boy came back with milk powder and sugar. "You have yours white?"

I nodded, yes.

"Have you got a new sim card for your mobile or should we get you one?"

"No mobile at all. I am simplifying my life."

"Have you eaten yet?" He turned to the boy and seemed to send him away with a new task.

"You are living in Kamalapur?" Belal puckered up his brows on hearing that our accommodation was located in one of Dhaka's poor areas. "I fend much better for my foreign visitors. The organisation should take better care of you."

Take better care of me? I shall ask him when I see him next whether poisoning a guest with a dodgy chicken sandwich was what he understands by that.

My body is depleted, my mind fuzzy and my heart in a curious state. I have been in bed all day - Fardin is still on my mind.

Even though my body is in Bangladesh, my thoughts are in England. It always takes longer for the soul and heart to follow. They have their own separate routes. Soon the faces, the petty concerns and dramas of England, will fall away and be replaced by the curves and angles of Bangladesh. But for now I am in a no-man's land where the old is gone but the new hasn't yet arrived - a place where I feel weightless and utterly free.

I miss Fardin's arms and kisses, but do I miss him? I wish I could say I do, but I don't. I merely desire his embraces, his kisses. They were addictive.

Wednesday, February 22, 2006

Starting work wasn't difficult in itself. The moment the first patient sits in front of you, you become a doctor. You take a history, conduct examinations and do your job as in any other place.

I am already used to our routine. Every morning at eight, without fail, we pile into a minivan that is already filled with the other team members: two interpreters and two care assistants, as well as Eshan, our co-ordinator. Then we set off to one of the five slums under our coverage, each slum on a specific weekday. Tanvir steers us through the frenzied traffic to our destination, which is past either railway tracks or murky, foul-smelling canals full of litter, carcasses and garbage pickers.

Locals are used to our weekly visits, yet children still get excited. They come running up to us with big smiles and rowdy choruses of '*alaykum as-salaam*'. Karl is frequently encircled by a swarm of children, especially at the end of the clinic. They manage to turn up just in time to snatch one of the lollipops Karl likes to buy and hand out.

After Tanvir drops us at the margin of the slum, we trek along narrow, muddy tracks, snaking through webs of houses: closely packed shacks made of bamboo, plastic or tin sheets. A few times my curiosity got the better of me, and I peeked into some of these open hovels - the door is mostly fashioned from a sheet or a curtain of nylon. Inside there is often a large bed that occupies half of the space; blankets, shirts and all sorts of clothing hang over a rope that goes across the room. It is life-packed, people-packed.

A putrid stench stalks us all the way through the daunting labyrinth.

"There are only a few latrines and water pumps in each slum," Karl told me today. "Aren't Bangladeshi women beautiful?" His words drew my eyes to the group of women squatting around a water pipe, some washing dirty dishes and clothes and some sponging their children.

"Yes, they are. But what I admire most is their ability to wash themselves with their saris on."

At times, there are up to a hundred patients flocking into our clinic - a hut of clay with two desks and some plastic chairs. Eshan takes a seat outside the clinic. He resides there like a custodian of the gates of Olympus, studiously scribbling the name and age of each patient on a green card, measuring their blood pressure and weight before letting them step in.

Most of our patients are housewives, beggars, cleaners, housekeepers, and workers in garment factories. They make quite a sight: women in colourful saris with nose rings and bangles, many of them with children.

"They eke out a living by sewing our shirts," Karl says. "Their burning eyes, chronic coughs and chest infections are a result of working in overcrowded and poorly ventilated factories."

For a week I had done my job with a sort of numbness and coldness, a matter-of-fact attitude in the face of the intense suffering I witness. No feeling whatsoever - until today.

The whole day through I saw mainly children. First there was a girl of four with the most striking green eyes I've ever seen. Big brave eyes in a softly-shaped oval face, her bald head emphasising her large forehead, bony arms emerging from short yellow sleeves. She sat on her mother's lap, quiet and motionless, and yet she exuded a fierce spiritedness. She has been mute for some time, but has never been investigated. Why, I wanted to know.

The interpreter didn't need to ask the mother, "When people are poor, girls come last."

There wasn't much I could do. We merely sent her to the healthcare assistant. She'll be included in our feeding programme; it's a simple regimen: *dal*, rice and milk powder spread over many months.

Then there was another girl, only twelve years old and by herself. She said she had left her village after her mother had passed away. Together with her younger brother, she had come to the city to live with their father and his new wife. And the stepmother had poisoned her little brother. There was no way to verify her claims; we didn't even try. Then she lifted her shirt, and I flinched. Thick scar tissue covered her torso like armour. Her two breasts were pressed flat. It was an old burn scar. When she was four, she was left unattended, and her clothes had caught alight at the cooking fire.

A girl with a pretty face but a disfigured body - what kind of future will she have? How will she ever qualify as a housewife or mother?

My last patient was yet another child: a skinny, quiet, nine-year-old boy on his own. I examined him thoroughly; he had pneumonia.

"Why didn't you come to see us much earlier?" I rolled my eyes in a show of criticism. From the panic in his eyes I could tell he had noticed the anger in my tone.

I was angry at them all. I was angry at them, at their lives, at their endless stories of sorrow and suffering.

The boy lowered his head, grasped the end of his unbuttoned sleeve and, with a cracking voice, explained, "*ami kajer shatheh basto chilam*" - he had been busy with work. His big black eyes lacked any childish sparkle, his tone was cowed and beaten. It was a sad sight. A sight that became sadder with the red lollipop in his hand.

A lump rose in my throat. I felt a void in my chest, and my eyes misted over. 'Not now,' I choked back my tears.

Karl, whose watchful eyes had taken in the whole scenario, beckoned the boy and sat him next to his own patient, a man with hennaed hair and beard.

I stormed out, straight into the latrine, and let those tears roll down my face.

Sunday, February 26, 2006

At this time of the year, Dhaka is quite hot and humid, and temperatures can rise above 30 degrees Celsius. The smog is a thick ceiling hanging over the city, suffocating and stifling. The air is so polluted that exhaust fumes settle on my clothes, face, even under my nails and in my nose. Not even the three daily showers I take alleviate the clamminess that clings onto my skin.

"Water and air conditioning are, in my view, the most humane and precious gifts in your part of the world." I announced to Belal from my seat on the black leather couch in the corner of his air-conditioned office today. He didn't think it safe for me to travel on my own at dusk, but it wasn't dark when I reached there. It must have been around seven o'clock when my Bengali class finished and I tumbled up the stairs to Belal's office. After firing a quick hello at him, I went straight into the ensuite bathroom to spruce up. This entailed washing my face, dabbing my armpits with a damp towel and brushing my messy hair. After this - the equivalent of a long bubble bath in London - I felt presentable to Vivek. Belal's closest friend was going to come later to dine out with us.

I could feel a sense of pride whenever Belal mentioned Vivek. It seemed important to him that we met. Vivek's father, a university professor, and uncle, a jute producer, were killed during the liberation war with Pakistan. He had studied engineering in England for a couple of years before returning home. Later on I could see for myself the trust and ease in the interaction between these two unlikely friends, a Muslim Bangladeshi and a much older Hindu, one married with family and the other living the life of a bachelor - an unorthodox lifestyle for a conservative country like Bangladesh.

As we waited for Vivek, Belal kept on working, whereas I - after checking my emails on his computer - read my book, Simone de Beauvoir's *The Second Sex*:

'*When she does not find love, she may find poetry. Because she does not act, she observes, she feels, she records; a colour, a smile awakens profound echoes within her...*'

Every so often Belal and I exchanged glances across the large black desk between us. He attended to his paperwork, made phone calls and dealt with the employees who dropped in and out of his office. He was wearing a navy suit, the top buttons of his shirt open and his dotted tie loosened; his sleeves were rolled up, revealing his hairy forearms. His pursed lips and puckered forehead gave him a focused look - exactly the way I am when at work. He seems to be the kind of man people like, admire and respect. He talked in a calm manner to his employees, but didn't smile at all.

'*...She rarely feels a bold creativeness, and usually she lacks the technique of self-expression; but in her conversation, her letters, her literary essays, her sketches, she manifests an original sensitivity. The young girl throws herself into things with ardour, because...*'

After a while, to turn my mind from my grumbling stomach, I set off searching the room for entertainment. There was not much to explore; even the most resourceful child would get bored in that place. The curtains were drawn and the walls were empty - though not quite: there was a large world map opposite Belal's desk. I studied it with my back to Belal. Holding one hand over Bangladesh and the other over Iran, I calculated that Bangladesh was only the size of one fingertip, whereas Iran took up three whole fingers. I twisted and turned my head towards Belal. He was watching me. My fingers on the countries, I moved one step to the side for him to see it for himself. I paused for a reaction from him. Mobile in hand, he flicked the ash from his cigarette and smiled.

"Do you have any pictures of your family on you?" he asked later on.

"The only picture I've carried around for more than a decade is that of Shariati." I grabbed my purse and showed it to him. "He was a controversial Iranian intellectual who studied sociology at the Sorbonne, Paris; he was too Western for many Muslims and too Islamist for many modernists." So went my well-rehearsed brief biography of Shariati.

"He looks old."

"He is probably not much older than us in this picture. Too much thinking makes one older than one's years."

"Give me a couple of examples of what he says." I had stirred his curiosity.

"A person's value is in proportion to the distance between where he is and where he wants to be," I cited the first thing that came to my mind.

"Now we know how valuable I am," Belal said with a playful nod.

"What do you mean?"

"I am content where I am," he said. "Give me another one."

"He also says that some people are like Coca Cola: a lot of fizz, but when the foam settles there is no substance left in the glass."

Before he could say anything, his phone rang again. He answered it but said little, mainly, *"Na", "Ji", "Acha", "Tik acha".*

With my legs stretched out on the couch, I examined his features: a gentle witty smile, long, soft, brown fingers that travelled between his chin and lips whenever he listened to me, and eyes that seemed to see through me; not particularly handsome, but certainly charismatic.

He lifted his head and gave me a puzzled glance. He knew I was studying him. Suddenly I heard some shuffling outside.

"Sit formally please." His serious tone took me by surprise.

Vivek walked in.

"Solmaz? From the land of roses!" Vivek was short, plump, bald and wearing a suit. He shook my hand and held my eyes with a smile.

Iran? Land of roses? We do have rose water and rose jam, but I didn't remember seeing many roses around. I thought we were famous for our tulips, the symbol of blood and martyrs, which were sung about and depicted frequently on television after the revolution.

"Iran is famous for its roses," Vivek declared again with a warm voice. I was not going to dispute it. Roses it was.

Sunday, March 5, 2006

Karl is in the church. He has chanced to meet some Chicago priests who run a nearby boarding school, which makes him thrilled at the opportunity to spend his Sundays at mass.

Having the whole morning to myself, I have climbed up onto the roof of our accommodation, a cup of coffee in one hand and my journal in the other. Relaxing in a rusty chair, I now tune in to the sweetness of the moment, looking over the adjoining buildings. The sun is setting over the horizon, and the sky has transformed into a palette of fierce red, purple and shades of orange. My Walkman is turned off, and I have taken off the earphones, surrendering to city noises and the muezzin's call for prayer.

There is one thing I have come to realise: one does not need to travel halfway round the world to a hot country burdened with overpopulation and pollution to do something good. We do it because under normal circumstances we are numb and sluggish. The extreme, however, shakes us awake.

I had romanticised the poor. People are the same everywhere: envy, greed, animosity - you find them here too. Take, for instance, one of our healthcare assistants - a middle-aged Christian Bengali woman with two grown-up children, who keeps asking for each and every item I am wearing. I have already given one of my earrings to her, but today, as the car was proceeding in its customary slow motion on Dhaka's roads, her eyes caught sight of something new.

"Your raincoat is nice. It would fit my son." She pointed at the army green Timberland jacket on my lap. Four of us, three women and Eshan, had bundled in the backseat so that I was boxed in by the two female healthcare assistants.

"Thank you." I smiled at the Christian woman to my left and, in fear of more demands, rapidly averted my gaze to the window, pretending to be preoccupied with something very important outside our minivan. I went on half listening to the conversation between Karl and Eshan about the high number of Japanese cars in Dhaka, while skimming through the titles of the pile of books a boy was carrying from car to car: Jeffrey Archer's *Sin of the Father*, Daniel Steel's *44 Charles Street* and *Expecting Adam* by Martha Beck.

"Solmaz, *Mensch*, look at that traffic officer." Karl yelled from the front seat. His hands snatched his camera to capture the man in his green vest and white sleeves with a whistle around his neck and a yellow umbrella with the Kodak logo.

"A very bizarre outfit," I said.

"*Dummkopf*. What a slacker. If it was up to me, I'd fix the traffic issue here by getting lazy bums like him to do their jobs."

"The poor guy. I wouldn't want his job."

"*Verdammt!*" He screamed at a crying old beggar clinging to his window, who was obscuring his creative moment. "*Baksheesh*? Okay, of course, alms." Karl rolled down his window and pushed some notes into his hand.

"You give it to him?" The healthcare assistant tapped on my shoulder, calling for my attention.

"What?" For a moment I was confused. What could she be referring to?

"The rain jacket! You give the rain jacket to my son?"

I pursed my lips and paused. "I am sorry, but it is my only jacket."

"When you leave. Okay?" she asked.

"Of course," I said with relief. In three months she will have forgotten about my jacket, I hope.

Then she started talking with the younger healthcare assistant to my right. The two women were giggling over my head.

"Do you want to change seats?" I offered the young woman.

"No, you can stay there. We are alright," and they continued speaking Bengali.

"Where is your family?" the young woman asked me all of a sudden.

"In Vienna."

"You mean *your* family?"

"No, I'm not married," I answered. "I am divorced."

And with that, everyone in the car, Tanvir, Eshan and the two healthcare assistants, went quiet, while Karl in the front seat was still puzzling over the bigger question of Dhaka's traffic, oblivious to the awkwardness around him.

"Are *you* married?" I enquired, unable to bear that judging silence.

"Yes," the young woman uttered with an audible pride. "Of course." Then they resumed their conversation in Bengali.

"Have you slept with your German buddy yet?" Eshan said out of the blue. His eyes had caught mine over the crouched head of the young woman, who had leaned over to whisper something to the older woman.

I cringed.

"It's no big deal anyway," he folded his arms across his chest. "Right?"

I was dumbfounded. Before I could gather myself, he shot me a smug grin and bent forward to answer Karl's question as to how women in slums made fuel from shreds of old garments and bamboo sticks to bake their breads.

"What a sick guy." I untied my hair and then tied it back again as I always do when nervous.

"Do you dye your hair?" The young healthcare assistant touched my hair.

"I do."

She shifted her attention to the older woman, conversing in Bengali once again.

Why Eshan's question all of a sudden, and why was it followed by 'no big deal'? Was it no big deal because Eshan is open-minded, or because I am virtually a Western woman, or because I am divorced - in other words, tainted so that a couple more touches don't matter anyway.

Still, the most illusion-shattering incident occurred some hours later, when I saw a granny snatching the free banana we give out with each prescription from her granddaughter's hand and eating it.

Yes, I had romanticised the poor. But not only the poor, maybe the East too. People here are not any better or worse than those in the West. Goodness and humanity don't correspond to geography, race or adversity. There is no spirituality in an imposed asceticism, no enlightenment in resignation and certainly no goodness in ignorance and naiveté. These are just normal people contending with daily hurdles and scraping by. Not all of them are grateful for our petty alms. Why should they be? Why should they feel indebted for what other people feel entitled to? They know they don't deserve this rotten life.

If I am right, why can I still sense grace here? Where does this come from? Here, amidst poverty, I see a life pregnant with possibilities ahead of me.

Does poverty do that?

Does poverty give you the gift of life?

How can poverty be terrifying and disgusting, yet graceful and bountiful all at the same time?

I hear thunder rumbling, and given that I am above thirty, hypothetically my chances of being struck by lightning are higher than finding a man, so I should really head back to my room.

Monday, March 6, 2006

I am finding pleasure in new things, trivial triumphs, such as writing emails to Peyman or Rekha and actually being able to send them. Computers are not only slow here, but we are also thrown off the internet on a regular basis.

"It's Bangladesh," the boys at the internet café say.

In the evenings, Karl and I have fallen into a routine. After work, he heads off to the German club in an air-conditioned cab - for which, by the way, he has my full sympathy. I would do the same if the car hire wouldn't add up to a fortune. Allegedly, not everyone can get into the German club, not even every German, but Karl has somehow made it happen.

I, instead, have taken to visiting the local cyber café to check my emails and engage in small talk with the nice twenty-something guys who hang out there.

Located in a shabby shopping centre, the internet café is really just a closet with four computers and a reception desk. A few days ago Karl tagged along to look at his emails. He didn't like the ambience, he told me. The Bengali music was "*ach Mensch,* too loud", the computers "*ach Mensch,* too slow," and the place "*ach Mensch,* too small," and the guys I have become friendly with were "*ach Mensch,* only kids".

I like it there. The guy I speak to most has a black shirt with a white Apple logo on it. I don't know why that struck me. Maybe because when I complimented him on it, he said he wouldn't exchange it for the world. Tonight he treated me to dinner at his house. He is the man in the family, since his father is dead and his older brother works in Dubai. His mother and two sisters greeted me with a warm embrace and appeared to genuinely enjoy playing host to me. Their friendliness and hospitality were the kind I remember from our distant relatives in Azerbaijan. Iranians are generally very hospitable, like Bangladeshis. Naneh Homa believed, "Guests don't come to your home for food, but for your kindness."

I would have liked to stay longer, but wanted to reach home before Karl. Alas, he had opted to stay home tonight.

I have never felt so married in my entire life. Karl expects us to take our meals together. He makes a point of always waiting for me to join him at the table. In the mornings, he passes the time with the newspaper *Daily Start*, while I do my exercises on the roof. When I come down to the kitchen, the table is set with a lavish breakfast: a range of juices - Happy Day orange juice, Pomegranate, Tipco mixed fruits - with wheat toasts and a couple of different jams, mango and strawberry.

Once a week on our way back from the slums of Gulshan, Karl asks Tanvir to stop at an upmarket store in Gulshan, an upper-class neighbourhood of Dhaka, where he buys his provisions. I have noticed the reproachful glances of our Bengali staff at the white linen bags characteristic of that shop when he walks back to the car.

"I am starving," Karl said as soon as I got home. "Where have you been?"

"At the internet café," I said. "What has Nalak rustled up for us?"

"A vegetarian curry. I'll warm it up."

"Thanks." I did not tell him I had already eaten. "Let me take a quick shower first."

"You want me to rub your back?"

"Yeah, sure."

"You are sure you don't need my help?" Karl said again as I was locking the bathroom door.

"Positive."

We both laughed.

At the dinner table I found out the reason for his cheerfulness.

"I had a phone call from my older daughter. She has decided to get married in a church. I'm very proud of her."

"Did you ask her to have a church wedding?"

"No, she wouldn't have listened to me. I kept quiet but prayed for it. I am glad she has come to this choice by herself." He told me how thrilled he was when she first brought home her now fiancé. "He is a good Christian."

Our conversations mostly revolve around him, his great house, his perfect family, his influential friends and, of course, his many accomplishments back in Germany. And I am his full-time audience.

Tuesday, March 7, 2006

"Do you beat your wife, too?" I threw at Belal point-blank. He had caught me in a very foul mood when he rang tonight.

The eyes of a patient were haunting me. She was a gaunt young woman - or rather a skeleton with protruding cheekbones, emitting a steady gaze from sunken eyeballs. There was no fat on her whatsoever. Her long black hair tumbled around her shoulders and over the red *dupatta* scarf, and her thin, bare arms were dangling by her side like two shrivelled sticks. There was no sadness in her face, only emptiness. Her parched lips didn't utter a word. Something heavy framed her whole body. Something that made me feel guilty and hypocritical.

My interpreter explained that she had seen Karl before; her chest x-ray had confirmed advanced TB. I couldn't believe she was a single mother. Like many other young mothers, she looked no more than a child herself. She had run away from her family to marry a man, only to be later abandoned by him. He had gone back to his village in order to remarry - just for the sake of another dowry.

And that is all an ordinary love story in Bangladesh.

I turned my gaze away, but still felt her large blank eyes upon me when I was stitching the cut on the face of another young mother. This one, though in pain, was smiling, a smile of shyness and embarrassment. Her husband had beaten her. Karl said I would get used to them.

Women with bruised eyes and battered limbs are a common occurrence in our clinics. Karl is a repository of knowledge about these things, much more so than me. He regularly reads the newspaper. Sometimes at our kitchen table he reads out certain sections to me, interesting news about Khaleda Zia, Bangladesh's prime minister, and her disputes with the opposition, but also reports about yet another village woman who has fallen victim to *fatwa,* or the woman who committed suicide after a public humiliation - they had shorn her long black hair like a sheep in the village square.

I had heard of honour killings, domestic violence and child abuse; I expected bad things to happen somewhere else, somewhere very far from me, in a strange country. I trusted their discretion to stay on the screen of a television or in a black print on a white paper. At most, those things should be a story, related by someone else's lips about an unknown person in a faraway land and time. I could handle looking at them, but not their eyes looking back at me. They shouldn't be so close to peer into my eyes.

Later Eshan shed some light on the issue. "Husbands work hard. They come home and see that their wives have been too lazy or don't appreciate them, then they get angry and beat them. Sometimes they do it because they are mad at their children."

The way he talked made it sound plausible, especially considering the few male patients I have seen so far: mostly rickshaw drivers who show up at our clinics, with weather-beaten and haggard faces; young men with old faces, suffering from back and knee problems.

My frustration must have been palpable on the phone. I wanted to blame someone or something.

"No, I don't," Belal replied, in answer to my question, sounding distraught over the phone. "I have raised my hand only once in my entire life." He told me that when he was fourteen years old, he had punched a classmate for having made a spiteful remark about his father. One blow from Belal had sufficed to knock out the boy. "That incident scared me for life," he concluded. Since then he has always shied away from fights.

His story perked me up; it reminded me of a funny incident from my own childhood. Like Belal, I too felt obliged to defend the honour of my family. I was no more than nine years old at the time. Maman had enrolled me in an all-girls' summer school for sports. Girls and boys, however, were thrown together in the school bus. One day, a boy a few years my senior poked fun at Baba's business back then - he had a bra factory. Fuming with anger, I snatched the water bucket the driver kept behind his seat and emptied it over the boy's head. Once I had finished my act of revenge, the empty bucket in my hand, I looked around and - not knowing what to do with it - shoved it over his head as a finishing touch.

When I was done with my story, I heard a chuckle at the other end. "You were meaner than I," Belal said.

I justified my action and reminded him that my victim hadn't lost consciousness - he had only been ridiculed by a younger girl and hopefully learnt a lesson for life.

Belal has invited me to join him and Vivek on one of his business meetings outside of Dhaka. En-route we'll stop at the old capital of Bengal.

I jumped at the offer - anything that takes me out into some green and oxygen is more than welcome.

Friday, March 10, 2006

There was the feel of a fairytale to today, from the beginning right through to the end.

If someone had told me how magical Panam City is, I would not have believed it. It is everything you don't expect in a country like Bangladesh: an ethereal oasis of dream, peace and nostalgia, only one hour away from the hectic soundtracks of Dhaka.

The journey takes more than the advertised one hour, of course. You have to battle your way, like the Prince in Sleeping Beauty, through a tangled bush of trucks, buses, carts and tin shops, past a harbour of boats loading bricks, before breaking through to Panam City, the golden village.

On entering it, you walk into a painting by a nineteenth century romantic artist: a depiction of narrow streets; decaying buildings in copper, blue and pink, adorned with vegetation; arched windows; patterned pillars and balconies; then a vast green field with palm trees, a pond with ducks and a woman in a sari washing dishes - the unexpected quiet. No honking. You could hear the birds and count the people on the road, for there were only a few. I had a sense that it could vanish anytime, the same way it had emerged - quietly and suddenly.

"I must say, you talk like an artist," Belal said when I shared my observation with him and Vivek.

"To me, it is only a large museum, inhabited by ghosts of a long gone elite," Vivek said. Puffing at his cigarette, he plodded behind us with his hands in the pockets of his slightly-too-large suit. He chose a spot for us to laze on the grass in front of an old mansion with two lonely figures on horses before it.

Belal's driver arrived a little later with a plastic box containing samosas and three bottles of water.

"Wow, I am burning." The samosas Belal's wife had made were too spicy for my taste buds. He handed me the water. The two men laughed while I gulped down an entire bottle.

"*Donnabat*," I bragged with a word I had learnt in the class.

"Bangladeshis don't say thank you. Westerners use *donnabat*. We only smile and you have to understand," Vivek said. "I hear you'll be going to rural Bangladesh."

"Yes. I'll be in Dhaka for three months to get training, and then I'll be transferred to a rural project."

"You'll like it there. That is the real Bangladesh."

"In what way?"

"People are nicer there." He dug his fingers into the box of samosas.

I looked at him; the neutral expression on his face - besides the suit and cigarettes - was something else the two men in my company had in common: faces that hardly reveal any thoughts or emotions, faces that are difficult to read. Apart from that, Vivek didn't converse much with me, and in that respect one could say that this was similar to my first encounter with Belal. Still Belal was the quieter of the two. Whenever Vivek said something to him in Bengali - he didn't speak to Belal in English - Belal's replies were short. However, this could have been on my account.

Driving back to Dhaka, Vivek sat in the front, next to the driver, and Belal in the back seat with me. Darkness descended on the bumpy roads outside; inside we were quiet, listening to Mary J Blige's *No More Drama in my Life* on the mix tape Fardin had made me. Belal fished out an aftershave from his bag and sprayed it on his wrist, then without a word he held his hand out for me to smell. I took his wrist, smelt the bitter-sweet fragrance on his skin and let go, but … he didn't. He grabbed my hand.

We held hands. We each gave only one hand to the other, for the rest of the ride. Our fingers came alive like never before. They caressed and circled around each other, ebbing and flowing to a primal rhythm, one time firmly locking, almost melting into one another; another time pushing away, parting with resolve but never losing that subtle hint of touch; one hand slowly and softly sliding up and down the palm of the other, twirling along the edge, reaching for the back and sensing the texture of the skin - his strangely softer than mine - tracing the bones and veins of the other with patience and curiosity; then one hand curling into a bud, allowing itself to be wrapped in an embrace, ever so gently, until one of us would stretch our fingers, opening them only wide enough to glide into each other's grooves, firmly intertwined.

I never knew hands could be that eloquent - delicate as well as explicit. My fingers were suffused with longing and passion, but the rest of me was wrapped in tranquillity and bliss.

Every now and then Belal would brush the nape of my neck with his other hand, or twist a lock of my hair around his fingers. Once he drew my face towards him. He was in search of a kiss. I turned away. *Not in front of everyone!* I scrawled on the back of my De Beauvoir book, and held it up for him to read in the light of the passing headlamps. Still he nudged my face towards his lips. I shot him a reproachful glance, turned my face away sharply and stared out of the window.

I did not let go of his hand.

Back in Dhaka, we had dinner before they took me home. The driver stopped on the main road; Vivek remained in the car while Belal escorted me back. Neither of us said a single word. But I could hear a hum in my head. It grew louder, more insistent, then it slipped out of my mouth.

"What am I doing here with the man of another woman?"

"Don't," Belal said. "Come on, Solmaz. Please don't." He sounded like someone who, in the morning, tunes out the

112

alarm, rolls over in bed, and pulls the blanket over their face, pleading with the day to start just a bit later.

We reached my flat, and he halted at the entrance as I stepped in. The dark hallway was only lit by streetlights. After a couple of steps, I turned back towards him. He was standing still. He looked outside the door and again into the hallway. I lifted my gaze and checked past the railings for anyone upstairs. We held each other's gazes, both wanting a kiss. There was no one, still it was too risky. It was not the right place.

"Go now," he said.

I pivoted on my heels, took a few steps, wavered and glanced his way.

"Go now." There was regret on his face, as there certainly was on mine.

I went.

'Morality is a lack of opportunity.' Karl often invokes this German proverb.

Wednesday, March 15, 2006

I rushed home after my Bengali class to wash my hair before Karl made it home. I was hoping to escape his jokes about us taking a shower together, which have turned into a nightly occurrence. The minute I got out of the shower the phone rang.

"What would you say to Chinese tonight?" Belal asked.

"Yeees? But didn't you say you were 'otherwise engaged'?" I repeated the words from his earlier email.

"Come and take a ride with me." He was outside, in front of the flat. First I thought it was daring of him, but then I remembered that Karl himself had mentioned to him yesterday that he would be in the German Club.

"See, your rich friends don't do anything for their own people," Karl growled after meeting Belal and Vivek yesterday

113

afternoon. He was curious to meet my 'Bangladeshi friends' before heading to his club. We spent only an hour in Belal's office. Karl urged me to close my ears and asked them about the availability of Viagra in Bangladesh. Belal and Vivek kept their straight faces and matter-of-fact tone

They invited Karl and me for dinner. Karl turned it down.

"I'll happily help them, but I don't need to get to know them. I don't want to eat with them or be friends with them," Karl said afterwards.

I, on the other hand, go to their homes, eat their food and like to get to know them - or at least one of them. Therefore, I lit a candle - there was yet another power cut - and groped my way downstairs to find him. He was on a motorbike.

"And you couldn't tell me that on the phone?"

"Is that a problem?" Belal raised his eyebrows.

I made a U-turn to my room, pulled my hair up in a knot and changed from a long skirt into jeans.

"I haven't ridden my bike for nearly five years."

He had taken it out of the garage tonight. It was the first time I had seen him dressed down in casual clothes: a beige shirt with sleeves rolled up, black jeans and a baseball cap.

We rode against a backdrop of clear, starry sky, a shimmering full moon and a cool breeze that kissed my face...or so I wished! It is Bangladesh, as the locals keep saying. There was smog, the stench of gasoline, a throng of people and vehicles mixed with dissonant honking and whirring noises - an ordinary weekend night. Our ride followed in the expected fits and starts. Nonetheless I relished every second the bike was moving, and along with it the rush of air.

People were staring at me. Once, at yet another imposed halt, three boys huddled on a neighbouring bike hollered some excited words in Bengali and took a picture of me.

"You are sitting on the bike like me," Belal said. "Not like a Bangladeshi woman."

I was sitting astride the motorbike. I looked at the other women. They had their legs firmly closed on one side. However, like them I too had my arms tightly wrapped around the rider.

There was something erotic in the texture of Dhaka's streets tonight. The swarm of bodies and the myriad of gazes, the anonymity and invisibility in the multitude as well as the reckless invasion of one's physical space, evoke a sense of panic and intimacy in equal measure - an intimacy that by the very nature of its imposition was charged with a sensual and intoxicating energy. One's ego dissolves into the crowd, into the darkness and into the heat - it evaporates into here, there and everywhere.

I slid my hand over Belal's shirt, my fingers lingering on the buttons. Feeling my hesitation, he released a hand from the handlebar, undid one button and, grabbing my wrist, pushed it further in. My hand worked its way up to explore his chest: warm, firm, and not much hair. He drew a deep breath and shifted back in his seat, so that our torsos pressed tightly against each other. I recognised his aftershave, a musky bergamot just like Omid's - Aramis. He was clean-shaven. He always is.

"When I said 'not in front of everyone', I meant Vivek and the driver," I whispered into his ear in an empty alleyway, and when shadows became darker, I pressed my lips on his face for a kiss.

"You are only a stranger," he tilted his head back for me to hear. "But many know me here." Belal gestured to the crowd, twisting his grip decisively and gassing the engine.

"Where will we find a place for a kiss?" The night made me bold.

"Most people are more subtle." He shook his head in delight. "I like your honesty. In that regard I trust you more than myself." He zoomed off, snaking the bike through the traffic.

It was the first time I had been on a motorbike. The subtle twists of my body, the way it instinctively responded to the shifts and bends of the bike, brought to mind the image of Sophia Loren, the personification of *sexy* to me. A sharp turn, and the wind blew off Belal's baseball cap, scribbling *Fine* on our movie - 'The End'.

Belal pulled over and went after his cap. I felt a gaze on me, and turned to see a rickshaw driver. He was leaning against a lamppost with electric cables dangling from it, his rickshaw before him on the other side of the open drainage ditch running between the pavement and the street. The streetlight shone on his deep wrinkles and red-stained, crooked teeth. He lifted his head, spat out some beetle leaves and then tucked his lunga between his legs to stand up. Munching on, he joined me in watching Belal. We both fixed our eyes on him as he raced against the traffic for his cap, seized it and brushed off the dust.

"Ha, country, Madam?" The man yanked me out of my fixation.

"Iran."

"Oh, Muslim?" His excitement was audible.

I nodded with a smile and turned my gaze to Belal. Beads of sweats were trickling down his forehead. I could see awkwardness in his face.

Later in the Chinese restaurant, we became sober and our conversation heavy. We talked for a while about my family. Omid's history of addiction and my parent's helplessness did not take Belal by surprise. He had similar stories on hand; stories about friends lost to and talents wasted on drugs. Strangely, our talk didn't include Fardin, nor Peyman. He was not curious about them and it slipped my mind completely.

Before leaving the restaurant, he pressed a paper into my hand. It was full of small black and white pictures pasted next to each other, all Shariati's.

"Now the walls in your room don't need to be empty," he said.

Sunday, March 19, 2006

A mosquito peacefully resting on my pen, the sun bathing me in her glow, my skin coated in a warm sweat, and every so often a gentle breeze caressing my body...

Maybe I am no beauty; maybe I am nothing special, but an ordinary woman who shines because they have turned off the lights around her - on the women around her.

I wouldn't stand out if you were let in to stand beside me.

We Muslim women are puppets, for the West as much as for the East. We are a measure of their power and superiority. They both use us. They both use us for their own agenda. Boys don't play with dolls, but grown-up men do: we are the dolls they dress and undress. They pull at our strings for the game they are playing with each other. It is not about us. It is only about them. It has always been about them. It has always been about their home, their property, their heir and their honour.

How needy a soul is for opportunities where there is no one. It is as if Shariati is speaking of the souls of women. That is what we need: no one to watch, no one to claim us, so that we can breathe, so that we can be.

"Women are precious jewels that need safeguarding." These words of a Mullah are burned into my memory. He had come to our school to give a speech on the occasion of Women's day - the birthday of the Prophet's daughter Fatima. I can see my eleven-year-old self among all those girls in their blue uniforms and dark blue scarves, sitting cross-legged on the carpeted floor in the big lecture hall and listening to his sermon.

"Islam is the only religion that respects women," the Mullah pronounced, drawing out the vowels while extricating the words. "It only asks of a woman to be a good wife to her husband, see to him when he comes home, tired, beaten up by the cruel world, be an oasis of comfort to him." A wave of giggling erupted among the girls. "Islam asks of a mother to bring up decent and good Muslim children. In return, the husband is obliged to provide for her. Women are precious jewels which need to be safeguarded at all times," he argued. In the same breath, he went on to confess, "I read all Western magazines. It is my duty to spot the devil's work. I warn my Muslim sisters…"

The message I heard was: I am a woman, I am tempting, I am seductive, I am desirable. My very being is the personification of guilt - no, in fact, the very embodiment of sin.

I don't fit into the respectable category of women that the Mullah was talking about. Yet, I am a woman.

Belal, you are another woman's man. You gave me the meal she cooked for you. I don't want you, and neither do you want me. You are too small, too selfish, too obsessed with yourself and your little world to be capable of love.

Now I am talking to you, his wife. I do not want him. If he doesn't love you, it's not because of another woman but because he is not courageous enough to love. I won't take him from you. There is nothing to take. I want for nothing but a kiss. Know that you possess him more than any other woman ever will. You have him in your bond because of his sense of responsibility and duty, because providing for you and your daughters renders his existence meaningful. Isn't that all a wife should be expecting from a husband?

Yes, I am a woman, Mullah! My beauty longs to be beheld. You believe I am dirty. You believe sex is a sin. You are filled with disdain for my body. You tell me only men have urges. You say it is always an offence for me, it is only humiliation and pain for me. You want me exiled from my body. Your devotion is to ideas, not feelings; to men, not women; to them, not me.

Yes, Belal knows how to look at me. My soul resembles the contours of my body. It has curves. It has cycles. It never stays the same. Something in Belal's gaze unravels the woman in me. Something in me comes awake, grows whole and real in his presence.

From my chair on the roof I let my eyes wander up to the clear sky. The vastness of it takes my breath away. Crows are roaming over my head. Are they the harbingers of doom? I don't care. Come what may. Come hell or high water. Today viva life, viva death!

Today I am not interested in Shariati. His voice is receding; instead a contemporary of his, a young woman, a poet, Forugh Farrokhzad is plucking on the strings of my heart:

> *"How much longer will you speak of love's agony*
> *If you ache for a kiss from my lips, seize it."*

Monday, March 20, 2006

By no stretch of the imagination could I have seen myself kicking off this Persian New Year in the German club in Dhaka. While in Iran *Eid Mubarak* wishes were exchanged, I was in the company of ten German men: tall, blonde and burly.

It started with Karl being cranky throughout the afternoon and refusing to talk to me - just because I had passed my lunch break at the internet café and not with him.

"You hang out with internet café guys in London too?" he had snapped at me. "*Mensch*, you are old enough to be their mother, you realise that, don't you?"

I bristled at his words. By now I know that he, like me, is quick to boil and as quick to cool. Still this insight didn't offset the sting of his tongue.

Having come down to his normal temperature after the afternoon clinic, he turned on his charm for reconciliation, and wouldn't let go until I caved in and agreed to go along with him to the German club.

"You and I have at least one thing in common," Karl said. "We are both headstrong." I took it as an 'I am sorry' or just a simple 'thank you', or a combination of both.

At Karl's request, Tanvir dropped us on the way back from the clinic. We climbed into a rickshaw for the short distance to Gulshan. The yellow passenger seat was too small for the two of us. Karl occupied the space for two and our bodies were pressing against each other. I felt guilty about the weight we imposed on the rickshaw driver. I looked at the wet patch on the back of his white shirt - the same sweat that drips down the back of a jogger, only he was engaging in the exercise to earn a living, not for living well. Now and then the rickshaw driver grabbed a green cloth - the colour of the scarf that was wrapped around his forehead - to wipe the beads of sweat from his parched face. Many times he got up from the saddle, leaned on the handlebar and pressed all his weight on the pedals to overcome our weight.

With one hand, Karl drew back the rickshaw hood to make space for his head - all the blue birds, pink lotuses and green leaves adorning it were pressed into an indistinguishable coloured rim.

"*Ach Mensch*, are they beautiful! Men in Germany would love to shag them." Karl was peering at some girls in saris getting into a car. "How can one tell the prostitutes apart?"

And why would he want to know? I swallowed my thoughts and acted deaf for the sake of peace.

Karl is a giant of a man, like a big American major, not just in his physical appearance but also in the way he towers over people in the street, with an air of superiority and ownership. We are a strange couple. The image that comes to my mind is that of a petite South Korean woman with a big American marine in documentaries or movies on the Korean War. I might not have the body of a South Korean woman, but Karl is definitely as large as any American soldier. I usually walk next to him with a sense of dread that one of these days his insolence will incite a fight. Today was a close call when three young guys on a nearby rickshaw smiled at me and I smiled back. They seemed to be having fun. Two were in black jeans and a shirt, and the other in blue jeans and a kurta. The one in a kurta took out his mobile and snapped a photo of me.

"*Shunduri* lady, beautiful lady," he turned his mobile towards me to show the picture. "Country?"

The moment I said Iran, all three asked simultaneously, "Muslim?"

"I like your president," one of them shouted. They were delighted to see a Muslim from the land of Khomeini. It was not the first time I had encountered respect and admiration for the drab-looking Ahmadinejad and 'his proud resistance against the US'. Even in England I had patients who would come to congratulate me, "They think they can trample on us, but your president is strong…. Good man." I am sure if they could they would give me a pat on the shoulder to say 'well done' to a person they thought of as the representative of their warrior.

"*Verdammt*," Karl's voice dropped. "Why are you encouraging those boys? Don't answer their questions."

"The two of us attract too much attention, Karl," I said by way of explanation, and continued in my own head, 'People surely wonder what kind of relationship we have.'

He glowered at the boy who was taking the pictures. "You okay?" Karl's voice sharpened. His jugular was pulsating rapidly under his tanned skin, which was now turning red.

"Yes." The guy smiled. "German?" The boldness in his voice set my heart racing.

"Ya. And you're from Dhaka?" Karl moved neither his gaze nor a muscle in his face - two rhinos locking horns.

"No. Rome," the boy said with a grin on his face.

"*Parlo Italiano?*" Karl asked.

"*Certo…*" The boy had flags of triumph waving in each eye as he spoke in fluent Italian.

Fortunately, our frail rickshaw driver pedalled faster than the boys', and we left them behind.

Karl got off the rickshaw snarling. "Your president, by the way, has the face of a monkey."

"So does Bush," I replied.

Unlike his usual generous self, he gave the driver the normal fare - collateral damage - and marched off. I hung back pretending to fasten my loose bun, and when I was sure Karl couldn't see, I poked the driver in the arm and pressed another twenty *taka* into his hand.

The sun was still blazing when we arrived at the German club.

"If it were not for me, you couldn't sneak easily into this sort of place." Karl took long cheerful strides through a large metal gate. The traffic noise was drowned.

The place he was touting emerged behind a tall brick wall. A tree-lined path sprayed with a heavy chlorine smell curved past an empty tennis court into a sort of English pub with a huge garden. I eyed the pool and the two female heads in it.

"*Gruess dich,* Karl." A voice beckoned us to a long table with about ten German men around it.

"*Gruess euch,*" Karl responded to the greeting.

I was introduced, shook hands with a couple of them, and finally settled on the chair Karl had pulled out for me. I was the only woman at that table. It reminded me of that old classic movie with Frank Sinatra and Sammy Davies Junior, and another actor whose name I don't recall. The three old friends meet after many years. Sitting around a bar table, they realise how estranged they have become and hum to the Blue Danube Waltz, '*Was mache ich hier, hier, hier?*' in the German version I watched as a child. If someone could have read my mind as I was sitting there, nodding and smiling, they would have heard me humming, 'What am I doing here, here, here?'

I tried to strike up a conversation with Florian, the man next to me. Not being able to come up with anything more original, I asked him what he was doing in Bangladesh.

"I am here for the tea," he said, and gestured to the cup in front of him. Unlike the others, who were drinking beer, he was having tea. "This is the tea of Gods."

"And you couldn't get it back in Frankfurt?"

"I measure rivers," he replied. "I am an engineer, and my friend here," he put his arm on the shoulder of a portly man next to him. "He deals with high voltage electric transmission. Do you know what that is?"

"Why should she when I hardly understand it myself," the portly man turned to look at me.

"I gather you are a doctor too?" Florian asked.

I nodded yes.

"Why though?"

"Why I am a doctor?"

"No, why are you here? People who do kindness are usually projecting their own need for it onto others. The locals here can help themselves best."

"Can they?" I was groping for an answer. Then I said, with a tone of irony, that I was 'fighting against poverty and injustice'. It was not a strong argument but I wanted to deflect a long serious conversation. I was worried neither my rusty German nor my skills at debating would keep up.

"Poverty and injustice are relative." Florian tossed a handful of peanuts into his mouth.

"A man beating up his wife is not relative." I was hoping that would shock them into silence. I may scribble all kind of ideas and opinions in my diary, but I shy away from entering into a discussion with someone who might glean my ignorance, someone who might work out that I don't have a clue and haven't thought it through to the end; the *juje* - the chicken - that Fardin had seen in me.

"He might beat her up, but she knows that he takes care of her," Florian said.

As I was mumbling some sort of a counterargument, I became aware of my hands gesticulating wildly, as if I was reaching for something somewhere beyond words, as if my fervour could compensate for what my rationale lacked. I consciously stopped my hands; they might see it as a sign of nervousness, I thought.

"They have their own system to look after themselves." Thomas exuded calm. "For example, the girl in Wolfgang's factory stays with her brother who is a driver for a middle-class Bangladeshi doctor. The money the doctor makes in his private practice goes into the driver's pocket; he supports his sister, and together they support the family in the village."

"Community gives stability and security," Florian added. "One can do more harm by meddling."

They looked quite likeable in their casual attire, with serious but amiable features - not at all the 'bad guys' one imagines when signing petitions against sweat shops. Their steady eyes were merely tired, maybe even frustrated and lonely.

Everyone I have met so far, no matter which corner of the globe they come from, is here either to give or to take, either to make money or to help. These seem to be the two main lures of poverty.

Later in the evening, when we were back in our residence, I had a call from Maman, Baba and Omid, wishing me a happy Nowruz. I couldn't help feeling melancholic and a tad sorry for myself. Peyman sent me an email. He couldn't get through to me on the phone.

Friday, March 24, 2006

His words are still echoing in my head. "Your choice," he told me.

Belal called an hour ago. These midnight calls have turned into a routine. I worry Karl might hear us; the phone is in the corridor next to his room.

"He is old. His hearing will be poor." Belal ignores my warnings.

I don't ask him what his family is up to when he calls. It is always past midnight, so I assume they are already in bed.

Tonight I moaned about Karl's improper manners. I told him of my daily torturous rides to slums, of my being sandwiched between the staff while Karl relentlessly demands my attention to his observations, meaningless comments and filthy remarks, and the fact that he gets cross should I fail to lend him an ear.

I was not detailed in my descriptions to Belal. Shame held me back. I worried Belal might think less of me if he knew that every single day before my shower, I permit Karl's impudent remarks about rubbing my back, let alone sharing the obscenities Karl pours out about Bengali women time and again.

His lowest point was today after the clinic, when he met one of the slum girls to whom I have been teaching English. I expressed my pride in and admiration for her curiosity, talent and rapid progress. Karl listened to me in silence. 'He must feel parental towards her too,' I thought. Then he glanced at her and stated in a nonchalant tone, "She is exotic, sultry. Men love that. It'd be easy for her to become a prostitute in Germany."

My stomach knotted up. It was plain disgusting.

I refrained from recounting any of those stories. I merely said Karl was a sexist and that every other word he uttered was about sex. I trusted Belal's imagination would read between the lines, but there was no comment from him. I pressed for a reaction.

"He likes you. It's easy to like you."

In and of itself this explanation was improper and ignorant, but not the way Belal delivered it. The tenderness and care in his voice tempered my dissatisfaction with the actual content.

"I am contemplating informing headquarters," I disclosed.

"You've worked hard to get where you are. Didn't you tell me yourself you have been planning this for years? Try to see it through."

Belal has a point. If I report Karl, I might jeopardise my plans.

"Sometimes you try hard to fight everything. Let it take its course and just focus on your work."

I could tell he was genuinely concerned that I might get into trouble by taking the issue any further.

"Solmaz, this is the life you have chosen for yourself," he said. "It is your choice."

My choice? What choice was he talking about? Me having problems with Karl? Me working in a foreign country? Or me being single instead of being protected by a husband? Or the choice that I was up late at night being comforted by someone else's husband? What choice?

Do I really have a choice?

Thursday, March 30, 2006

In a period of five hours we did sightseeing, ate dinner and had our first fight. In brief, we made the most of our time together.

Shaheed Minar was a must-see according to Belal. He parked the car near the Medical College, and we ambled the short distance to the monument. As we drew closer to Dhaka university, the traffic became sparse and the roads larger. The last beggars we encountered were a blind boy led by an old man in a long white lunga and a Muslim cap. Belal placed some *takas* in their hands.

The university campus was a district of its own, dotted with clusters of students. It was the familiar scene of any university life: boys and girls, books and backpacks, the serious intellectual face, the laughing charmer, the romantic, the cool guy with his

Playboy bunny T-shirt and a cigarette, the animated discussions, the group of girls lounging on the grass, and the couples. However, the city life invaded it with its rickshaws, coconut and melon vendors, and a few cars. Amidst a group of neatly dressed students, a teenage boy was lying in a corner. He was in a yellow lunga and an open red shirt. With his knees pulled up to his chest, he had curled up himself in a foetal position, his face, shielded by his arm, turned away from the crowd. Through the open shirt I could see his soft brown skin, but his hands and the soles of his feet were rough and thick with layers of soil.

This is Bangladesh. Everything is lumped together. There is no perfect and pure moment of peace or privacy. You can't artificially separate lives. Life spills into life. Public life overruns the private space, and the private happens in public, like the little girl on our way who was defecating in the raised barrier between the two traffic lanes.

"We are the only nation that fought for our language." Belal was referring to those students and intellectuals who rose for the right to speak Bengali and were defeated by the Pakistani forces. "We are not just a poor country." Like other Bangladeshis, he was proud of his country.

"I know there is more to your Bangladesh," I said. The truth is I don't. I said it only because I somehow felt for him.

If cities raise monuments for the same reason we put pictures in our homes, if they keep a particular memory alive because it defines them, then the few statutes on the way to Shaheed Minar told the story of struggle, suffering and sacrifice. Its red circular plate rising behind the white marbled columns was a token of rising hope as much as of bloodshed.

Shaheed is the same word we use in Farsi for 'martyr' - I'm pretty sure it is Arabic though. The East seems to declare those martyrs whom the West calls heroes. One shines the light on the pain and the other on the glory.

Yet the past didn't impress me as much as the glance Belal shot at me the instant I got into his car today; a quick scan of my blue jeans and beaded black kurta, followed by a smile that said,

'You are beautiful.'

He drove me to Banani for dinner. It's one of the smarter parts of Dhaka, but the restaurant was quite simple, furnished only with plastic chairs and square plastic tables covered with white linen. When I went to wash my hands, I caught sight of a folding jute screen separating a section of the room for prayer. There were even special facilities for washing the feet as part of the Islamic ritual before prayer. That is Bangladesh too: religion and all life's essentials hand in hand.

At dinner, Belal told me of his first love. Last night he had rummaged in his old boxes, looking for her letters. She was a Bengali and also a Muslim, a girl of twenty whom he had met on the college campus. Their love story had spanned over five years. There was a mixture of joy and melancholia in his tone as he spoke.

"Our families didn't match." He meant that she was richer. Her family was moving to the States and she had asked Belal to join them. "Basically, she said that her father could secure me a job, but my life was here. I had my parents here." He shrugged his shoulders. "I am selfish. Love is important to me, but it is only one part of life. I wouldn't give up everything for it."

Our gazes turned to our neighbouring table: two men and one woman, all three Bangladeshis, who were speaking English with an American accent. He cast his eyes downward and shook his head. For a moment I sensed he was wondering how a different choice would have shaped his life.

His vulnerability put me in a dreamy frame of mind.

"Imagine you and me far away from all this; another time, another place, marooned on the sandy beach of a stunning Greek island, walking, a cool breeze on our faces. Utterly carefree, light ..."

"You talk like a sixteen-year-old girl."

I blushed. His comment was as sobering as the burning sun

and the smog of Dhaka that we had left outside the closed doors of the restaurant.

"Sorry." He knew he had embarrassed me.

I sulked and he apologised. I went on sulking and he went on apologising.

"Never change. This very ability of you to dream is what I love most," Belal said in the car.

"Women dream while men are ruling the world," I protested. *"God, deprive me of all the talents that are not of use for people,"* I quoted Shariati.

"It'd be the end of the world if women stopped dreaming."

"Then let's start with the end!"

I couldn't help laughing at the apocalyptic tone of my words. That was it. I had spoiled my own drama. So I did the only appropriate thing. I threw in the towel and, still laughing, suggested we forgot the whole incident.

"You say it now, but tomorrow I'll get an angry email from you." Now it was his turn to mope.

"Being angry becomes you; it makes you sexy."

"Oh, God, deprive me of all the talents that are not of use for people," Belal citing Shariati like me set me off into another bout of laughter. When I finally managed to look at him, I saw him gazing out of the car window, facing away from me.

"Hey, Belal." I tapped on his shoulder.

"Silly girl." When he turned towards me, there was a big smile on his face, a boyish smile, not his usual enigmatic one.

Next we headed to Vivek's place. He had asked Belal earlier to take me there to examine one of his two children.

Vivek led us to the lounge, which was his bedroom at the same time. I was curious to find out more about him. Yet, his flat didn't tell me anything about its inhabitant; it was a generic space without any individual features. The sort of furniture, decoration, books and music that would reflect idiosyncratic traits were missing. The items were merely necessities, their value was in their function not in their aesthetics.

129

Sitting on the floor, Belal and Vivek chatted in Bengali, enjoying a cigar with whiskey, while I assessed the rash of Vivek's younger daughter. Together with her sister and grandmother, they are Vivek's adopted Muslim family. A series of fateful incidents had led them from slums to the shelter of Vivek's home.

Before we left, he gave me a picture of my face that he had sketched on a serviette. He had accentuated my large eyes and eyebrows that seem typically Persian to him. There was a rose next to my portrait.

"You know who my favourite Iranian poet is?" he asked.

"Rumi? He is every foreigner's favourite Iranian poet."

"No. It is Omar Khayyam. He, like me, revels in women and wine," he laughed.

"Awake, my little ones, and fill the cup
Before life's liquor in its cup be dry…"

He took a sip of whisky and recited louder.

"Oh, come with old Khayyam and leave the wise
To talk, one thing is certain, that life flies,
One thing is certain and the rest is lies;
The flower that once has blown, forever dies."

Vivek was very forthright; he stated he had never been with a woman more than six months, as thereafter every woman starts to bore him. He preferred cigars, alcohol, art and his male friends.

And he is Belal's best friend. What does that say about Belal?

…It is not love though, is it? Love is a child of reality and fantasy. There's no place for fantasy here. And the reality?!

Thursday, April 6, 2006

Today I saw more than a hundred patients in two different clinics, taught English to fourteen students in our slums, sat for my first Bengali exam and kissed Belal.

How was it? I don't know...

I have a headache now; his breath smelt of nicotine, his lips were too soft and yielding, nothing like Fardin's strong and firm kisses... In brief, I did not feel much.

The images of two women I had seen earlier today were bouncing around my head. The first one was an old-looking woman - she appeared old, but was not necessarily old; here even the young can look old. A frayed brown sari covered the woman's head. She was squatting on her haunches breaking bricks, while the child by her side was playing with pebbles and gravel.

"They break the bricks into smaller pieces and then mix that with sand for construction. We don't have natural stones. You can only find them in the hills, and it would be difficult to transport them to Dhaka - and also expensive," Eshan explained.

"How comes there's no man around arguing that the fair sex is not made for that heavy a task?" I said.

"This is Bangladesh."

It would appear that poor women here are more equal to men than their richer sisters. Ironically, poverty grants them some freedom, some equality. They are the ones who also easily divorce - as opposed to the middle class, which is in charge of custom and tradition. The middle class is the one agonising about good reputation, but their strict moral codes don't apply to the poorest and the richest in this country: the latter because they can afford not to care, the former because they cannot afford to care.

This realisation was made more disturbing by the sight of

131

another woman slumped at the side of a busy highway. Middle-aged with long grey hair, she was completely naked. Her bare breasts were sagging, while her genitals were somewhat protected by a ragged raincoat. She was holding out an emaciated hand, begging. A bright sunny day, streets awash with people and cars, but nobody even bothered to look at her. Poverty had robbed her of her femininity, of her sexual allure.

A Muslim woman. Naked. In a Muslim city. Do people ever wonder what their prophet Mohammad would have said to all of this?

As for me, I was done for the day. All I wanted was to forget. So I lounged in Belal's office, this time sitting on the chair in front of him while he flicked through some documents, occasionally taking a puff on his cigarette. He kept shifting in his seat. There was a restlessness in him I hadn't seen before. Something was different. I dismissed it and attended to the book on my lap, until the heave of a loud sigh drew my attention back to him. I caught his black eyes - they were on guard.

Belal put out his cigarette and rose from his chair. He walked across the room towards the bathroom - or so I thought at first. Soon I heard a key being turned in the lock.

Belal's office became safe.

His warmth, the mingled smell of nicotine and Armani, reached me seconds before he placed his hands on my shoulders. They slid down and closed just below my neckline in a soft embrace. A shiver went tingling down my back.

"Does that mean we are alone now?"

"Yes," - loud, certain, and relieved.

I took Simone de Beauvoir from my lap, got up and put it down on the chair. Behind the closed curtains the sun must have been retiring one more time. As the light sank, the muezzin's chant rose, "*Allah is grace, I bear witness, there is no God but Allah.*"

Belal grasped my arm, and we swayed backwards until my back was against the wall.

"Rise up for prayers, rise up for salvation," the speaker in the mosque was calling to devotees.

Balal let his slender fingers wander along my lips, like a pianist playing an octave. They followed the shape of my upper lip and then moved to the lower lines of my mouth. I could sense the hum of anticipation in his fingers. All my desires, longings, and the frustration of the last weeks surged onto my lips. I wanted the waiting to come to an end.

His finger slid in between my half open lips. I lightly bit on it.

"The time for the best of deeds has come," the muezzin was pouring into the silence of the room.

"I love you," Belal whispered.

"I can't hear you," I smiled, trembling inside.

"A Muezzin from the tower of darkness cries,
Fools your reward is in neither here nor there."

I could hear Vivek reeling off those words of Khayyam as we kissed.

Friday, April 14, 2006

Rain is pouring down from the gutters and heavy drops are beating on my windowpanes - their sounds overlaid with children's laughter and screams on the streets, and the rickshaws honking...

The ceiling fan drones steadily. I am on my bed, half-naked so as to let the sweat dry. A smile persists stubbornly on my face. My eyes wander down to my chest. They linger on the words written by Belal: 'I Love U'.

We were lying on the couch in his office, talking and kissing. He grabbed my pen from the table, pulled down the collar of my shirt and scribbled something. I didn't read it at that time, but later in the bathroom, while splashing water on my neck and chest, I caught sight of his scribble. "Oh," was all I uttered.

We had arranged for Belal to pick me up from the Sheraton Hotel. I intended to have some me-time with a large coffee in an air-conditioned place, but it didn't work out the way I had planned. It took me too long to put my embarrassing rickshaw ride from earlier behind me.

On the way to the hotel, I asked my rickshaw driver to halt briefly by a supermarket to buy a jar of Nescafe coffee. When I came out of the supermarket I saw a myriad of rickshaws, all of them colourfully painted with pictures and inscriptions and all the drivers looking the same: short and slim, with worn-out shirts and lungis wrapped around their legs. It would have been a perfect snapshot for a travel magazine praising Dhaka as the rickshaw capital of the world, but a somewhat puzzling scene for me. One of the drivers smiled at me, giving a reassuring nod. I got on his rickshaw and shoved my heavy rucksack onto the floor. I was busy looking around, checking out the boys and men of all ages with a *taqiyah* - a prayer cap - on their heads and in long *fatuas* - shirts - returning from *jumah* - the Friday prayer - when the usual exchange took off.

"Country?"

"Iran."

"Oh, Muslim!"

Why was he asking me the same questions again? Something was amiss. Instantly I became aware of a desperate yelling behind us. It was another skinny rickshaw driver who was speeding behind us, like a small boy whose ball had been snatched away from him.

Muddling up my drivers, I had jumped onto the wrong rickshaw. I was not really any better than Karl, whom I constantly chide.

My cheeks turned red and, with my head down, I changed

rickshaws. Ashamed of my blunder, I tried to gloss over my ignorance with a generous tip and a good amount of smiling to both drivers.

When Belal emerged at the Hotel lobby, I was still not done beating myself up. Belal was wearing a long brown *fatua* with a *taqiyah*.

"Have you come from the mosque?"

"Whenever I get time, I go to the *jumah* with my father."

He looked sexy in this mixture of modernity and tradition.

"Coffee?"

"This is not the real Bangladesh. Let me take you to a real Bengali place with real Bengali food."

We drove to a small stall with rusty chairs and tables, in the basement of a dark old shopping market. Loud Bengali music was booming from a nearby shop. I don't know whether that was the real Bangladesh but for sure I would never have found that obscure place on my own. An old man was cooking in one corner, while a young boy was serving.

Belal ordered tea with *dosa*.

Torrential rain had set in as we left the car park and rushed into his office building.

"Race you to your office." I shot up taking two stairs at a time, followed closely by Belal. We mostly ran neck and neck.

"Not bad for a man who doesn't exercise at all," I said on the fourth floor. I too was gasping.

Belal showed me on his computer the pictures he had taken of his house. I had asked him for them, as I wanted to catch a glimpse of his life, and he had taken me literally. There was even a picture of the toilet, but none of his - or rather their - bedroom. I liked him even more for this discretion.

"I would have taken you home if there was not some work being done at our house."

"Really? Would you have introduced me to your wife as 'this is the woman I kiss'?"

"Stop it, Solmaz."

He slipped a blue bag into my hands. I peeked inside. There was an MP3 player.

"Walkmans are out of fashion," he said, his tone less troubled. "I've downloaded some songs for you."

I unwrapped another gift. It was a watch, a watch with two different displays.

"This way you can always have both time zones, Dhaka and London."

He had remembered what I had mentioned in one of my emails from London, namely that I had kept my watch on Bangladeshi time for several weeks after my return.

I also had a gift for him. From a shop at the Sheraton Hilton I had bought two identical T-shirts with a quote by Gandhi on them: *You must be the change you want to see in the world.* I had straightaway slipped into my new shirt in the changing room at the hotel - his I held out to him.

"No, give me the one you are wearing."

"But this is sweaty and soggy."

"That is the one I want."

I turned my back to him and, holding the new shirt tight between my knees, I pulled off the other one over my head. It smelled of my sweat mixed with a musty odour. I half-turned my head. He was still standing in the corner away from me. His gaze was fixed on me. I put on the clean shirt and left mine on his desk.

"In the last few weeks I've spent more time with you than with my wife in the last seven years." The earlier playfulness was gone from his eyes. They had turned wistful. "You know today's joy will be tomorrow's pain."

"Yes, but I can handle it," I said firmly, trying to convince both of us of its truth.

As we left the building together, we had a moment of privacy in the lift. I wanted to kiss him one last time. Belal, however, pulled back and reached for my face. He cupped it in both his hands, locked his eyes on mine and didn't utter a single word. I smiled; he had an earnest expression. Like a photographer, he was framing my face with the touch of his fingers. I had a sense he was mummifying the moment.

"Come on, Belal! Don't look at me like this. I am not dying," I tried to conceal my own melancholia.

"Let's take the rickshaw tonight." He left his car in the office.

Saturday, April 15, 2006

"I am not going to lie to you to please you, Solmaz," Belal didn't look at me. "No. I don't."

That was the premature death of our romantic rickshaw ride last night. Upon my return home I omitted those words from my diary, yet it didn't change the fact that yesterday's tenderness had fallen prey to some unexpected ogres.

Belal doesn't believe in gender equality.

I was not surprised. I didn't scream out, 'Et tu, Brute?', like a stabbed Julius Cesar, yet a fatal wound was what I felt.

"No big deal," Eshan would probably say.

I had friends in Austria who didn't like foreigners, but they liked me. "You are different," they'd tell me. If I ask, Belal might say the same, then he'd regurgitate a passage he's heard in his mosque: *Men are in charge of women because Allah has made one of them (men) to excel the other (women).*

I am sick and tired of religions that fail to make me, the woman, their *mokhatab,* the one addressed in script and speech.

Does anyone address me at all?

'Father, Son and Holy Spirit'. I feel like jumping up and down, waving and shouting, "Hello Father, I beg you! Here is your daughter. Take notice of me too. And while we are at it, what happened to Mother? Seriously what did you do to Mother?"

Thou shalt not covet thy neighbour's wife, nor his servant, nor his ox, nor his ass...

What self-respecting woman, reading the tenth commandment, can take religion seriously? Finding excuses for religious insults is no better than a woman who explains away the blows of her abusive husband.

Religions are made by men for men. They speak only to men. I am through with them, really through.

I need God in my life, but not the God of religions. I need the real God, the One who sees me, the woman, the One who respects me and considers me competent and valuable, the One that entrusts me with great responsibilities, assigns me to significant tasks and also grants me rights. The One who doesn't speak *about* me but *to* me. The One who also recognises my sexuality, a sexuality that is not just in the service of men, to give them pleasure as a wife, to produce their heirs as a mother or to be the daughter who will produce even more heirs for them, male heirs. The One that acknowledges my ageless sexuality which does not cease with my periods. I DO NOT stop being a woman, I DO NOT become sexless when my reproductive functions end.

It seems God is an invention of men. They have the monopoly on Him. Men have taken out a patent on God.

Is a woman not doomed to feel alien when the One she worships is always referred to in terms of her opposite gender? It is no wonder that women feel subordinated to men when even their God, the Almighty, is male. How distorted and pathological do we women then become?

Maybe it is not 'penis envy' that women have, as Freud thought, but 'God envy'.

Sunday, April 23, 2006

After Sunday mass, Karl and I met outside the church. We intended to try out the pizza place Karl had spotted in Gulshan.

"Stop, *tamun*. There is a Pizza Hut there," Karl called out at our CNG driver.

"Don't scream. He doesn't need to know where we are going," I said.

Karl didn't give a snappy comeback. He was a changed man, courtesy of his first Bengali mass today. He told me he was touched to tears by 'the simplicity and purity of his fellow believers'.

"If I were a widower, I would have sold everything in Germany and moved to a village here."

Throughout the evening Karl remained charming. No more picking on me for my poor general knowledge of politics or my afternoons spent in the internet café. Instead, he looked at me with fondness.

"Solmaz, *Mensch,* you are attractive. If only I were twenty years younger," he said. "Though you have an impulsive temperament. I can imagine you planning to go out to the opera one evening and, after getting dressed and all, changing your mind at the door and deciding to stay home for a lazy evening."

In Pizza Hut, we received five-star treatment. Two doormen eased our path, first to one door, and then to another which opened into a cool and immaculate space, the exact opposite of the outside. The chilliness of the restaurant made cold drinks redundant. A Westerner at the table to our right wore a green sweater and had a shawl around his neck. I also spotted a jacket next to him; he clearly moves from one air-conditioned place to the other.

Doors always separate space and ambience, but in no other place is this separation so tangible as in Bangladesh. These are not merely plain doors, but fairytale doors in the way they separate contrasts and leave you open-mouthed after passing through them. These are transformative doors - not just for space, but also people, for their very posture, mood and the way they carry themselves; one becomes soft by entering, and tough on leaving.

My gaze fell on a young man in a red kurta, his chest thrust out. He was taking large strides, whereas the woman next to him, probably his wife, walked almost on tiptoe. At the adjoining table, three young girls were batting their eyelashes at two boys who threw them smug smiles. At another table, a young Bengali girl in a fashionable *churidaar* caught my attention. Snuggled against a boy, she opened a heart-shaped locket and showed the inside to him. She looked enchanted. He, however, gave a faint smile and looked down at his mobile again.

"I don't believe in love," I said.

"What is that supposed to mean?"

"Oh, nothing. I had an email from a Bengali friend in London. She is having an arranged marriage." This was true. Soon Rekha is coming to Bangladesh to get married. I am invited. But it was not so much Rekha who preoccupied my mind. I was still mad at Belal.

"I do." And this coming from a man whose every gaze and word belied this.

"Do you love your wife?"

"Of course," Karl replied right away. "We have been married for thirty-five years."

"And you have been loyal to her over all those years?"

"That is beside the point."

"Then I take it you haven't."

He shrugged his shoulders in a manner that said he didn't care what I thought. "You don't stop travelling or thinking after you get married, so why should you stop looking at other women, or even coveting them. Only a man who is content can be there for his family. An affair doesn't mean that you don't love your wife."

140

"But what about trust? When I am with a man, I need to know that I am special."

"*Na ja* - well - that's what I'm talking about." He leaned back in his seat. "Women only cause themselves unnecessary suffering. It is about moments. Sure, in that moment you are special to him, maybe not the most special person, but he has chosen you. That makes you special. It is always a special moment unless it's with a prostitute."

"I couldn't sleep with a man who is also with other women."

"An affair is temporary, but a marriage is something solid: planning a life together, having kids; these things are sound and reliable foundations. Your problem is you don't like men."

"What? No, I do."

"No, you don't." Karl shook his head.

"How did we get here anyway?"

"It started with you asking me whether I am loyal to my wife. A question I would never ask anyone, but I still didn't want to let it hang in the air."

Karl was right. My question was inappropriate, but there is a voice in me that doesn't leave me any peace; it propels me forward despite my shivers and fears. It leaves me unsatisfied. It doesn't let me rest and accept reality, the way life *is*. It demands beauty. It demands love. It will not settle for anything less. That voice is a wild horse. I don't know how to tame her. I keep tumbling from her back. These falls are tiring me, yet she pressures me to mount her, again and again, paying no heed to my aches and bruises. She scares me. She is fiercer than I. How do I draw the rein? How do I break her in?

Monday, April 24, 2006

It's hard to believe. Karl is leaving in five days!

"Even my dog in Germany has a better life than these

141

people." Deep frown lines formed on his forehead. Our eyes were burning because of the smoke rising from the shack in front of the clinic.

There was yet another public strike, something of a trend in Dhaka. Eshan had cautioned us against taking the car - that could be interpreted as breaking the strike.

Today Karl's mood was like mine: sour. Early in the morning, shortly after we had opened our doors to patients, a woman ran into our clinic, howling and whining. Her teenage son is dying from bone cancer in the hospital. She screeched with pain, beseeching our help, her face contorted with desperate impotence. Between the sobs was her story: a few weeks ago she and her husband had left their village and came to Dhaka, so as to be closer to their son. They had to pay for everything; in fact, they had to buy morphine from the black market - and now, with their savings dried up, her husband couldn't afford the hospital bill.

"Why can't my son go to India for treatment, like all the rich people?"

No amount of vitamin tablets, cough syrups and antibiotics we prescribe will do away with this inequality in Dhaka. It only lulls our conscience. On the one side there are the countless poor and on the other side the very rich, and only an insignificant number of middle class. There are shops, cafés and restaurants exclusively designed for the elite. If it wasn't for this mismatch, this enormous gulf between the classes, the elite wouldn't feel privileged and special.

I barely like myself here. I sweep away others' misery: a girl flinging and pushing her broken, loose-hanging arm through the car window begging for money; a beggar shuffling along and carrying his friend - a trunk with a head - in his arms; disabled people sprawled on the pavements. Now I only say *joteshto* - enough - and turn away.

Is it a symbiosis? Do the poor stay poor because everyone

is, in one way or another, deriving some benefit from it? How does this social make-up shape people? What marks does it leave on the soul? The souls are like the city itself, growing chaotically and aimlessly. Poverty is a cancer; it eats away all beauty. I might not be on speaking terms with religions at the moment, but I cannot help recall a quote from Imam Ali: *Poverty comes into a house through one door, through the other faith goes out.* Islam has never glorified poverty.

My patients sometimes don't seem poor just in money, but in hopes, dreams and desires.

This afternoon Karl, bent on opening my 'naïve idealistic eyes,' as he said, took me on a tour through the government hospital. When we arrived at the Medical College, he ventured, without any permission, into various wards. Giving the staff a withering look, he self-righteously opened the door to one clinic room after the other, holding it open for me to peek inside. He did this with an air of arrogance, not the slightest unease or any sign of shame, not even when the doctors on a gynaecology ward shook their heads and threw him a harsh stare.

"See there are probably five hundred beds, but they admit five times as many patients. Patients lie on the floor of the intensive care unit," he filled me in. "We are not responsible for them; their own people are."

"I am not any less responsible just because I was not born here," I said.

"*Ach Mensch*, open your eyes. You are an idealist - no, you are only sentimental."

Saturday, April 29, 2006

His last day, and I finally mustered up the courage to blurt it out. There was no particular trigger other than Karl's 'Oh, you have already showered? Weren't we supposed to have a last shower together?' There was something in me that couldn't let him go without telling him what I really thought of his conduct in the last months. I worried I wouldn't be able to look at myself in the mirror if I let the chance to stand up to him pass me by.

"You do realise that you've been sexually harassing me over the last months?"

"For God's sake, you are my daughter's age." His voice was shaking. His white teeth were literally gleaming against a tanned complexion. "I have always been very generous to you." His face darkened. "The only problem is I am German and you Iranian."

Part of me wanted to let it go, but I had vowed not to waver in my resolve. "That is not true. For a woman I have quite a high threshold for sexual jokes." My heart was pounding in my chest. "Don't try to tell me that any European woman could have stood being subjected to your obscene remarks on a daily basis. I have come here to work, not to be treated like this."

"*Mensch*, what are you going on about? I have always respected you professionally, although it's not like me to trust younger doctors," he replied. "You are impulsive and ungrateful. No wonder your husband divorced you."

Our argument transpired in our lunch break. The rest of the day passed in an awkward silence.

After dinner he knocked at my door. I was resting on my bed.

"Let's forget and forgive. I am leaving tomorrow." He gave me a hug. "After much thought, I found the reason for your outburst. It was not easy but I figured it out, it was predictable." His face expressed satisfaction. "You are more of a man than your husband ever was, so you are taking the frustration out on me."

I said it was okay. And it would have been had he not come back for more hugs.

"We are alright now, aren't we? I like you."

"Yes, no problem." I was starting to feel uncomfortable.

"Your ex was stupid to let you go. Next time find yourself a proper man, a German man." And one more hug.

"Oh, *der kleine Karl hat sich gemeldet*! Wow, I am much younger than I thought." 'The little Karl said hello' - he was smirking with triumph.

Now he's finally gone. I pace through the flat, go to his room, then to the living room, then to my room and back to the living room, announcing first in a whisper, "He's gone," and then rather loudly, "He's gone!"

Tears pricked my eyelids. I almost cried, not out of joy, but because I was sad. I felt sorry for myself for having had to put up with him for such a long time.

By the time Belal called - just before midnight again - I was relaxed and a different person. I lay on the floor in front of Karl's room with only a shirt on and chatted with him. Meanwhile a couple of cockroaches were crawling up and down my sweaty legs. Unlike my early days, I was oblivious to them. I didn't find them hideous or revolting. I merely shook them off each time they came back.

Belal and I got down to talking about how we met and when we felt what.

"Peyman doesn't approve of us," I told Belal.

Last week Peyman had managed to get through to me on the phone. When I told him I had kissed Belal, his response was, "Him too?" He meant after Fardin. "Belal is a married man; what he's doing is wrong."

"Peyman is right. But we didn't plan on this," was all Belal said.

I wanted to know what he would have done if he were not married; he said he might have proposed to me.

"Just might?" I teased him, saying I wouldn't have married him anyway as he was not loyal.

"Loyalty depends on the woman," he fell back on the old chauvinistic reply.

In other instances, I would have spewed fire like a dragon. Last night was not one of those. "Yeah, yeah...sure...."

We lost track of time. It was 5 a.m. when, with great effort, we ended our phone conversation.

I managed to get two hours sleep before going to the airport with the driver to pick up my new colleague. Marie is a pleasant French woman, a brunette with short hair - after Karl that's like fresh air.

Monday, May 1, 2006

It's strange, almost unbelievable, how the mood has changed in our little apartment. Just subtle changes like how Marie always puts up a foot on her chair, her slender shin with the bony kneecap boldly pushing against the table edge; or the way she wraps her large yellow towel around herself, her hair dripping wet on the wooden floor and the scent of summer trailing behind her as she dances from the bathroom to her room; or how her large, dark sunglasses watch over a serene, happy smile at all times on the streets. And the way she speaks English, rolling the r's, drawing out the vowels.

Marie is the exact opposite to Karl. Women are so much better. They know how to be comfortable in their own company without spectators and applause. In her presence, peace and sanity have settled over the rooms.

Tuesday, May 9, 2006

"I sinned, a sin all filled with pleasure
Wrapped in an embrace, warm and fiery
I sinned in a pair of arms
That were vibrant, virile, violent.
In that dim and quiet place of seclusion
I looked into his eyes brimming with mystery
My heart throbbed in my chest all too excited
By the desire glowing in his eyes.
In that dim and quiet place of seclusion
As I sat next to him all scattered inside
His lips poured lust on my lips
And I left behind the sorrows of my heart.
I whispered in his ear these words of love:
"I want you, mate of my soul
I want you, life-giving embrace
I want you, lover gone mad.
...
I sinned, a sin all filled with pleasure."

Every once in a while Belal would slide his hand under my kurta and I'd pull it out.

"Please," Belal pleaded with me.

He slipped the straps of my bra from my shoulders. My skin was numb. My eyes were glued to the door. I couldn't dismiss the awareness that the office boy was somewhere in the building. He lives in a back room on the same floor. And there is always Belal's driver waiting outside by the car. What if one of them popped in for some reason or other? A locked door might avert explicit embarrassment, but it doesn't grant privacy.

Our touches were hurried, our kisses sneaked and our lust fearful.

'Not this way! No!' My body was screaming. 'Not in this trivial manner.'

I pulled down my kurta and kissed him more - not passionately, but desperately. I wanted the kiss to shove away the confusion that was bearing down on me.

His hand grabbed the belt of my jeans and descended behind it. I was shocked. I grabbed his wrist, and pulled it firmly away.

"What was this?" Anger suffused me at the dinner table. "Just take me to some place and let us get it over with."

Tonight has been a bad compromise, settling on a halfway intimacy; we hadn't made love. That was the complete opposite of the dance of our fingers. We were clumsy teenagers. Above all we hadn't done it in style.

"Why the rush?" he said.

"Isn't that what we want? Then let's do it."

"Do you have to plan that too?" His voice was full of sorrow. "You constantly put me in a pigeonhole." He attempted to take my hand; I pulled it away. "You easily get mad. I am not like you. I can't express myself the way you do." He drew back to his seat and stared out of the window into the dark street.

"Sunday is my last night here. Let's go out for dinner with Vivek." That was the only sentence I could get out.

I *sinned* a thousand times more than you, Forough.

I dug out Forough Farrokhzad's poem, *Sin,* at the internet café. This courageous woman writing so explicitly about love is another Iranian genius who died long before her time - decades before I was born.

I *sinned* by not *sinning.* I *sinned* by not having the guts to *sin.* The *sin* was more than I could hold. I was afraid. I was mortified to become annihilated by this thing, this enormous thing that is dark, messy, weird and powerful.

That is not to say that I didn't want to *sin,* Forough. I wanted him like you wanted your lover and did not want him at the same time. I wanted him, but not only for one night. It wouldn't have been enough for me. I wanted all of him.

Sinning was not enough.

148

Friday, May 12, 2006

Our senses are stirred by beginnings and ends. Sights, sounds and scents that were just about to become ordinary for me have turned extraordinary. It is in dawns and dusks that we are kissed awake, in all those first times and last times. In less than forty-eight hours I'll be leaving Dhaka, heading to my project in the rural areas.

Little things make it impossible to dismiss the approaching end. Like today, when I taught the last English class in the slums. I arrived with a handful of books and stacks of chocolates and biscuits for my pupils. At the end of the lesson we took pictures. Each of them thrust their way to the front, eager to stand next to me. Walking out of the school, I resembled a rock star being mobbed on leaving the stage. My little fans came over to me for hugs and kisses. "Do not forget us, Madam," I still hear them shouting behind me. Most of them handed me their own drawings as gifts. In their drawings - mainly village scenes - houses were orange, trees had yellow trunks and green leaves, lakes were blue, fish brown and boats purple.

I recall the Italian lady who, looking at the pictures in our clinics, had described them as 'simplistic art'. She was a minor royal, someone rich who was visiting our project to assess whether it was worth her money.

"How is the intelligence of the people here?" she asked Marie. "Is it like in Africa, where I had the impression they were provided by nature with the basic necessities in order to survive and could also improvise well, but they were not capable of learning anything new?"

"Actually they are very curious and keen to learn, especially the women," Marie explained calmly, as was her way. "You even notice how their walk changes after they've learned something new. They hold their heads up and step out with pride."

149

That evening, with the lights turned off on the stage, Marie and I took a break from this relentless saga and stepped up to the auditorium, the rooftop. The air was humid. Karl had just once set foot on the roof; he had come to see for himself what kind of exercises I did every morning. I suppose he didn't like it - he never made another appearance.

"Beautiful, huh?"

"This is breathtaking," Marie exclaimed.

Marie and I propped ourselves against the water tank. She recounted her life as a widow in Paris, her children and grandchildren. Marriage was not on her agenda; she had planned to work for *Medecins Sans Frontieres*.

"As chance would have it, I met Henri at the interview. He was supportive of my dreams, but before I knew it I was pregnant." They got married and life unfolded differently. "But now I'm a widow. My children have their own families. I finally have time for my original plan."

"There might be a universal male conspiracy against women."

My response amused her, making her burst out into fits of laughter. I wonder whether she felt the same affinity to me as I did to her.

"Seriously, they seem to have a distinctive attention-a-woman-is-up-to-something radar. The moment their collective mind receives the signal, one of them is given orders to manipulate that woman, wipe out her aspirations by weapons of female destruction: love or children," I said.

"It is a lovely weapon," Marie managed to get out between laughs.

"A woman can conquer the world, but as long as she does not have a husband and children, she is a failure."

"Do your parents expect you to get married?"

"No, but everyone from the medical staff to the rickshaw pullers in Dhaka does. Marriage and children, they think, is the only worthy achievement in a woman's life...."

She laughed again. I smiled over my earnestness. I did mean it. The one conversation besides the usual questioning 'Country? - Iran - Oh, Muslim' that I often find myself exposed to is, 'How many children?' My nonchalant answer is, 'None. I am not married. I am divorced.'

Then a bewildered 'NO' drops like an aftershock to a severe quake. Eshan told me that girls marry at twenty-two and guys at twenty-eight in Dhaka. And Belal warns against imparting this bit of information here... Why should I conceal it? I haven't killed anyone. I am just divorced.

Next they usually want to know my age. Thirty-one is my reply. Then if I am lucky I am acknowledged with a pitying silence, but if the enquirer is less sensitive I hear him proudly declaring, "Oh, I am younger, but have four children!"

"You have a knack for mixing seriousness with the comic." The light of the stars fell upon her face, lending her eyes a quiet glister. "Well, I don't have any regrets." She certainly didn't.

"Don't give up. You are still young. My hunch is that one day a man will come - *someone who dances you to the end of love.*" She pointed with a chuckle to my diary - it has images of Vettriano's paintings, amongst them *Dance Me to The End of Love.*

This takes me back to last night.

I was in a coffee shop, waiting to see Belal briefly amidst his full schedule. He didn't want me to go to his office as people have started to talk. I understood he was worried.

"I'm not worried for myself, but for you," was his response.

Interesting, isn't it? His reputation wouldn't be tarnished by this affair, but mine would.

That day in the café I was wrapped up in making plans, big plans, of how to lead a realistic and rational life, when Belal approached my table.

"May I sit down?"

"Well, I am actually waiting for someone." I turned my head and scanned him from toe to head. "But if you happen to be more interesting, I'll take a chance on you."

"Remember good things come to those who wait."

The jukebox was splashing out Modern Talking beats - *You Are One in A Million, You Are My Soul, My Love* - in the nearly empty café, harbouring only two tables: at one, two parents with their chubby son devouring burgers, and at the other, us. Belal snatched my diary and flipped through the images. Soon we were rating Jack Vettriano's paintings according to our liking. *Dance Me to the End of Love* scored ten for both of us. Then he suggested we play tic-tac-toe. We joked and talked for another half hour before going back to our own places.

I told him he wouldn't get a goodbye gift from me.

"You kissed me. That's the best gift," Belal said. "I won't give you a gift either, but I'll have a surprise for you. I'll give it to you when it's definite."

I don't know what surprise he is talking about. The only surprise would be... I don't dare to think it through to the end. I know it now and I have known it all the way long: this is a dead-end relationship.

Monday, May 15, 2006

He had said something about a surprise, hadn't he? I have been curious what it is, but last night there was no mention of it.

I am waiting in Tanvir's car at the dock for John, the coordinator of our rural scheme, to board the boat. The day I've been dreading; my final day in Dhaka has come and passed.

Let me try to recapture it in sequence.

We met in Belal's office. By 'we' I mean Vivek and myself. Instantly I registered the dark circles under Belal's eyes. At the restaurant he spoke little. He lit one cigarette after the other. Vivek and I engaged in roving dialogues. Vivek had offered to put some of my belongings in his flat so that I knew I had a place to stay on my leave and long holidays.

"Don't be a stranger." He hugged me for goodbye. I promised I'd email him.

After dropping off Vivek, Belal and I were alone in the back seat.

I was waiting for the surprise.

He seized my hand and held it firmly. "Do you recognise the shirt I'm wearing?"

I nodded yes. It was the same shirt he had been wearing in the car to Panam city - when he held my hand in the car.

When I saw us passing the posh shopping mall, I realised the driver was taking me to my accommodation, not Belal's office. Horror gripped me.

"Are we going to say goodbye on the street?" I withdrew my hand from his grip. "Without a last kiss?"

His eyes said yes.

I had thought there was an unspoken understanding that we would say goodbye in his office, behind locked doors.

"Our last evening, and we spent it with Vivek?" My voice was creaky. "Why didn't you feign an excuse so that we could be alone?" Tears rolled down my cheeks. Something was stuck in my throat. I couldn't breathe. He moved closer to me.

"Solmaz…" His words were short and broken. My memory is jumbled. He tried to explain how busy things have been for him and reached out for my hand. He touched the tip of my fingers, I hurriedly crossed my arms in front of my chest.

When we arrived at my flat, he asked the driver to get out. "I am as unhappy as you are, but…"

I refused to listen to him. I wiped away my tears and leaped out of the car. He followed me.

"Let's get on with our lives," I extended my hand.

Our eyes met only momentarily, his were staring at me in disbelief and pain. He seemed to be at a loss for words.

"I'll walk you home."

"No!"

"It is very late. You shouldn't walk alone in the dark."

"No!" My hand was still outstretched.

He gave me a loose handshake and walked behind me until I had reached the flat. I hastened into the building, without looking back, and ran up to the roof, bursting into tears. A crescent moon and a few stars were dimly shimmering from behind the clouds. I recalled the evening, his every move, his smile, his shirt - deep sorrow encroached upon me - a grief for a last embrace that we were denied.

I went down to my room and tried to call him over and over; the line was dead. Exhausted, I drifted off to sleep for maybe a couple of hours. The muezzin's call to prayer awakened me. *As-salatu khayrun minan-nawm* - prayer is better than sleep - resonated twice from afar. It was only about 4:30, and yet I had last night's anger in my heart and a constant 'you arrogant selfish asshole' on my tongue.

I sought refuge on the roof. Dawn was beckoning life to move. The morning air had a chill and fresh scent after last night's drizzle. The streets of Dhaka had taken on a quiet and slow beat. The rush and sounds hadn't started yet. Flocks of crows were swirling around one of the shabby buildings opposite our apartment, and a few pigeons were perching on our roof, but flew away before I had any chance of getting a proper look: as fleeting as happiness.

Did I provoke a fight to stave off the pain of goodbye? For hours I held onto my anger for dear life. I know how to handle anger, but not that inexplicable terror that was welling up in my body, crushing everything in its way, twisting my head and digging a hole in my chest.

When saying goodbye, I took off my silver earrings and gave them to Marie. She gave me a warm hug and promised to come and visit.

On our way to the port, I asked Tanvir to stop at a call centre.

I called Belal.

"Thank you." He heaved a sigh of relief. "I didn't sleep at all last night."

He had tried to ring me several times, but couldn't get through. He had thought of coming to the port and seeing me off, but had been afraid that my colleague might be there.

"There was nothing I could have done. It was a last minute meeting that was shifted to my office." It had been difficult for him to get the evening off. "Ring me when you get there."

"Sure. I'll do that."

"I'm wearing the Ghandi shirt you gave me. It still has your scent. I love you." He sent me kisses over the phone.

Forough's words came to mind:

"Remember the flight, the bird is mortal. "

Monday, May 15, 2006 (p.m.)

"The West is a real mess, too materialistic and money orientated." I have no doubt that John's first words will stay with me long after I have forgotten his name, in the same way today's river trip will anchor in my memory as the one cruise I took on waters reeking of rotten eggs.

Our bespectacled, grey-haired project manager was hunched over his backpack when Tanvir spotted him at the port in old Dhaka, introduced me, and then instantly left the *Sadarghat* terminal. I hurried one step behind John as we crossed the ramp alongside hundreds of Bangladeshi passengers to board the triple-decked ferry. We were flanked by rows of boys, bare slender trunks stretched out under the shade of the gangway, laid out with exhaustion, faces turned away from the travellers toward the heap of garbage - old tickets, papers, plastics, mangos - floating on the grey water. A bunch of barges was moored in front of the ferry, and ashore I could see a

155

handful of street vendors with their carts or baskets, as well as beggars, all squatted over the waste, searching for a living. Yet what stood out was a boy of ten or twelve and a limping, emaciated dog, both foraging_in the sewage for something edible. All the muscles of my face, from forehead to chin, contracted as I screwed up my nose, building a barricade to halt the stench rising from the water, but in vain. Natural elements in Bangladesh know other ways than the conventional senses to reach one. They stick to your skin like glue - the heat, the smell, the man.

With one hand I clutched the backpack on my shoulder, and with the other I pinched my nose as we made our way to the top deck, where John and I found our seats in the back row of a cabin stacked with theatre-style chairs in front of a small TV screen.

"Either we have to be dull to bear this world or we need a God," John said, early into our five-hour ride. He is affiliated with the Bangladeshi Baptist Church, which runs twelve centres in five districts, ranging from adult literacy and training activities to water quality and health-related issues. In the latter they collaborate with my organisation in Khulna. Apart from that, he wasted no time on the details of our individual stories. He was not curious about mine, and not chatty about his. "Science has already been thought out, whereas the spiritual and religious worlds are still mysterious."

If there was any topic that could bring me out of my preoccupation with Belal, it was the God theme. "Tell me about your missionary work," I prompted. "I don't know much." To me, missionaries are synonymous with colonialism.

"My Baptist church promotes social justice, which is faith, truth and spirit." He paused. "You asked the question. I am not imposing." He stressed the last words, which came on a bit too strong to me, bordering on paranoia. Then again, who knows what type of folks he associates with.

"Don't worry, just go ahead. I won't accuse you of proselytism."

"Of course, I'd like you to convert to Jesus. I don't say Christianity as it has right wing American associations. Jesus has said, 'My disciples should go out into the world and spread my teachings and baptise people.' The Baptist church was started after Luther's Reformation of Protestantism…" As he summed up the history of the church, sweat drops emerged on his lean face. "Albert Schweitzer used to say he had two paths: one to show the source of love, which is Jesus, and the other to restore the wrongdoing of the past. At least this is my interpretation of it. People ask me what I do here, and I can't answer it without talking about religion. My kids think we are here for God."

John has five children and many grandchildren back home in Australia. I suppose they would consider it selfish if their parents were here for any other reason than Jesus.

"I am not a fan of religion. Doctrines cause separation," I interjected.

"You mean exclusion," he rephrased me. "All humans do. We divide. I believe in all paths. They all preach that there is a Creator, but I additionally believe that God has a son, and Jesus is his son. He is God." He paused again. "And I don't want you to kill me for that."

I didn't respond. I was working out whether I should tell him that the only community some odd ones like me might ever know is the human community, hence my resentment of all those tribes that make me an outsider.

"But I don't want you to shut up either," he said, with a tone more sarcastic than thoughtful. He must have acquired that sarcasm in his youth when, as a young college student brought up in an agnostic family, he set out in search of something, a strong foundation to hold on to. I imagine him a depressed young man until Jesus came to his rescue.

"No one can shut me up." I turned to face him. "There is

no point in arguing with you. With Jesus as your gatekeeper, I feel an outsider."

"I don't see it that way. I'd like to believe I can relate to people on different levels," he objected. "Still, I believe there is no value-free justice."

"There is then no value-free development work?" I exclaimed.

"We all talk about unity and diversity, but it is silly. You don't want to be in a house and argue all the time. We all look for like-minded…" His sentence hung unfinished. The loud laughter of other passengers hushed our conversation. A group of children were running around, back and forth between the cabin and the deck, while most of the adults were watching a Bengali movie.

"Films here always have the same story line: a good and a bad guy, and a girl in-between. For some reason, she goes first with the bad guy and then ends up with the good guy."

"Why do you think that is?" I had exhausted my arguments and wanted to shift the gears of our talk.

"She is helpless," John said.

On that note I got up and went to the deck for some air - but the air was static, and the foul smell even more intense under the scorching afternoon sun than in the cabin. I looked over to the riverbank: bricks, factories and smog as far as the eye could see. In the middle of my stomach I felt a stirring vortex. Oh no, not another vomit. I rushed back in and sat down. The veiled woman in our row had zoomed in on me. I smiled, but she didn't twitch a single muscle in return. Was she studying me like an object? I can never think without an air conditioner in Bangladesh, let alone in that reek. So, I focused my attention on the man accompanying her. He was eating a snack wrapped in newspaper.

"How can they eat in the midst of such an offense to the senses?" I asked John, who was now dozing. He opened his eyes and followed the tilt of my head. He threw the man an indifferent glance and shut his eyes again.

"My stomach is turning," I said, leaning back on my seat.

"That is pollution for you, another souvenir of industrialisation." John smiled. "We are on the second largest delta after the Amazon. Isn't the boat smooth? It is as smooth as the Titanic!"

'Right, here is a dark-humoured man,' I thought.

Only as I disembarked from the ferry did I realise the luxury our cabin was: the smell was even worse in the lower decks. Sigmund Freud must have generated his notion of sub- and unconsciousness, the soul's dump yard, travelling this repulsive river and this triple-decked ferry almost a century ago. Well, maybe I was learning to think without air conditioning at long last.

A woman in *burka* shuffled to our line of seats with a black-and-white photo of a boy on a hospital report. The veiled Bengali neighbour checked it and reached for her pocket.

"From the softness of the feet I can tell the class of a veiled woman and from the eyes the age," John said, beckoning to the beggar. "Poverty is never out of sight. My pain doesn't feel important amongst all the suffering around me." He slipped some coins into her palm. "They lost a generation of individuals during the war and now the country is suffering," he said, referring to the war with Pakistan after partition from India.

I pondered whether he was here out of sentimentality rather than compassion. If John could have heard me, he would have replied that it doesn't matter as long as one is here. I know that because he told me himself that he didn't mind if he had to bank on guilt to motivate people back home to donate. "If guilt is what it takes, then guilt is what we need," he reasoned.

Maybe there is a place for religion here. Not being religious, not having a God, is a luxury most people can't afford. Affluence doesn't only express itself in things one can have, but also in all those things one can do without, such as God, hope and other people. Affluence brings the ability to do without.

Tuesday, May 16, 2006

Yesterday, soon after sunset I retreated into my room downstairs on the first floor. The hospital and staff accommodation is constructed on a campus encircled by dense tropical vegetation. It is hidden at the end of a cul-de-sac off a dirt road, closed off from the small local kiosks by a large metallic gate and a paved walkway with overgrown hedges on both sides, taking one to a pond at the centre of the campus - all the other buildings orbit around it. The volunteers inhabit the four floors of the guesthouse; John's residence is on the top floor. That is also where we will dine every evening, like we did last night.

John's wife, Judith, has such a softness about her that it could have put me at ease, were it not for all the other people at the dinner table, a cross-section of Western benefactors: three British middle-aged women; a physiotherapist and two midwives; an American couple, both English teachers, with a baby and a three-year-old boy, and a rosy-cheeked, Jewish Dutch nurse, whose brother has stopped by on his self-discovery odyssey through South Asia. After the sweet-faced Judith, Nathan, the Jewish brother, instantly became my favourite in the group. His curly hair comes down to his small, bony shoulders; he said that he had neither shaved nor - wait for it - looked into a mirror, for six months. Of course, in comparison to this weirdo, the rigid and average-looking American couple didn't have any chance with me. It doesn't take much musing to establish why I took such a dislike to them.

For a start, after greeting, the first thing the American

woman said to me was, "Please move up to the other chair."

Not knowing who was who, I had sat on the first empty chair, next to her husband. I got up.

"Where should I sit?" She looked around and suggested the one in the corner; she wanted her husband close to her, but then she rearranged my seat twice more until she had her family around her, the son between her and the husband and the baby on her lap. She couldn't have been older than me, maybe even younger.

"Where are you from?" she asked.

When I said I came from the UK, John interjected, "Solmaz is Iranian."

"I know I confuse people."

"No. You should just introduce yourself as Iranian." John's voice had an irritated tone.

"Oh, you look more Western than any of us," she said, pushing a spoon into her baby's mouth.

That was when I realised that all the women at the table were dressed in *shalwar kameez*, while I was in a shirt and cotton trousers. I was on the point of saying, 'I'm sorry to disappoint your exotic notion of Iran, but what you call your own clothes, are indeed what I grew up in.' Instead I said, "I'm afraid we don't have traditional clothes in Iran like they do here: no saris or *shalwar kameez*."

The new imperialism romanticises aspects of my past or notions about me, bottling them and shoving them down my throat as who I am, even if that is nothing like me at all. Cultural stereotyping is where new imperialism and lazy liberalism cross paths.

Luckily, at that exact moment Judith came out of the kitchen. "Oh thank you, Solmaz. This is so lovely." She was carrying a small plate with the Emmentaler cheese I had bought them in Karl's supermarket.

"Cheese! That is very fancy." John's comment made me see

what an indulgence eating cheese was to them in their modest lifestyle.

After we were all seated, they folded their hands in prayer. "Thank you, dear Lord," Judith bowed her head, "that Solmaz has arrived safely. May she feel at home here and be of service to Bangladeshi people."

They all said amen. I also mumbled amen. I hadn't prayed since my divorce from Peyman. For a fraction of second, I felt the prayer. Something like joy softened my heart and I remembered what it was like to have a God residing in me. And then it went again.

They opened a bottle of wine for the occasion. When Judith poured some into my glass, I didn't object. While I don't drink, I have always loved the colour of red wine. As a child, whenever Maman and Baba were out, I used to pop open a Coke bottle and empty it into one of the crystal wine glasses we kept on display in the cupboard in our dining room.

"It is the first time I've had alcohol," I said, turning to the American matriarch. "What an irony: a Muslim girl raised in Europe having her first alcoholic drink in a Muslim country alongside Westerners." I lifted my glass. Her stern look told me that it had been a poorly thought-out remark, so I hid my face in my fish curry and rice, swallowing down the second funny line that had come to me, 'I hope you're right with your Jesus, or else I'm drinking my way into the Muslim's hell.' Belal and Vivek would have laughed at my joke.

"Solmaz." Nathan, the Jewish Jesus, was shouting my name.

"You need to speak louder. English is her second language," John was talking to Nathan about me. I blushed.

"I was saying, there was a call earlier," Nathan went on. "A gentleman was asking whether you had arrived safely. He sounded Bengali."

Once the reference to Belal had brought him to our dinner table, I didn't feel lonely anymore. My confidence was restored.

Friday, May 26, 2006

Good morning. I keyed in Belal's number on the work mobile John has lent me.

How would I stay sane if not for these regular text messages? We text 'good morning' or 'KLM' - kissing, loving and missing you.

In the first week after my arrival, he called me a couple of times. I had a cold and my voice was hoarse, which he found very sexy. To his disappointment I got better, the voice went back to normal and our communication back to the written word. These simple and ordinary texts are little illusions we weave for ourselves. Their function goes beyond making the separation bearable. They remind us we were not a dream. We happened. We hold on to them for the illusion too, the illusion of closeness, as if the separation had never happened. Goodbye shouldn't have the last word. We even talk about what we eat, or what music I listened to the previous night, or what film he watched. That is all we exchange. We don't say anything else; we don't want to - not yet. Still, he sent me this email today:

Whatever you say, you are right. I should have written much earlier. Solmaz, you mean a lot to me. I love you because of who you are. It was very difficult to separate from you that way on your last night. I only controlled myself with effort. My feelings won't change even if we don't sleep with each other. If I wanted sex, I could have taken you somewhere to be alone, but I feel you are not sure. When it happens, it should be special, neither of us should have any regrets…Sorry for the delay. You might laugh, but it took me two weeks to write this email. I am no good with words. I spent much time on it so that you know how valuable you are to me.

He had struck out the text and written at the end: *If you don't like what you read, you can delete it.*

Delete it? How could I?

I have a surprise for you, very soon. KLM, his email ends.

Sunday, May 28, 2006

I work on five outreach programmes with a focus on women and child health, as well as on the gynaecology and medical wards in the hospital. My role is mainly clinical. It is Dr Khan, the clinical coordinator, who holds managerial duties. I'm glad that he and the other local doctor, Dr Parvani, are working with me closely. They are not volunteers like the foreigners here, but paid staff.

"I feel comfortable with you, you know, because you speak English with an accent, just like me," Dr Khan, an anaesthetist, acknowledged at the end of my first week. He too lives in the hospital accommodation, but not in the guesthouse. I recently found out, on one of my afternoon walks through the campus' green alleys, that there is a separate building behind the training centre just for Bangladeshi staff: doctors, physiotherapy trainees and nurses. Dr Khan's wife and his two young sons live in Dhaka with his parents.

This afternoon, at the end of our working day, he walked me around the rehabilitation ward. It was a long hall bearing two lines of beds, similar to pictures one sees of wartime emergency hospitals. The patients didn't look acute like in the movies, with bleeding wounds, but they were all disfigured. Everyone had at least one limb missing.

"Most of my patients have suffered injuries at work. Others were involved in road traffic accidents," Dr Khan said. "We have a lot of accidents here in Bangladesh. Sometimes, people just fall off the top of overcrowded buses and acquire spinal injuries." He showed me a young man with no arms. "For example, this one has been electrocuted at work, but the company refuses to pay compensation. They changed his identity and claimed that he had never worked for them."

A life so easily wiped out and declared for naught.

Both Dr Khan and Dr Parvani seem to genuinely care for

their patients, although I get a sense that Dr Parvani is here more out of commitment than for the money, unlike Dr Khan. Maybe it is my prejudice, but surely as a man he has to provide for his family, whereas Dr Parvani has more liberty to be idealistic.

"I owe these people my education," she said. She is a gynaecologist in her fifties. With her eloquent gestures she has an air of grace and kindness about her. I like her humble nature and her compassion at work. Her husband is a surgeon, working in Dubai. Their only son is in the States, following the footsteps of his parents into medicine; they also have a married daughter in Dhaka.

When I asked when they saw their families, they told me that they don't have any custom of holidays in Bangladesh, but as staff members of IMC they are entitled to holidays.

A few days ago, while taking pictures of the hospital's wards, I found Dr Parvani and Dr Khan dining together in the canteen.

"You want to show the world how uncivilised we are?" Dr Khan's words drew my attention to their plates. They were eating their lunch with their fingers.

"Come and sit with us, Solmaz," Dr Parvani said.

"Dr Khan and I are going to a couple of villages tomorrow. He will complete his survey, and I will have a meeting with the village community workers and traditional healers. We were just saying you might be interested to come along."

That was a boon to me. Tomorrow being Friday, I need something to stave off boredom.

Friday, June 2, 2006

On the ride to our satellite clinic, our van cut through a woodland of jackfruit, coconut and bamboo trees. We lurched on a meandering mud track, past roadside stalls, cows, chickens, schoolgirls in white *shalwar kameez* and blue scarves, boys playing cricket on the plains. At Dr Parvani's request, the driver paused at a small pond so that I could take pictures of a group of laughing and playing boys who had caught my eye. I was cornered by a dozen boys in white *shalwars* with *taqiyah* - rounded caps - on their heads, all giggling, then shying away before coming back to giggle some more. All of those boys had big coal-black eyes with the sparkle of an excited puppy, smiles of a mischievous Buddha, half innocent and half wicked, and an aura of curiosity about life like that of an exploring toddler. The breeze and brightness of a new morning was as tangible in their faces as it was in the quivering grass. Whatever they touched with their twinkling eyes sparkled too. Their excitement, so trusting and real, could have disarmed the most ill-tempered contemporaries.

Still, there was something else in their eyes, something I don't see in the eyes of children in the West. What was it? There was a particular kind of wisdom emanating from their souls through the windows of their eyes into the world, something of a-light-at-the end-of-the-tunnel kind of hope in those black pupils, that kind of trust - no, that kind of knowing. I asked them their names and found out that they all started with Muhammad and some appendage. A generation of Muhammads!

I stayed most of the morning with Dr Parvani. I suppose I was trying to avoid Dr Khan. He irritates me. In the car, while the three of us were talking about the survey, he suddenly told me, "You are always very serious when talking about work. You are so British with us. Just be your Iranian self."

"That is who I am. I am being myself."

It is perfectly possible that he meant it in an affectionate way, but there is something about him that tells me to steer clear of him, something that brings Karl to mind. He knows I am avoiding him, but doesn't seem to care. He went about his survey business, and Dr Parvani and I spent our time in people's small huts eating *chotpoti* - mixed spicy snack - and drinking sweet tea with them. Dr Parvani never refused anything offered. She explained that it would have been rude, and that these people enjoyed being hospitable.

Later we visited a terminally ill patient of hers. She had been left by her husband. She explained that in Bangladesh women were usually blamed for a divorce; even if the man was unfaithful, the woman was seen as the guilty party - she must have done something wrong to push her husband into the arms of another woman.

"There is nothing but morphine that I can give her. I mean strictly speaking in medical terms. What I can do is be a witness and walk the journey with her," she said. "Solmaz, I have come to learn something they didn't teach me in medical school: that is, not turning away when you can't fix it. If you ask me, that is when, for a doctor, the rubber hits the road. We doctors always want to fix. People also expect that. They want me to fix things, and they think if they could only see a proper doctor, all would be fixed. I can't always cure but I can always be there, just simply be there. That is the toughest lesson to learn."

We ate with them. Then she looked at her patient's medication, suggested a few changes and we left.

"They liked seeing you there. They wanted me to discuss their medication with you. I did so to please them." She said people in Bangladesh believe a foreign doctor might be able to save them. "I never trample on their hopes. I never say there's nothing I can do. There's always something I can do. I mean again just being there and going there, again and again. Listening and allowing them to feel sorry for themselves. There's nothing wrong with that." Then she relayed a story to me. "I have learnt everything from these people - even this I learnt from a patient. He kept coming to see me for his knee pain; it was osteoarthritis. One day I lost my patience, I threw up my arms in resignation and asked what do you expect me to do? And he said, 'Nothing. I just want to moan and then go, doctor.'"

Dr Parvani's visits took longer than we thought they would - no, longer than I thought. They are used to that. Neither of them rushes from one duty to the other, the way we do in the UK, scurrying through our hours. In the UK, we don't just live or work, we binge life and work. We work to the extent of getting sick and then we binge on our holidays, then the cycle continues. No wonder they can do without holidays here. Work and life don't seem to be separate things. They do their socialising while working. I would get sacked by the NHS, or at least get into medico-legal issues in the UK, if I were to befriend my patients or accept gifts, let alone sit and eat with them. It would be unprofessional. I learn to talk in terms of evidence of treatment, boundaries with patients and efficiency of work. Everything is regulated and controlled in the UK. We control it by milking the soul out of medicine. The more I learn how to manage my patients, the more I unlearn relating to them on a human level.

Dr Khan and I left earlier than Dr Parvani, as Dr Khan had received a call that his uncle had passed away. He has to go to Dhaka for tomorrow's funeral. Our driver went and found a CNG, an electric rickshaw, because Dr Parvani, being a woman, couldn't be left on her own and had to drive back with our driver.

In the car, I discovered something that only a local could know.

"Here we think that NGOs are loaded with money," Dr Khan said. "They don't have a good reputation in Bangladesh because of their expensive cars." He then told me about the importance of family and community, and that freedom and individuality are deemed Western ideas, hence dismissed by

Bangladeshis. "People need community. Community is for an individual what sun is for a flower; without that one dies," he said. "Isn't it selfish of you being here instead of taking care of your own family?"

"Selfish?..." My mobile buzzed. It was a text message from Belal: *KLM.*

"Your boyfriend?"

"No."

"Then, what is that smile?" he said. "You've been checking that mobile all day."

He was right. I can't wait to find out what the surprise is that Belal has been going on about.

"So, you were saying," I said.

"See, serious again. Very British."

The bumpy roads have left me with back and shoulder pain, so I am sitting tired but wide awake in my bed now. It took me half an hour just now to compose an email for Peyman and Omid and send it off. Before leaving Dhaka I had emailed them my new contact details for emergencies. They can call me on the landline as it has a better reception than the mobile. Peyman tried to call me up on my mobile in the first week, but it was hopeless. After the email I busied myself with a shower, but the cold water makes my showers rather short. When I went out to fetch a cup of coffee in the kitchen, I spotted the Dutch siblings perching on a sofa in the large impersonal common room, watching a movie. It's just the three of us on this floor. Four rooms and a shared kitchen skirt the living room.

"Solmaz, do you want to watch *Kingdom of Heaven* with us?" Nathan ducked his head into the kitchen.

"Thanks, but no. I want to grab a book and read something."

It was a lie; therefore, I had to pretend to flick through the stack of books in the living room, a collection of books left behind by people who have stayed here over the last twenty years, traces of history: *Bible Commentary*, *New Bible Dictionary*, *The Saffron Kitchen*, *Flesh-market Close*, *Flight of the Dragonfly* and many more. After seeing those books, it makes sense that John is not curious about me. He sees far too many people coming and going and is probably saturated with stories.

Sunday, June 4, 2006

1 a.m. Belal rang me on my mobile.

"Now I can tell you the surprise I have been harbouring."

My heart raced. For a moment, I was one of those Muhammeds at the pond.

"I am emigrating to Australia."

My body froze. So did the room.

"Say something."

I must have held my breath for few seconds. "Wow, I mean... When?" I stuttered. "You alone?"

"Me and the girls." He referred to his wife and daughters as 'the girls'. I remembered that just as 'London' was the word for 'England' for many South Asians, a man's 'I' was the word for 'we' in Bangladesh.

"You are the first after Vivek I'm telling this to."

His voice faded off. From then on everything became muffled. I think he said something to the effect that he didn't wish to leave Dhaka, but Vivek and his father had been pushing him and saying that it'd be a good move, that he should think of the 'girls' and their future; they'd have a better education and health system there. He has a few friends over there; he'd be working in a shop for one of them.

"Is that your good news?" The air was stifling. "What about us?"

"You are my best friend."

170

"*A friend?*" My voice broke.

"A very special friend," he lowered his voice.

I hung up.

Thursday, June 8, 2006

I won't pretend I am fine when I am a wreck. For days I've been ploughing through, trying hard to focus on the project. Just work and nothing else. I am bordering on the obsessive, but it is good; I need that.

Yesterday, just before midnight, I was called to assist with an emergency caesarean section. I threw on my jeans and a long kurta and gulped a couple of ibuprofen. My migraine was very bad and my eyes all puffy from sobbing. I followed the theatre nurse up a path lit by her torch.

We cut open the abdomen of a woman who, unlike the majority of my patients in the UK, did not really have any layers of fat at all; just a tiny cut and we were already in her uterus. There was not much bleeding either.

"All women here are severely anaemic." Dr Khan's teachings were the last thing I was interested in.

The light in the theatre went off at intervals. All of this seemed to be completely normal to them, and by now to me too. Also familiar were the jokes and gossip in the operation theatre. They asked me the standard questions.

"You have children?"

"Not yet, my husband and I want to wait a little." An answer to please them. I couldn't handle a confrontation.

"Is your husband a doctor?" Dr Khan's assistant asked.

"Yes."

"What sort of doctor?"

"A surgeon."

"Iranian?"

171

"Yes."

"Ah, an Iranian surgeon in London!" Dr Khan broke his silence. There was admiration and respect in his voice. "When will you get settled and start having children? You are really being selfish leaving your husband alone in London." Then he drew nearer and murmured, "You know you are not getting any younger."

I could sense in their expression, hidden behind the surgical masks, that now I was something of worth. Before that I was merely a female doctor with no particular significance, but having a Muslim penis waiting for me in London made me valuable, it gave me a life. Before the penis, I was only represented by my own sex: the disposable, the passive, not-worth-a-penny female sex, but now that I was tied to a male I became visible to them, I became part of the human race, still inferior, but not outside of the community of humans; a lower version of humanity, but human.

I was birthed by a penis.

My second birth. My mother's vagina brought me into the world, but the penis brings me into the human race.

I wonder whether they would have been happier if I had said my husband was English. I guess not. An Iranian penis is better than an English one. The English one would have endowed me with an aura of authority and superiority, but the Iranian one makes me one of their own. They will sleep in peace tonight. This vagina knows her rightful place and duty. This vagina remains within the big Muslim family.

Saturday, June 10, 2006

What an irony. Here I am, looking for happiness in the East while he is moving to the West in the search of the very same thing. I can still hear him: 'a *special* friend'. Does he still love me? He is so quiet. Whatever question I put to him hits a brick wall. Tonight I pleaded with him at every second sentence to say something, yet the only response he contented himself with was, "I don't know what to say to make you happy."

"How did you expect me to react to your news about Australia?" Heat rushed into my head.

"I thought you'd be happy to hear it," his voice indicated a genuine disappointment. "You have been behaving strangely lately."

"Strange!" He couldn't hear the loud throbbing of my heart or see my lips trembling, but my voice broke from restraining tears. "Is that all you've noticed?"

"It doesn't seem that I can make anyone happy anyway," he said with resignation.

The thing is that I need more. I don't know what, but I need him to talk, to say something, something to draw a little comfort from. It rips my heart that he makes no effort to see me again; neither does he ask when I will next go to Dhaka.

What should I do?

Sunday, June 11, 2006

Tonight I woke up gulping for breath, drenched with cold sweat and a heart racing mad. Then my whole body broke out in convulsive sobs.

My stomach feels empty, as if I haven't eaten for a week; my chest is not tight, but I can't breathe. In my own world, deep down inside, being with Belal feels so normal, in fact the most natural thing on earth, so that the outer reality - of him being where he is and me where I am - becomes absurd, a sort of nightmare.

I am still in utter disbelief about what happened. I need to speak to him. I need to see him again. What should I do? The ground is trembling under my feet. I need his help to steady myself. I need him to say something. I don't know what he wants. I don't know whether he wants me at all. Maybe his love was only built on an illusion about me. If I don't contact him, he won't contact me.

I am afraid, and I feel ashamed in so many ways. I cannot and do not want to be the woman lingering and waiting for a man who is not hers; not one of those women who, like a beggar, bargains for crumbs from a man. I don't want to be the woman who is a puppet in the hands of a man - a despot torturing me with his silence, as with many of his gender. His silence is not only unfair; it is cold, it is crueller than death. His silence is a sandstorm tossing me about and making my senses even more obscure than this terrifying fear can. I can't battle it alone. I can't battle the fear alone. I wish there was someone who'd tell me that it is okay to feel the way I do.

I have to let him go. I don't see any other choice, but the thought of it alone takes my breath away. Maybe the question is not what I should do, but rather how do I summon the strength to do what I have to do?

Tuesday, June 13, 2006

Judith, John's wife, came downstairs to see me tonight.

"I've been worried about you, dear. You haven't had dinner with us for three nights now. Are you alright? Is your family alright?" She inquired with a tone full of warmth and tenderness.

"Oh, yes." I choked back my tears. "My father hasn't been very well recently. It is his lungs, but he will be alright."

Afraid she might not be content with that, I fumbled for more to justify my grim face at work and the regular retreats into my room. For all my discretion, it was unavoidable for the

174

Jewish siblings to notice my changed behaviour. They must have said something about me spending most evenings alone. At times I even get anxious they might hear my sobs, though I try to shed tears in silence or in the bathroom under running water.

"The weather is so sultry here that I have lost my appetite and suffer from constant migraines."

"I put a plate of dinner in the fridge for you."

I forced a smile.

"You let me know if you need anything, won't you, dear?"

"Sure. I'll do."

Then, as she was leaving, I had a second thought. "Can you please say a prayer for me?"

"Here?"

"Yes, please."

She came and sat next to me on the bed. "Dear Lord, I pray for this child. She is an adult but she is still Your child. Protect her and guide her with Your wisdom. Shine Your light on this precious child of You. Let her feel Your presence in the dark night. I pray that with all my being. In the name of the Father, and the Son, and the Holy Spirit. Amen."

After she left, I felt peaceful.

I need to distance myself from you for some time, I texted Belal.

I love you and don't want to lose you. Whatever and wherever you are I am always with you. Missing you a lot, he texted back.

I envy Judith her faith.

I miss speaking to You. We used to be close when I was a child, but then I lost You. I just couldn't stay in touch anymore. Your name was tainted with blood, hypocrisy and misogyny. I told You I could not accept You without understanding You. I, Your old passionate lover, promised You I would come back once I had the answers I was seeking. If anything I have just drifted further away from You. I haven't found any answers. I haven't found anything to justify those laws attributed to You. But I miss You. I so miss You now. I miss speaking with You.

'Thee do we worship and thine aid we seek,' Muslims say this prayer daily. I would add, 'Thee alone I speak to'. You are my only *mokhatab*.

Mokhatab - what a lovely word! It is said that the miracle of Islam was 'the word'. And the word is uttered by one with an addressee, a *mohkatab*, in mind. The one we speak to is the one who speaks with us. Words are not the sole making of the speaker, they are made in the dance with the *mokhatab*. There are words that are never spoken as they haven't found their *mokhatab* yet; they are souls waiting to be born. They are not even in the mind of the mouth that will give birth to them. They first need to be planted there by the right *mokhatab*, to be kissed awake by the *mokhatab*.

I am tired of the earthly *mokhatabs*. They are flawed. I need the one *mokhatab* that impregnates me with divine words, words to make me whole, words to take me home.

You are my only worthy *mokhatab* - Thee alone I speak to.

Wednesday, June 14, 2006

"You have lost your spark, Solmaz," Dr Khan remarked today.

I feel ashamed. I feel ashamed because I feel exposed. Can it be that Dr Khan sees the helplessness in my eyes, that he can read the anguish in my tone?

It was a long day.

We left early for one of our villages. Dr Parvani's daughter is visiting and came along too. Somehow the heat of the day, the humidity, the sun, everything felt more intense than on other days. Our clinic, an empty schoolroom, was packed with chatty young women with black eyes thickly ringed with kohl, wearing colourful saris, like Dr Parvani's daughter, cheerful withered grannies laughing, snot-smeared children with flies buzzing around their heads. And many more waited outside under the frying sun. At the end of the day my throat was dry from repeating instructions, and I felt nauseous from the intense smell of urine in the toilet where I had to perform gynaecological examinations on a mat we had spread. The odd thing is that the image that is in the forefront of my mind is the beautiful pink bra of one of my patients and a sense of envy about it.

Once Dr Parvani's daughter had me to herself, she related her marital issues in detail under the long shadows of the afternoon sun. It started with me rambling something about her elegant sari, as a way to apologise for my lack of warmth and engagement with her all morning. Upon this she opened up and spoke at length about how her husband was the one choosing her outfits whenever they went out, and her father-in-law requested that she wore a sari all the time, even at home. Moreover, she was hardly ever given permission to visit her own parents. Her in-laws believed she didn't have any responsibilities and obligations towards her 'old family'. She also complained that her husband has so far denied her a declaration of his love; he has never said 'I love you'.

Apart from the exhaustion, I don't feel much. Gazing out through the car window I was thinking there is nothing special about Belal. Now I see that many Bangladeshis have his eyes, his posture, his hands, his arrogance and pride. He is an ordinary Bangladeshi in almost every way. Many of his countrymen think very highly of themselves, and so does he. Many of his countrymen treat women as inferior, and so does he. Many of his countrymen lack courage, and so does he.

Where are You?

I am looking for You everywhere. The only beauty I feel is my thirst for You.

Friday, June 16, 2006

We had to catch a CNG as our driver was off sick again. It was almost midnight when we stopped at a local restaurant, still open. I ordered a dish with fish to evade any more comments on me looking so pale and thin. The waiter brought a huge meal and other plates.

"This is too much for me."

"This is Bangladesh. Here you order for the family and they bring food for everybody," Dr Khan explained, and John smiled.

I was only half-listening to their conversation. By now I know that both these men are used to deciding the direction of conversations. They only want to know the pieces of puzzle relevant to them, otherwise they leave you alone - fortunately for me.

"Everyone has sacked someone at some point, but we have compassion," John was talking about the driver.

"I'd like to take a few days off to go to Dhaka," I said and turned to John. He and Dr Khan had their heads down in a large black folder, studying something. John didn't respond.

"John, did you hear me?"

"I can't multitask."

"Of course, you can't. You are a man."

"I can handle the remote controller."

"You already need a vacation?" Dr Khan grinned. "I like her, but I don't like the restlessness in her. She is not like this with her patients." Dr Khan turned to John, speaking about me in the third person. "I have watched her closely. With them she exhibits bottomless patience." Then he turned his gaze to me. "You can't travel alone. Where will you stay?"

"Nathan is leaving tomorrow to meet his family in Dhaka," John said in his typically laid-back tone. "Why don't you go with him to Dhaka?" He threw me a sidelong glance. "It is actually a good idea. There is a 5-day workshop in tropical medicine in Dhaka. You could attend that too. I'll sign you up. We'll pay."

"I can stay in a hotel?"

"You can pay yourself for the hotel. Just tell them you want to throw away your money," John said. "You won't need the mobile in Dhaka. Make sure you return it."

He will book a room for me in the same hotel where Nathan's family is staying in Dhaka.

Monday, June 19, 2006

Before me, Dhaka is rolling out in sounds of roaring traffic and barking dogs. I get up and dawdle through the huge hotel room, brushing my hands over the desk, the brown oak chair and the TV. I didn't expect John to choose this expensive a hotel, but that is what falls into one's lap when going for accommodation in a nice, safe area in Dhaka.

It was that expensiveness that spurred me on yesterday, just shortly after my arrival.

Nathan was really sweet. He carried my suitcase to the room and suggested I dine with him and his parents. I said no. I intended to pay a visit to the tropical hospital before the workshop. Belal's office, I soon discovered, was within arrow's-range of that building. The next thing I remember is making a U-turn at the hospital entrance, taking off my ill-fitting flip-flops and marching barefoot, fuelled by a carnal rage funnelled into an amber-red laser beam aiming for him. My mind was blank. The traffic and people around me became blurred. I could feel curious gazes fixed upon me, but did not care. With the same fierce steps, without check, I fired up the four flights of stairs and went in. All stayed still for a split second. The film roll got stuck on the reel and we froze: I at the door, he sitting behind his desk on his familiar leather chair, Vivek opposite him, both in suits, with cigarettes in hand and coffee cups before them.

Belal was the first to turn to me; a shade of surprise passed over his face. They both rose to their feet, Belal stood aside as Vivek hugged me, then I extended my hand to him for a frosty handshake.

"Have you had lunch?" Vivek asked, and got the reel going.

Belal hardly spoke, while Vivek inquired about my project and accommodation; I remained vague on both subjects. Although I don't recall much of the detail of our conversation, I am dazzled by the lethal flame burning inside me during that half hour in Belal's office.

After less than twenty-four hours my head is still vacant, but I am starting to feel the soreness in my feet. A fresh breeze is coming in at the open window, which faces a beautiful garden. Its coolness is soothing.

My phone rings.

"I couldn't sleep last night. What about you?" Belal asks.

Just the opposite. I slept through for the first time in weeks.

My eyes wander to the chair where Belal was sitting last night. Why did I change my mind? I don't know. Once I had left his office and returned to my hotel room, I called him. He was very grateful.

"Can I come to see you please?"

I gave him the address. And he came.

It was the first time ever that we were alone together without fearing that somebody might drop in. It was *our* place. I quickly popped into a pair of jeans and a white T-shirt.

When the receptionist rang me for my permission to let him come up to my room, I felt a shiver spiralling down my spine. 'Breathe,' I tasked myself with closed eyes. A soft knock at the door. I turned the knob and let him in. He was still in the same suit. Our 'hello's were exchanged with as little eye contact as possible.

"Can you adjust the AC on this remote control? I am a bit clumsy with it; either it gets too warm or too cold."

A practical exercise of the helpless-woman-and-capable-man seemed the best means to overcome that initial awkwardness. It worked. I stepped away and breathed in the scene, his standing there before me.

"Sit down." I showed him to the corner with seats and the bed. I sat cross-legged on the bed. He chose the chair, upright and tense, with one leg crossed over the other, his hands placed on his lap.

Soon I was telling him how trying the last weeks have been on me, the despair I went through on hearing he was leaving Dhaka, my inability to focus at work and finally my recent panic attacks. He didn't make a sound. He merely listened. To be frank I did not want him to say anything. I just needed to be heard - by him.

"Come to bed." His eyes widened at my suggestion. "Don't worry, I don't want sex." I only wanted him to lie next to me.

As if in conflict, he heaved himself to the bed and lay down, his body rigid, like a petrified animal. I rolled over on my side and, resting on my right arm bent over him, placed soft kisses on his forehead, then button by button I undid his shirt - he lay motionless - I rested my head on his bare chest and listened to his heart, beat by beat, his life happening beat by beat - vulnerable, precious. Then I kissed his chest, right above his heart. Slowly, I buttoned up his shirt again.

"Now you can go back to the chair."

On that note, he jumped off the bed, took back his seat opposite me and exhaled deeply, as if he were just releasing the air he had inhaled before coming to me.

"I don't want you to stay here all by yourself. I'll speak to Vivek. He meant it when he invited you to his flat."

"I don't mind being alone so much, but it is just too expensive."

"I'd feel better if I knew you were at Vivek's. Tomorrow I'll send my driver to take you to his flat."

By and by we stood facing each other and holding hands. He kissed my forehead; I gagged at that, flung myself in his arms and burst out weeping, tears as hot as the sun of Dhaka flooding my face. He squeezed me tighter, his breath on my neck.

"Solmaz, please try to understand."

"I thoroughly understand. Even better than you do. This is why it hurts so much."

With tears in his eyes, he pressed his lips firmly on mine. It was not a romantic kiss, but a kiss of agony.

Tuesday, June 20, 2006

Now I'm sitting in Vivek's shabby, two-bedroom bachelor flat.

A couple of his married male friends are visiting. They are crammed in the small living room, playing poker, smoking and drinking alcohol, a trivial scene - and memories come rushing over me.

They bring back images of my own childhood; my father getting together with other male relatives, playing cards, smoking, laughing and debating politics while football was running on TV; the women huddled in the kitchen, cooking, gossiping about sex and men. I feel oppressed and nauseated. I admit my greatest fear is that I might be in love with a man who is just like them, a Neanderthal incapable of love.

Earlier I went to the terrace to erase those memories, but my train of thought was interrupted by Vivek's adopted daughters; they sat before me and started massaging my legs. Then their grandmother joined us. They kept casting prying looks at me, talking and chuckling.

"Can't you see that I am actually a *conscious* human being

feeling discomfort with those looks and giggling into my face?"
I said the words aloud. They didn't understand English. It only
caused another bout of laughter.

Men in a smoky room on a Saturday evening, women on
the balcony pursuing their meaningless and naïve lives, the
descending sun over the smoggy, stifling city. I felt suffocated,
stuck, and hopeless. There was no escape. I could change
countries, go to college, earn my own living, but the past still
haunted me.

I returned to the living room to prove to the men and
myself that I no longer was that powerless child. They kept
teasing me, and I responded with what I thought were answers
witty enough to defeat them; they simply laughed off my
aggressive tone, turned back to their cards and made me feel
even more frustrated. I was an object of amusement and
entertainment to them. My biting remarks, my opinions, my
judgment of them, my whole being was not of any significance
to them. All was futile. I dwarfed into David before their giant
Goliath-like egos, throwing pebbles at them, which they turned
into smoke with a puff.

Back on the roof terrace, I glared at the poignant face of
Dhaka's moon. In the West you cannot see the stars for the
clouds, and in the East they are invisible because of pollution.
All you can do is have faith, faith that they do exist out there,
shining on your path.

Wednesday, June 21, 2006

Last night I had to share a room with Vivek; he gave me the
bed and slept on the floor. I told him that I did not mind
sharing the bed with him.

"I do," he said in an apathetic tone.

It was boiling hot in that small room. The heat and Vivek's

183

snoring didn't make it easy for me to fall asleep. I went out into the corridor, which was an extension of the living room, and stretched out on the old creaky dining table, but once again the heat, the humidity, the mosquitoes and the cockroaches did not give me any peace. Then the grandmother came and saw me. She muttered something in Bengali, grabbed my hand and led me to her tiny room. To get to the bed we had to step over the head of the two daughters, who were asleep on the floor.

As soon as I lay on the bed, next to this elderly woman, I became aware that she was not wearing any blouse under her sari. She put one arm around my shoulder, exposing her drooping breasts, one of them touching mine above my shirt; before long she dozed off. I had come to Dhaka pining for the arms of a Bengali man and now here I was, lying next to a naked Bengali granny. It seemed the stars had granted me what I had wished for, but with tiny changes due to miscommunication, perhaps a result of poor reception because of the infamous air pollution - an example of how we all, sooner or later, pay for what we do to nature. But seriously, I was very grateful for the darkness in the room because I was not eager to know what kind of sheets I was sleeping on. Nothing in that flat seemed to be really clean. Lying on those sheets, soaked through with sweat and hearing the trickling of the tap in the corridor and the buzzing of the air conditioning over our heads - there was too much disruption for me to go to sleep.

When I was sure that the granny was in a deep sleep, I freed my body from her embrace and left the room. It was 3 a.m. I called Belal. He was awake as usual. He felt bad and guilty that I could not sleep, but also infuriated that Vivek hadn't fixed up a room just for me. We chatted for a while, and he promised he'd come up with another solution. I decided to go back to the snoring man. I made enough noise to wake him up and temporarily stop the snoring. Soon my exhaustion got the better of me and I dozed off.

Thursday, June 22, 2006

Unbelievable! Yesterday I moved into Belal's house.

His mother, his grandmother and his younger brother…I met them all. I am in Belal's house, and I've met his family. Just unbelievable.

His family received me with warmth and kindness. His wife is away with the girls, visiting her own parents in Sylhet. And Belal thought it best if I leave my luggage in his house.

Their house is a two-storey, well-presented townhouse with four bedrooms; the grandmother shares one with Belal's children and brother, and his parents use the one downstairs. The entire second storey is girded by a balcony, which overlooks the courtyard and a small garden. It's a simple household with mainly Bengali artwork.

I was given Belal's bedroom to sleep in for the time being. When I went to the ensuite bathroom, I saw his ashtray with few cigarette butts next to the toilet seat, his shower gel, his aftershave… I went under the same shower and thanked God for finally being so close to him and his life.

I didn't ask Belal how he had convinced his family to take me in by simply telling them that I was a friend. I assume as the breadwinner of the family, he didn't need to explain. They might also be used to him working with foreigners. And my being a Muslim Iranian, alone in a big city and requiring support, may have helped too.

Later in the evening I played cards with his brother, Osman; he's a chubby boy who has just turned thirteen. Belal's grandmother and mother were wearing simple saris, their hair tied loosely at the back with a central parting. Before dinner, they pulled some photo albums out of a closet and showed me pictures of Belal's childhood, various holidays in Sylhet and Calcutta, and also of his wedding. I saw pictures of his wife as a young bride next to Belal, as a married woman with babies in

185

her arms. I saw pictures of his daughters, cute babies sleeping, smiling, and also as small children playing and posing for the camera. It felt good. I needed to see him, to see his life and all that made up his life.

Belal came home late; the family waited for him for dinner. At the dinner table, I sat next to him. He looked proud to present me as his guest. He encouraged me to tell his family of my project. As I was talking, he rubbed his leg against mine before suddenly pulling it away. The reality of our situation must have hit him.

Friday, June 23, 2006

God, help me.

> *"I am cold*
> *I am cold, and it will appear*
> *That I will never be warm again."*

Only two hours ago I was in this very café having a good time with Nathan. He had seen me from afar having my lunch, and come up to my table. He told me that they were leaving for Calcutta this evening, he and his parents. Then we marvelled at photos he had taken here: a rickshaw driver grinning in front of his upturned rickshaw, two transvestites hugging, and a banner in red with the large black letters of Development on it, below it a girl of about four or five, defecating. I laughed at that picture.

"Development - I ask myself what we are all actually developing here," I said.

"I personally think locals have the best capacities to do well," Nathan replied. "Projects should be run by locals, not foreigners. There are far too many NGOs here, all willing to help, but they are going about it the wrong way," he continued passionately. "Bangladeshis want to be heard, and only when they feel heard do they believe that others care."

We could have been two academics engaging in an avid debate on our findings. I liked that. Debating things makes you believe you stand above them, and moreover that you are better than those you are examining. You distance yourself to watch, thus this sweet sense of superiority - unlike love: degrading, humiliating, earthly love.

That fusion of youth's confidence and optimism in a Jewish Jesus in Bangladesh lifted me up into a good mood. So I hurried up to Belal's office and found him in his customary state: behind his large office desk with the phone in his hand, and smoking a cigarette.

"Let's do something nice and fun tonight." My enthusiasm was that of a cheeky childhood friend, not a heartbroken lover. "Let's go out for dinner."

"I am busy." He glanced at me from the opposite end of the desk. "Go home and have fun with my brother." His voice was detached - no, it was aimed to sting.

"What's the matter with you?" I snapped. I waited for a ripple, nothing. I searched his face for something soft - nothing. He made no sound. He gave no sign. His eyes were fastened upon the papers on the desk. We were in our space, in our most intimate space in Dhaka, the same spot we had teased, caressed and confided in each other so many times, but all he let me see now was a stern grown-up disrupted by a whining child, and all he let me hear was, 'You are a nuisance, I want you gone'. I was gripping the edge of the cliff, below me the void, I was clutching the corner of those lips that had kissed me, hanging on those eyes that had blazed for me, reaching for those long brown fingers that had held my face, below me nothing. I was hanging on that lifeline of a man; just a 'sorry', just a cup of coffee, or even a 'have-you-eaten-yet' could redeem me - nothing.

"Look at me!" An immense force was building up in me. Though seated, my knees were wobbling.

Belal sank against his chair and looked up at me.

"Why are you being so cold towards me? You don't talk to me. You haven't said anything relevant about us since my return. You act as if nothing has ever happened between us." The volume of my voice was changing with each sentence, from disappointment to agitation to anger. "You are acting arrogant. You are not being fair." I paused and then yelled, "Is there any heart in that chest of yours at all?"

"No, there isn't." His gaze locked with mine.

I jerked myself from my chair. He flinched. I dashed to the door. He ran after me.

"I am out of here." I reached for the doorknob.

He seized my arm and turned the key in the lock.

"Open the door." I yanked my wrist out of his grasp. "I want my luggage here by 8 p.m." He was standing between me and the door. I was not looking at him, but at the key in the door. "Open the door or I'll scream."

"Be reasonable, Solmaz!"

"Open the door."

"You are being childish."

I opened my mouth to indicate I was going to shout. He threw his hands up in a gesture of surrender and unlocked the door.

He let me go.

Dhaka has morphed. This reckless coldness. A hot wind was blowing and the sun still glowing on the horizon ahead when I left his office, but it was and stays cold - cold and dark. The city was mocking me, the disfigured beggars were laughing at me, and the crowd of children, those miscarried souls, were haunting me. I cleaved my way through this underworld of spirited skeletons, the rubble of snubbed childhoods, uncherished women and shameful men, to creep under a shelter. I am gulping down espresso after espresso. A burst of terror goes off in my heavy chest. My jaw is tightened and my teeth firmly clamped, erecting a barrier to dam up the fountain of tears that are trying to erupt from my constricted throat.

The clock has started to count down. What if he really returns my luggage? I dare not to think.

God help me.

My head is throbbing.

Please help.

What should I do?

Saturday, June 24, 2006

"Be reasonable, Solmaz." Belal kept his voice low on the phone. "Are you in my office?"

"It is 8. Where are you?"

"Please don't do this. My family is expecting you at home." He was appealing to my reason. How ignorant of him. The last time I consulted that faculty was five months ago at Heathrow in London. I must have sounded resolute, but inside I was terrified to death - for the first time in my adult life, now that I think about it.

"I want my bags here."

"You easily get angry. My family will be upset if you don't come home tonight. What am I supposed to tell them?"

"I want my stuff."

"I am on my way to a meeting in Srimango. If you really insist, I could ring my driver to drop it off at the office."

That was not the way I had mapped it out. He should come and get me. He had no business to be on the road to Srimango. He should be here to reconcile with me. What should I do? Where would I go on a Friday night? My mind raced, but my lips said, "Bring me my bags." I didn't want to lose face.

"Please, be a bit normal," he implored.

"A bit *normal?*" Before I knew it, I had hung up in the heat of the moment.

My head span. No - how could I undo this? Of course, I wanted to go back home to him. It was just a bluff, but now I had played myself into a checkmate. I should have grasped the chance when I had it. There was no way back. With tears locked up in a tight chest, I raced up and down in his office, my ears and eyes on high alert, just like someone holding a vigil, praying to see him walk in through the door, waiting for the phone to ring. I must have resembled a scared, wounded animal. Yes, that is literally what I was: a scared, wounded animal. The rain started beating down. Suddenly the creaking of the floor in the corridor drew my eyes to the door.

"Bags, madam." It was the boy, the driver.

Panic gripped me. If it was a nightmare, that was the part where one escapes by forcing oneself awake. I looked at the clock in his office. It read 10 p.m. The boy was waiting for my next move. I dialled Belal's number again.

"How could you? I can't believe it. You really did send back my bags. Are you leaving me on the streets of Dhaka?" My fear eclipsed all the other emotions.

"Solmaz, please. Don't do that."

I jumped on that hint. "Ok, I'll return."

I followed the boy into the car. Only a couple of minutes later, turning into a road to bypass the Friday night nose-to-tail traffic, we were brought to a halt by an officer. The boy got out. I watched him from the side window in the back seat. The policeman started shouting and wagging his fingers at him. From their gestures, I realised he had steered into a one-way road. I had never looked at Belal's driver before, but in that moment I was seeing him as he was standing with his face illuminated by the car's lights, in front of that dark silhouette of an officer, whose back was to me. The boy had the face of a girl, delicate-looking, with bold, bony features and the subtle glitter of ambition in his eyes.

Being a foreigner and a woman, I was obviously best suited to defuse the situation. I ran to them, and with me the crowds of on-lookers - only men at that time of the night - doubled. There, in the middle, stood the boy and I, side by side, trying to talk our way out of it.

"It was me who asked him to turn. I am so sorry," I addressed the officer, but he didn't spare me a glance. He only turned to the boy and slapped him across the face - just like that.

"Why are you beating him?" I yelled, and I drew nearer to the boy. So did the men around us. The circle tightened. They were all staring at me. I must have looked hysterical. I was hysterical. Tears were streaming down my cheeks and I was screaming, "Why? Why on earth did you do that?"

"Madam. Okay." The boy stayed calm, exchanged something in Bengali with the officer and then, placing his hand on my back, pushed me gently into the car.

"Madam, this is Bangladesh," the boy peered at me through the rearview mirror. The expression on his face told me he knew more than I gave him credit for.

I was still sobbing when we arrived at Belal's house. The driver told the family about the earlier incident. They all greeted me with warmth and sympathy, probably thinking I was just an over-sensitive woman brought up in the West, who couldn't handle the ordinary reality of Bangladesh. They gave me Belal's room again and brought me dinner and tea. Belal's father offered me two of his sleeping tablets, in vain, and his grandmother came to sleep in the big double bed to keep me company in my distressed state - I cannot help attracting Bengali grannies into my bed.

Finally, at 2 a.m., I slipped out of the room and walked down to the living room. I knew Belal would be there. He was

191

in a long and loose white kurta and black *shalwar,* sitting on the floor, his legs bent and the laptop resting on his knees - above him the ceiling fan rotated and in front of him the news channel showed dead men in their white *shalwar kameez,* covered in blood.

He looked up at me while I sat down, huddling up against the wall at a right angle to him. "What are you doing here? Go to bed. They might see you."

"Who am I in this house?"

"You are my friend."

"Do we have a future?"

"I don't know what the future holds." Belal's eyes were fixed on his laptop.

"I can't remember anymore who I was and what I wanted here. I didn't come to Bangladesh looking for love. See, I understand it better than you do. What about your wife? What about your daughters? I do not see any way out."

"Go to bed, Solmaz."

And I did as I was told.

Tuesday, June 27, 2006

For two days I haven't been able to write; I simply couldn't. I was just surviving, running on default. Now I'm trying to record the facts. My memory of last days is faint. He packed my stuff and sent me back to the hotel. There is no grace or respect left in me. Rekha used to call love a sort of obsessive-compulsive disorder.

I feel abandoned and humiliated in this country.

I am sitting on the roof of the hotel, and the sun is setting over Dhaka. Life looks bleak, as if nothing changes here but the vegetation and weather, and I am thinking about suicide. I could cut my wrists or jump off the roof, and that would be that; no Belal, no Omid, no Peyman, no Maman and Baba, no more searching, no more chasing for…what anyway? I could really do it. All these struggles could be over in an instant. You wouldn't even try to hold me back, would You?

Wednesday, June 28, 2006

Last night was awful. Lying in bed, my chest tightened, and I couldn't breathe. My mouth went dry and I broke into a sweat. Next thing I knew my stomach was churning and I felt like throwing up, but I was too weak to move.

I want to die.

Peyman rang. I sobbed on the phone. He told me Belal had tracked him down in the hospital and given him this number.

"Come back."

"No."

"Solmaz *joon*, I beg you to come back."

"I don't have anywhere to stay. I don't have a job to come back to."

"I'll handle everything. Send me a copy of your CV and I promise to find you something soon."

Thereafter, I did everything without much thought. I emailed the organisation, saying that my father had been diagnosed with lung cancer and I was needed at home. I also sent John an email to inform him and asked him to say goodbye to everyone. I told John to keep my books. They will be added to the bookcase in the living room.

Friday, June 30, 2006

I don't know, maybe I just wanted to see him one more time while feeling clear in my own mind, when I was not doped up with medication and in complete despair.

We sat facing each other with two bitter espressos between us. He sat with his elbows firmly pressed on the table, leaning forward, his head bent over the letter I had composed for him. I knew that talking to him wouldn't give me the required result so I had penned him a letter instead, requesting some answers and explanations. He would read a few lines, then stop, let out a deep sigh and look up at me, and then continue. At times he took little breaks to shut his eyes and rub his temples.

In that letter, I had once again expressed my love for him, but also my disappointment in him - *You don't leave the woman you love with all her belongings and with no one to turn to in a foreign city in the middle of the night.* I needed to understand why he had been skirting around the elephant in the room. I had written that I could not be friends with him anymore, not after the last week's events. I had pleaded with him to stop being vague about us and our relationship. I had played along with his game so far; in fact, I had been happy for things to stay vague, as vagueness had given me hope. But now I'd had enough.

He finished the letter and looked up at me. "What you want is impossible."

I really did not wish for anything, no promises or requests.

"Have you ever really loved me?" I asked.

"We are friends, and friendship is love too."

"Come on, you know what love I am talking about. Not a platonic one, but the way a man loves a woman."

Again no clear answer. He kept repeating that friendship and love were the same.

"They are not one and the same. Belal, do you know what I actually want to hear?"

"Yes, I do," he said.

I wanted to hear a *no*. I needed to hear it from him. I wanted a no, so that the pain would die. There was no holding me back this time. It was my last chance.

"Answer in plain English, please," I pushed him. "Have you ever loved me?"

"You are special to me."

"No. Hear me. The question was: Have you ever loved me?"

"No. Of course not," Belal yelled.

"Thank you. That was all I wanted to hear. You can go now."

He stooped his head, covering his face with both hands, rubbing his eyebrows and cheekbones and then keeping his face concealed for a long time. When he finally removed his hands, his eyes were filled with tears. Or so I thought at least.

"No friendship?" he asked pleadingly.

"No, because I am in love with you." I gave a cynical smile. "You lose a friend, but I'm losing... I would have waited for you if your answer to my question had been a yes."

"I never gave you any hope."

We stared at each other in silence.

"I won't wait for you," I said.

Belal continued pressing his fingers against his temples, looking to his right, left, and then again at me.

"Let's go," I said, and I got up.

We stepped out, and he stopped on the top of the stairs to take a cigarette from his pocket. I embraced him; he didn't move his arms in reaction. He was still and rigid as if frozen on the spot. We called a rickshaw and rode in silence to his office. Wherever I looked, bricks of promises: *Housing and Finances Investment, Cuppa Coffee Club, Have Everything Your Way in the World of Icon* - depicting a handsome Bengali in a grey suit with a mobile in his hand, *City Bank, The Perfect Electric Shop, Burger World, Chicken King, The Weston Dhaka: a place where you can be at your best.*

Belal got off the rickshaw; we were in front of his office.

"Please call my family. My brother is asking for you. My mum and grandmother are missing you too."

"I am not friends with your family."

"At least call my brother. He is young; he doesn't understand."

I just nodded.

The rickshaw driver did not stop in honour of our moment. Actually, nothing stopped. The next second came after the one before, time carried on. Shameless time.

"Country?"

"Iran."

"Oh, Muslim?"

"Yeah, Muslim."

DREAM THREE

Total apocalypse on earth. Cities lying in ashes, buildings crashing, smoke towering above the ruins. The end is imminent, I realise and walk to two people who are standing in a corner. We embrace each other, whispering soothing words. Azrael, the Archangel of Death, is with us, in the middle of our little circle. Then in a flash we are transferred into a large hall with round tables; smartly dressed people are sitting quietly and waiting with awe.

We are dead, it dawns on me. We are dead and waiting for God.

No, I whisper. No, I refuse to sit and be still. I get up. "Let Him come," I yell with the full power of my lungs. "Let him come," I hear my angry voice reverberating through the hall. "I am going to talk to him about this bloody mess He put us through. Just let Him come."

LONDON

Friday, July 14, 2006

It is 1983. The clock on the wall shows past midnight. The phone rings. "Since then I am terrified of phone calls coming late at night," Maman always says. "Phone rings are not all the same."

Maman is right. Their timing reveals much about their content. Up to that time she knew the late morning calls from aunts, cousins or female friends; the afternoon ones could sometimes be phone stalkers - a common occurrence in bored Iranian lives - and the evening calls were usually addressed to Baba. These days she also knows the Sunday morning phone conversations with her children. But that particular phone call came in after midnight. Not that we never had late night buzzes. At least a couple of times a month some relatives would decently ring after 10 p.m., before dropping by for a social visit, whereas others would just ring the house doorbell, expecting dinner or maybe even to be put up for the night.

That one was not any of them.

Baba answers the phone. His face cracks.

"Naneh is not well. It is her heart. We have to drive to Khaleh. Now." Baba's voice quivers like autumn leaves.

Naneh Homa sounded the same when she last visited us two weeks before. "My breath is weak today, Solmaz *joon*."

Walking from the door to the living room had rendered her breathless and pale. When she stretched out her legs, I noted her puffy ankles. Omid and I played with them by squeezing deep pits in them and counting the seconds until they filled up again. That was a game she suggested to replace our routine hide and seek around the house. Then she put a pillow on those ankles, laid Omid on her legs and, by swaying them, rocked him to sleep. Maman hunched over a large silver tray of lentils, sorting the good seeds from the dirt.

"Last night I had a nightmare. I woke up panting. God forbid, I dreamed you were dead."

"Tears are joy in a dream and death means a long life," Naneh interpreted.

"Yes, it is *Insha'Allah* good," Maman replied.

Dreams are another of Maman's curses and blessings, like the white fleshy thighs that compelled Baba to ask for her hand in marriage. Maman dreams of exams passed and failed; she dreams of marriages and births long before they come to pass. She also dreams of people's deaths. Nowadays, not only she but even all who know her, from acquaintances to close relatives, dread when she announces, 'I had a dream about you the other night.'

Dreams are not taken lightly in my family. That is another of Naneh's legacies.

"Sleep on your right side to have a good dream," Naneh taught us. "When you sleep in a new place, make a wish or ask a question and the answer will come to you in dream."

She taught us that it was Prophet Mohammad's tradition to heed one's dreams. They could guide you or be a prophecy. Not only is the dream itself important, but also its interpreter, hence good care should be given to whom one turns to for advice. If it is an unwise person, who interprets the dream in negative terms, it becomes a self-fulfilling prophecy. One day someone had gone to the prophet about a bad dream that had come true and the prophet had commented that this was not the true meaning of his dream but it had manifested that way by virtue of the unfitting interpretation.

"When you have a bad dream, you go to pure running water," Naneh told us. "Just open the tap in the kitchen and say your dream to it, not to any other person. You say, 'I had a dream, Ya Allah. It was good, Ya Mohammad. Interpret Ya Ali.'"

Baba carries Omid half-asleep into the car and puts his head on my lap. Baba doesn't look at me, but I see deep wrinkles carved into his forehead.

We drive from the North to the South of Tehran, a long drive from our grand house to the modest house of Khaleh in *jonube shahr* - south of the city, the part of Tehran with most martyrs.

Baba takes deep breaths from time to time. Other than that he is quiet. He has always been Naneh's favourite son-in-law. It may be because of his generosity of spirit and his ability to provide for Maman, Naneh's little girl, and her favourite grandchildren. We know it. Everyone knows Omid and I are her favourites.

Maman too is quiet. She is not crying, only sitting with her palms pressed into each other in front of her mouth, pulling on her lips occasionally and rubbing her face before closing her hands again. I can't tell whether she is praying or trying to keep herself from falling apart.

When I tell her that today, she says she doesn't remember it. As an adult I came to realise that both our memories from that night were patchy, but differently patchy. Like terrified animals we had to shorten our vision. That was not a time when you wish to take in every detail, to behold it for good. You live in horrifying anticipation. You shield yourself from as many painful images as you can.

My recollection of that night is tinged with fear; still, the horror in the eyes of my cousin is burned into my memory to this day. She is surrounded by other figures, shadows whose faces fade next to the bewildered look on my cousin's face the instant the headlights of our car fall on her skinny teenage figure. Her brown *chador* with flowers has slipped to her shoulders, exposing her long, brown, curly hair - an alarming signal, considering the pious girl she is. She is pacing up and down. Her mouth is moving, but we can't hear her. The moment the car's engine becomes quiet and Maman opens her door, we hear her screaming, "Naneh Homa is dead. Naneh Homa is dead."

Maman shrieks, pounds her head with her fists and runs into the house. Baba quickens his steps, silent tears flowing down his face. Omid and Baba are alike. They never cry. But if they do, it must be really hurting.

I feel a pang in my stomach and the loud beating of my heart. They seem to have forgotten about Omid and me. Omid is now also awake. He in his Zorro pyjamas and I in my Inspector Clouseau nightgown with a black *chador* above it. As a child I looked cute whenever veiled, so much so that strange women on the street came up to me and pinched my cheeks. Tonight, the streets are veiled in a dark sorrow too. It is late autumn weather, chilly and foggy. Tehran prides itself in doing justice to all four seasons.

I am holding Omid's hands. My cousin kneels down to kiss us, then she takes Omid in her arms and grabs my hand. She pulls me through the metal door into the yard. Light from the living room penetrates into the garden. It is barren now. Last spring it was covered in roses. We climb up the stairs, eleven of them. I kept count since I competed with my two male cousins last summer to prove to them that a seven-year-old girl could do whatever seven-year-old boys did - I was a better jumper than them. We go inside. We are in the corridor now. My cousin draws me closer to her waist. Khaleh's house, usually a place of family gatherings and joy, is flooded with lamenting women and men. I am petrified we might need to see the dead Naneh. I don't say anything. Adults know better; if we have to see the dead, that is the right thing to do. My cousin turns upstairs to the second floor, but slowly enough for me to dart a glance into the living room at the white sheet with a hump underneath.

Once we are safely upstairs, I feel this strong urge to see my grandmother. I want to see her and they don't let me, the adults don't let me see my grandmother. There is this sense of a hole in the middle of my chest that sucks the rest of me into itself.

"You knock the pebble three times on the grave to announce your arrival to her," Baba teaches me a couple of months later when we visit Naneh's grave. He pours a bucket of water on her grave so that the words shine: *Homa Zaklaki, daughter of Hossein Zaklaki, 1300-1362.*

She is laid before sunset in Qom, the city where the Shi'a Mullahs are trained. On the way there, I shudder in the back seat knowing that Naneh's corpse is being carried in our car boot.

Women wash Naneh's body in the mortuary and wrap it in a white sheet that she has sewn for herself during her lifetime. Once a month, she would get into that sheet as preparation for death.

"Maman, I hate it. Why do it?" Maman would protest.

"Go out, you don't need to see it," Naneh would say in reply.

Naneh is laid to rest with her head towards Mecca. They put a stone on her head before filling the grave with soil. They say the dead don't know that they are dead for a long time, until everyone is gone. Then she will want to get up, hits her head on the stone and realises all that mourning was for no one else, but for her.

"We mourned as custom is for forty days. I cried for a long time, much longer than forty days. I couldn't eat, and felt I was dead. At times in life you experience things which seem to be beyond you, but life has to move on as before, you have to move on as before. Thank God, one forgets things. It would be impossible to live if one could remember all that pain," Maman often says this, then she adds, "But inside me, for a very long time, the world didn't feel the same anymore."

That was Maman. For my part, back then I started to devise all sorts of things to hold on to a sense of control over - no, to deceive - that large merciless world. Later, as a grown-up, I determined that making plans was the best way to hold the reins, but back then as a seven-year-old I didn't know of plans. Instead, I became friends with the archangel of death, Azrael, and made a pact with God: I say my three prayers a day and in return, God keeps Maman, Baba and Omid alive from one prayer to the next. I thought Allah could manage little demands like that.

Which pact do I need now?

It is the first time I am writing since I've come back. I am afraid of pinning down my feelings. Words breathe life into feelings. That might also be how God created life: he breathed words into us.

I miss Belal. How am I going to live without him? After all, they were right about the chances of a single thirty-year-old woman being struck by lightning.

Whenever I was with him, the world still wasn't all right, but I did feel the strength to face anything whatsoever. I felt the same way in Naneh's company; whenever I walked with her on the streets, I walked tall.

As the plane took off from Dhaka, my heart was being ripped out from my chest. I cried to Belal to hold me tight, to never let me go.

It feels as if any minute my heart could stop beating; it feels as if the lump in my throat would not release the inhaled air. In his arms I felt at home.

Wednesday, July 19, 2006

No honking and no gazes in London. Here men are clean-shaven and in suits, women short-haired and in high heels, and dark colours are universal - as is the sight of earnest faces, with no one looking at anyone else, as if they were grievers with rushed steps. Over there the colourful, flimsy clothes; the blowing of car horns; the green of trees, smoky green; the blue of sky, smoky blue; and the roads full of potholes. Yet it is as though one place is celebrating and the other mourning; one is Alice having her adventures and the other is orderly kids in a schoolroom. Here everything seems ready-made, cut to purpose, even the people, but there lives the messiness of opportunity and the unexpected.

Today I woke up early again. Armoured with my diary and the *Oxford Handbook of Oncology* in my rucksack, I walked the eight miles from Finchley to work. When I arrived, it was hardly past seven. Sun was beating down on the large hospital windows. The building appeared still - what a contrast to the frenzied mood inside.

My gaze fell on a black porter in a blue uniform, leaning on the wall beside the sliding doors to the A&E department, sunglasses on his bald head, blowing the smoke of his cigarette into the air and chatting with one of the ambulance crews. I could tell from the relief on their faces that they had finished their shifts. I thought of Omid. I didn't pick up the phone last night. He left a message.

"Hey *gherty*, I haven't spoken to you in a long time. Anyway, just wanted to say hi to me angel. Love ya and a big kiss from your little bro."

It must now be the end of his shift too. He doesn't have to wear a uniform behind the reception at the youth hotel, and he can smoke indoors in Vienna.

A text message was all I could muster: *Sorry I missed your call last night. Busy with work. Take good care dash.* With Baba and Maman in Vienna, I don't need to worry about him feeling lonely anymore.

The porters smiled back at my nod. I walked past them. I couldn't go inside. The size of the building was stifling; its spaciousness could swallow me. So I went to Starbucks.

There is no familiar face left in the hospital. Now that Peyman and I work in different hospitals, we can't see each other that easily. Still, he has been texting every day since my return, and last night he rang me up.

"Are you alone?"

"No, I am with Fardin. What a question! Of course I am alone."

"You shouldn't be alone. Call Rekha."

I reminded him that Rekha is still in Bangladesh, getting married.

"Don't you see what you are doing? It is impossible." Poor Peyman sounded genuinely worried.

"I'm not stupid. You don't need to point out again and again how impractical it is to love Belal, but I do. I love him. What am I supposed to do now?"

"Be realistic."

"Don't you see I'm hurting? I just need hope. Please!"

"I don't want to give you any false hope."

I hung up. I didn't want to hear what he had to say. Peyman means well, but he is clumsy at comforting. The only way he knows how to console me is with revolutionary slogans or Persian poems, no words from himself. In revolution they don't teach personal relations. He rang me back with an Iranian saying.

"*Neither are you old, nor is the world miserly.* God is gracious." There was pity in his voice.

God help me. Time to head off to work.

Sunday, July 30, 2006

When night sweeps through the hospital wards, we focus on sustaining, not intervening - that is for the daylight. In about twelve hours the ward will be filled with shouts of 'good morning'. The bubbling and whistling of kettles in the kitchen, patients' coughs and the sounds of suction machines will mingle with the smell of coffee and antiseptics, against the backdrop of patients being walked or pushed in their trollies to the next investigation. Black and brown women with blank faces and short-sleeved uniforms, their trollies stashed with towels and bin bags, will mop the floors until disrupted by the masters over life and death. Doctors will then crowd around their metallic grey trollies containing patients' files - at the centre the consultant and next to him the nightshift doctor, who is recognisable by the shirt hanging out from his creased trousers.

For now, though, this theatre stage is quiet. As soon as the night nurses were huddled for the handover, I sneaked out to my on-call room.

A civilised on-call, Rekha would call this one. In a strange sort of way, I enjoy doing oncology. Maman doesn't understand though.

"I can never go near a hospital, let alone cancer patients," she said when I rang them up this morning. That was after her big news, "I met Mrs Maryam the other day. They still live in Vienna. She said Atrin - you remember her eldest son is married to an Italian - she said his wife is warm like us Iranians. They have two kids, one girl and one boy. And her younger son is married to a Russian. She says they are in and out of each other's houses. She said, 'Wouldn't you want Solmaz to be near you?' I said, 'Of course I would. A daughter is special, especially my Solmaz, she is like a man, independent and strong.' She asked whether you were married. 'A woman needs a man over her head,' she said. I said Solmaz has other priorities. Life has changed, not everyone gets married nowadays." Maman continued. "How are you? Why didn't you return our calls this week?"

"Sorry. It is because..."

"Oh, I know you work round the clock."

"No, I feel low lately."

"Do you think it is good for you to work with dying patients? It is depressing."

There was no point in disagreeing with her. Clearly, she didn't want an answer. She wanted to skip over the murky waters and I needed to dive in. We didn't do either. Our conversation was drowned.

What I would have told her was that, of all people, I feel most comfortable in presence of the dying. It comforts me to be around loss and death, to be close to it. Out there, there are people who are living, but I am not one of them. Here, I am close to mystery, to people without any masks; here people are like me, all resembling trees in winter with all their leaves gone, vulnerable and completely exposed, at the mercy of winds, no shields to hide behind.

Depressing? The reverse applies. I can only breathe with them. All others live in fear of things going wrong, whereas they are sitting amidst their own ashes. It has already gone wrong for them. Here, I am in Forough's land:

"Then
The sun grew cold
And blessing left the lands

And the green shoots on the plains withered
And the fish in the seas dried up
And the earth, from then on,
No longer accepted the dead onto itself."

Eva took an overdose when things went wrong. She was told the treatment hadn't stopped the cancer cells spreading to her liver. With her eighty-four years, she was not the typical self-harmer I was expecting; a surprise that became a shock at the sight of her tiny body on the large bed. She looked fragile, but her eyes were young and strong. They hadn't aged with her.

"I like your ring." She pointed to Naneh's ring on my finger.

In the half hour I spent going through the admission routine with her, there was no hint of sorrow. I couldn't say whether it was her smile or the sun that put such a glow in her room.

Eugene the Irishman doesn't take any interest in jewellery. His blocked urinary catheter was the only reason I left Eva's irresistible charm. Contrary to her, Eugene doesn't smile. Ridden by Parkinson's, his exterior doesn't reveal much about his interior. His face is blank and his eyes steady. I look at him and wonder why. Is it his cancer that frames his face with agony or the Parkinson's that robs his eyes of sentiments and his movements of vigour, or is it because he lost his wife of fourty years two months ago?

Eugene and Eva are both loners - a word I learned in the multidisciplinary meeting this morning. An Iraqi Kurdish man, Ali, was referred to that way by his social worker. He'll be transferred to our care this week.

Loner - it sounds frightening.

Wednesday, August 9, 2006

Eight o'clock in the morning in Dhaka.

When the heartbeat of the city slows down, my restlessness sets in. It must have been 2 a.m. when, after lots of tossing, I finally succumbed and slipped out of bed to shake off my anxiety by pacing up and down in the living room. The full moon was following my steps like a spotlight - seven steps diagonally and five vertically, I was counting.

My landlady didn't hear me. I don't doubt her solid night's sleep, given the cheerful and dynamic vibe that I perceive in this seventy-year-old widow. From where I stand, the stream of her life flows through a wind-free grassland in an everlasting summer. I look at her as a woman who has been nestled on the edge of that stream - not dipping her toes into the water or diving in, only watching. In her five-bedroom North London house, life is never loud and dissonant.

You'd think I would know the English by now - I don't. Those who say you grow to know others haven't met the English yet. My understanding of my landlady is unlikely to have a second growth spurt after the first few months. BBC Radio 4 is her true companion, entertaining and educated. Her daughter, son and grandkids visit for Sunday dinner; she and her boyfriend of one year - who lives in Manchester - come together one weekend a month; she goes to her gym, helps out with various activities in the local community and does good quietly, without boasting - the way she drinks her afternoon tea and votes Conservative. It was in keeping with her commitment to this unpretentious altruism that she took me in. When Peyman was asking around for a place for me, an Argentinian nurse in his clinic suggested her. She had lodged in her place as a student nurse.

My landlady might have a big house, but I bet she could also make do with less. At this stage there exist only two groups of people for me: those who make you feel at home, and those who make you a foreigner all over again. My landlady teams up with the latter.

We are two women silently living side by side. I leave home when she is taking her morning shower, and bump into her only occasionally in the kitchen in the evenings. I always take my meals in my room. It's not that she minds if I stay in the kitchen, but I don't want to. Sometimes I share my fruit with her or give her half of a cake. She seems to much appreciate it. 'Bless you', 'Oh, dear me' or 'Oh, my goodness' - these are her habitual responses to both me and Radio 4. At times when I feel overwhelmed by the intensity of the pain, I need someone to talk to, but no way would I open up to her. To every generation, to every tribe their own pain. My story would sound *cheesy* to her, the same way the light of the day laughs at the sentiments of the night; in similar vein, her preoccupations appear as trivial to me as the rushing of the day does to the silence of night.

At daybreak I tugged on my trainers and went running. My heart and lungs feel in a constant state of rushing - the exercise is a sheer necessity for my muscles to synchronise with the rest of my body. On days like this, my heart is already racing and my lungs hungering for air long before I set foot on the street. If it were not for the running, I couldn't bear days like this. The rain came on and rinsed the tears from my face. I could tell my tears apart from the raindrops; the rain was sweet, while my tears were sour.

The vanilla scented candle sways its flames to the sad tunes on Classic FM. I fluff the pillows on the bed and lean back on them, writing at one moment in my diary and at the next skimming over Forough's poems.

"And I think the garden can be taken to hospital
I think…
I think…
I think…
And the garden's heart has swollen in the heat of the sun
And the garden's mind, little by little
Is becoming emptied of all green memories."

My bedroom has adopted a Spartan, no-nonsense look. I used to have a calendar on a large board on the wall, a calendar with red and green circled dates: red for the family planning clinics and green for the public health seminars, and so many other plans and goals - not anymore. Most of my stuff remains unpacked in my landlady's garage. Even Shariati's books are there. I still have his picture taped on the cupboard above my desk, and next to him is a picture I have chosen from the dozens of drawings my slum students showered me with at our goodbye. It depicts three houses, one red and two purple, separated by green palm trees with yellow branches. There are three tracks leading from the houses to a river with fish. A man and woman the same size as the houses are standing in the middle, next to a meadow covered with orange dots for flowers. The woman has long black hair, a red shirt and a pink skirt. The man is in a purple lunga, smiling and reaching out for her. At the corner of the picture is written, *Don't forget me, Sharmin, I Love*. My eyes shift to the two pictures of Belal on my desk. In one he is a ten-year-old boy in a suit. He sent it to me in response to a joke I made in his office one day.

"I bet even as a boy you wore suits," I said.

"You think?"

"Yes, I do."

He kept his legendary silence, but next day I received this photo attached to an empty email. In the second one, I captured him in his kurta one Friday afternoon. He is smiling shyly into the camera, tilting his head as if he feels exposed without his generic suit.

On days like this, all I want is to be held by Belal. I need to see him, caress him, smell him...How can I go on? On days like this my judgment becomes poor and I feel overwhelmed by things I have to do and decisions I have to make.

I don't see myself capable of doing a shift tonight. I will call off sick with a migraine.

Thursday, August 17, 2006

Just as I thought I'd give up on Eugene, he cracked open. Ten minutes before my on-call ended came a request from the night nurse to assess Eugene for chest pain. Up to now I have found various excuses to dodge visiting him, and have left him under the care of my colleague with the big diamond ring - engaged to be married.

I never quite know how to help him. The multitude of his problems make me feel incompetent. In addition to his frequently blocked urinary catheter, he has lost his sense of taste, which bothers him most - even more than the swallowing difficulties; his tremor is also out of control and he struggles to articulate words, so that I struggle to decipher what he wants to say.

This week the soon-to-be-bride is on leave and his care is on me. Each morning on ward rounds, when I draw the curtain around his sadness, I try my hardest to ensure that he doesn't see the hurried and helpless expression on my face. I am anxious he might see through me and realise that medically we have run out of tricks to bring him any more relief.

A cloud of pain has settled on Eugene's face. It weighs down on him, making all his features heavier even than Parkinson's does. Time and time again the staff have suggested he see a therapist, but being from the old school, he has objected.

"I don't have anything to tell a stranger."

He seems a man who, even without his Parkinson's, would have put on a brave face, a man who buries his wounds or endures them in silence.

I drew open the curtains. He was sitting on the chair. I suggested I could examine him there, but he insisted on going to bed, precisely what I was trying to avoid. He closed the book he was reading, and with trembling hands put it on his over-bed table. I held still as proof of my patience. My gaze drifted to the picture of a woman with short curly hair and timid eyes, on the table next to his bed. There were some blotches on it - from his drooling or tears, it crossed my mind.

He was still struggling to get up. I reached to help him, but he shook his head no. Instead he reached for the Zimmer frame and put his weight on it to pull himself up. It took him four wobbly, heartbreaking steps to cover a space that I would have covered in one single step. He walked the way a child runs, with the trunk ahead of his legs, so rigid that you'd think he could drop anytime like a wooden stick.

I did my usual examination, and confirmed that he had yet another muscle spasm and not heart pain. I gave him a reassuring pat on the shoulder and started to reassemble my equipment to leave. He has one son who comes visiting first thing in the morning, and I wanted to go before he turned up and made enquiries.

"We used to do everything together," he said. When I lifted my gaze, tears were running down his grave face. "She had dementia for the last ten years. I used to do the chores around the house. I cared for her too. We never had a single fight."

I put my hand on his. He didn't pull away.

"She was a kind and strong woman." He uttered the last words with a pride that said, 'She was my wife.'

Gazing into space he continued talking as though to himself.

"I used to feel strong too, but now I am very small. I think women are stronger than men." He sighed. "There are two trees in Queen Mary's Garden in Regent's Park that are hugging, that is our spot."

"That is beautiful." He hadn't come across as a romantic to me.

"I am a lucky man, aren't I?" He stared up at me.

"Yes, you are."

I thought of all those years I won't have with Belal. I won't grow old with him. I won't be able to take care of him. His wife will.

"Yes," he gave my hand a weak squeeze. "Yes. I am indeed."

How wrong of me to assume that Eugene wanted a cure from me. All his physical pain was dwarfed by the grief in his heart. Over and above any medical miracles, he needed my time and presence. He was not expecting any answers. I like it when not having answers is all right. It makes me human.

Monday, August 28, 2006

People become more real when they live on the edge; they are more honest when the façade is gone, when they can no longer afford the luxury of pretence.

A burst of sunlight was casting sharp shadows on Eva's bed. She was listening to Barry White's *My First, My Last, My Everything.*

"He is my favourite." She had her eyes closed.

The fullness of late afternoon light illuminated her beautiful face - a beauty that is accentuated by an unceasing warm smile, deep blue eyes and an intense resolve. She possesses the amiability of a baby. Liking her is easy and instantaneous.

"How are you managing your prognosis now?" I was exploring any ongoing suicidal thoughts after her recent attempt.

"Well, I manage to cope with it, but I don't manage it."

"Are you afraid?"

"Of course, I am - not of death, but of dying. Anxiety should be a flavour though, not the whole person."

Eva and her husband had come to England from the Czech Republic in 1968, following the Russian invasion. She has a bowel obstruction secondary to ovarian cancer. The community nurse had wanted her admitted for a long time, but she was adamant she wanted to stay home and 'tidy up her stuff' - until one day the nurse found her unresponsive on her arrival.

"I lost all my family. I was the only survivor. Yet, I had a good life." She ran her fingers through her short grey hair, pushing some locks away from her long forehead. "God was kind to me." She recounted her work as a nurse and the large circle of her rich social life.

"I have buried them all. There won't be anyone to bury me." She clasped her hands, caressing her fingers as if to comfort herself. "You know, my dear, as a young woman I cared most about being loved, but the older I got, the more thrilled I've become at the prospect of loving than being loved."

On her chart, we have only her name under the family tree. My colleague with the big diamond ring says that's sad. Why write off a whole life as 'sad' because of a name without any arrows going down from it? Eva is loved. Even now she is surrounded by people who adore her. She is the darling of all our nurses. She is not dying alone. She is dying a darling.

The other one with a lonely family tree is Ali, the Iraqi Kurd who was transferred to us last week. He is dying all alone at the age of fifty after having lived more than twenty years here. He is a man with no country of his own, no one to call his own. I met him - the loner - on one of my weekend shifts. His family is scattered all over Europe, and he keeps silent about himself and his past. I heard from one of the nurses that he used to be a bodyguard. He is now only skin and bone with a moustache and spectacles. No matter how much the social worker urges him, he refuses to contact his family to tell them of the seriousness of his illness.

My patients are a stubborn bunch. Eugene can't eat and still rejects a nasogastric tube, Ali opts out of chemotherapy, and Eva turns down morphine injections.

Ali was in a lot of pain today. He was sitting on the edge of the bed, his legs hanging down, bent double and holding his abdomen.

"God, what is happening to me?" he whispered, and then in the same breath he added, "It might look sad from the outside, but I am not alone. God is with me."

"I am you, you
And the one who loves
And the one who suddenly finds
A vague connection within herself
With thousands of unknown, unfamiliar things."

Friday, September 1, 2006

This pain - I thought I'd be able to trick it, go to the edge of pain but not really fall, not submerge in it. I was wrong.

I have good days when I receive it with cynicism, 'You can't do me any harm. I have risen above you,' I cry, 'I am in charge.' I bask in the sun and call out into the world, 'Here I come.' I am Julie Andrews, singing and dancing in the Alps, as though I don't have a care in the world. But then in the next moment, all of a sudden I'm seized and weighed down by that pain again. I don't even know when and how it has encroached upon me, but it is here.

How can something that heavy tread with such light steps?

I turn my back on it, yet it is there once again; I avert my eyes, still its relentless presence startles me. It walls me in, it is everywhere around me. Try as I might, I can't fight it. I give in and watch it getting hold of all of me, streaming into me as freely as the air I breathe, going deep into my soul. Now it is inside me.

What should I do? Will I crack to pieces? Should I smash my head against a wall to rid of it?

There is only one option left: waiting until it is satiated and slackens his hold.

When the pain grows too intense, as it is now, then I write.

Writing: the witness to my existence, hopes and fears.

Writing so as not to die, so as to keep faith. Writing, trusting and hoping - in defiance of everything.

Writing so that the fear loses its horror. Writing so as not to go weak at the knees. Writing to survive yet another day. At times we write in order to avoid the pain; at other times writing means to meet the pain head on, to give it a name, to give it a face. And the moment the pain has a face and a name; it becomes part of our lives, an inescapable part of our journey.

Sunday, September 3, 2006

"God is my witness. I didn't have any make-up on, only my scarf was a bit down."

It always amazes me how Maman's brain makes associations between the most unlikely things. This memory, for example, was evoked by me mentioning my Kurdish cancer patient who has withdrawn into himself. Once she had started, I knew I had to hear the familiar story all over again. It was about how, on her visit to Iran, she spent three hours in a prison. She was in the middle of sewing at home and ran out of thread, so Baba drove her to *Meydan Mohseni* and waited in the car while she plodded to a haberdashery. The *Basij*, the morality police, happened to be carrying out one of their random raids on that upper-class market, which landed Maman - along with a dozen chic and heavily painted young girls - in their minibus. She didn't have to spend the night in the prison. Baba paid bail, but she was still taken to the Mullah to display repentance. She had to promise she'd never put on make-up again.

"He was holding rosaries and having his dinner. He pointed

to your Baba. '*Haji* looks like a good hard working man,' he said. 'For his sake I let you go.' He was devouring a large chicken with his podgy fingers all the while. You know I don't like meat, but the way he was eating made my mouth water."

I was still trying very hard to comprehend the connection to Ali. Thank God she closed her narrative with, "Who knows what your patient has experienced. These Mullahs are very scary."

"What do you do then, nowadays?"

"Not much. My life is dull. Troubles have become more, and equally friends have become less. Sometimes I busy myself with doing some exercises with the aerobic video you have bought me." She sighed. "Your Baba is trying to snatch the phone from me. He is dying to tell you something about Bangladesh."

She put Baba on the phone. I was curious what urgent message he had for me. He hadn't asked me anything about my visit to Bangladesh so far.

"Are you well, *gizi*?" When Baba is affectionate he uses the Azari word for daughter. "You have a good heart helping these poor people. God will reward you for this." He was clearly in good spirits. "Do you need any money? I am going to Iran in a couple of weeks to finish the sale of one of the flats. I can send you money."

I knew he wanted to demonstrate tenderness by offering money. The reality was, he didn't have any extra to give away.

"Thank you, but it is not necessary. I am a grown woman and earn my own money now, which is enough."

"You are just like your Maman. I always tell her I hate *I* and *mine*, don't use it, but she never listens. *We* is right. The warmth in a house depends on people; it is not about *your* and *my* money. My father always told me two things, 'Firstly, never work for anyone else but yourself, and secondly, never be alone.' It is no good. You can't succeed alone."

218

"Yes, Baba," I said. "How is your arthritis?"

"Much better. It was the cinnamon. I told Dr Zamani, 'Doctor, I am taking cinnamon and my pain is much better.' He is just like you, very humble. He said, 'Yes, why not.' He is a good man. As you always say, being humane is important, not possessing a degree."

I didn't remember saying that, but I agreed.

After hanging up, I turned to the virtual world for company. It's funny how you can ask Google anything and it churns out a multitude of answers. I put 'heartbroken', and 'does he still love me?' and got various pages coming up. Then I tried an online questionnaire for depression. It found me to be mildly depressed, but displaying a high anxiety level. I tried out some of the suggested coping techniques last night when I almost called Peyman to take me to A&E. It didn't work. What helped was sobbing my heart out and screaming - my landlady is away with her boyfriend.

Tuesday, September 12, 2006

Starbucks. 3 p.m. London. 9 p.m. Dhaka.

The days are ruthlessly long without Belal. When feeling calm and sane after a long run or a night's meditation, I promise myself all kinds of things, but in the gruesome brightness of the day I am blown away by the first breeze. I feel ridiculous. Only teenagers lose their minds over love, not mature, level-headed women. Even Belal would poke fun at me. He would laugh at my trembling for his love.

The golden light pouring in through the Starbucks' window doesn't feel warm, but cold. I am hurt by its indifference to my pain. The streets are crowded with people. They like the long summer days. To me it is an insult. Everything is an insult. People's cheeriness, their banter, even the sun - all is sheer pain.

219

How do they laugh when I cannot even breathe? Joy without him is agonising. I long for winter. Winter would shelter me.

How am I supposed to live day after day without him? I am holding my breath. Breathing means living and living means feeling the pain of not being with him. I want to die and am sentenced to live.

...Just a few minutes ago an Afro-Caribbean man walked into Starbucks; he started going around and asking for money. I reached for my purse. He saw that and moved up to my table.

"You a'right?"

I glanced at him. I was met with a sincere gaze. It was not a casual question. The intimacy in his look broke up the cloud around me. My eyes stung. My heart pounded. I felt naked. How come he could see it? Was it that obvious? I forced an awkward smile and buried my face in my bag, hastily fiddling in it. The search for my purse became urgent. Tears started running down my face.

"Is it because of a man?" He kept his voice low.

I quickly gave him some change.

"There are more out there, love." He touched my shoulder.

I looked at him briefly. 'You gotta get out of here,' my eyes urged him. He obeyed. I looked around. All around me were going about their business. Slackening my shoulders and unclenching the grip on my bag, I heaved a sigh of relief. No one had witnessed the scene.

Monday, September 18, 2006

The first thing that had caught my eye was her wedding ring, and my first thought was, 'A married woman. What would she think of me and my pining for a married man?'

The first two sessions with my therapist were spent with me sobbing and filling her in on my story. She listened and I spoke nonstop, as though I was in front of a judge and needed to argue my case thoroughly before her verdict. I was terrified how she would react.

"I'd like to challenge you in this session," she said today. "Is that alright?"

I nodded yes. I was ready to take whatever was offered. I was desperate for help.

"Can you recognise any parallels between your father's addiction to gambling and your pattern in love and romance?"

"You mean I see love as a gamble?" I asked her.

"We hear only what resonates with us."

I was still not getting her, but then she started picking on Belal's resemblance to my father in his infidelity. Interpreting me and my story in the light of her books and training, she expounded on Freud's old bullshit theory about projection, transference and the father complex. I had projected thoughts and feelings for my father or mother onto Belal, she clarified. I wanted to be loved because I had a powerful feeling of love for my father, so I had transferred all that love to Belal as if he were my father.

"Therefore it was false, not an emotionally adult love," she concluded.

"I didn't choose to fall in love with him. I was not looking for love. I am in fact furious that this has happened," I exclaimed. "I am heartbroken, not pathological. Why can't we simply treat it as a natural course of love and loss not requiring any expert's help?"

"You are the one who came to me. Part of you must have thought that an expert was required." She stared at me. "The absence of the father sets up an inner rage to call father into account, a desire to gain power over a man, like saying I am not going to be like other women but will mess about as much as you do." She paused to blow her nose - rhinitis, I thought. "Why do you think you are attracted to the world's dangerous places? Could it be that you are trying to attract your father's attention?"

"No, it is not true. I have always had this dream of working somewhere that made most sense. I feel I am an adult trying to make a child's dream come true."

"That's profound, and romantic. But abandonment by father leads to strong longing for him to be present. One does all sorts of things to attract father's attention."

In her view I had looked for a distant and cold lover because I believed I didn't deserve love and wanted to reinforce that feeling.

"There is no reason why you should feel guilty. You haven't killed anyone."

Whoa. That was pretty harsh. My so-competent counsellor repeated that nonsense twice. "No need to feel guilty. You haven't killed anyone." Being in love with a married man seems to be less of a crime than murder. What a relief! That was of course very helpful and reassuring. Ironically, guilt was not plaguing me - maybe it was her own projection.

Why are we so suspicious of romantic love? Its temporariness evokes in us disgust, and its intensity horror. There is this fear of doom and madness attached to it.

I brought up the analogy of the abandoned child, and again she quoted Freud. I was experiencing 'an extreme sense of rejection and abandonment because daddy didn't love me'.

What is wrong with feeling like a child when in love? Like a child, because you are vulnerable, hopeful and faithful; like a child, you love deeply, and you want to be loved in return. Oftentimes in life when I feel good, I feel like a child.

I left the office of this mastermind of life and love being glad to have come off better than a murderer. It was not a hard decision to drop future sessions with her. When I called the clinic, I told the manager about my disappointment. I complained that I found her a bit too rational and intellectual.

"I assumed you being a doctor yourself would appreciate her rational approach," she replied.

Wednesday, September 20, 2006

In my dream I was driving, but facing backwards. I had to look at the mirrors, and could only drive with extreme difficulty. The car got faster and faster. I finally managed to bring it to a halt, then I changed my seat and faced the front, wondering why I hadn't thought of that earlier.

I rang up Peyman; I needed to talk to someone. He simply listened.

"You always know what's best to do. I am sure you can pull yourself through this," he told me.

"Did you eventually tell Shirin the truth?"

"What do you mean?"

"You picking me up at the airport?"

"No." He was still keeping it secret that he had helped me to move into my new place. When we had met at Heathrow on my return from Bangladesh, he had let me in on the fact that Shirin believed him at the library. It had crossed my mind that it was unlike him to lie, but I hadn't said anything. After all, Shirin and Peyman were not my chief concern at that time.

I remember I had my head resting on the passenger seat, my red eyes closed, holding both hands over my nauseated stomach. My period had come on after two months, and I was glad that I hadn't gone into premature menopause. I have seen enough odd things caused by stress to worry that a broken heart would shut down my ovaries once and for all. Belal and my period were my main preoccupations during that ride, while Peyman was transfixed by my new hairstyle.

"You look like a naughty little boy." He ruffled my short hair. I had cut it the day after saying goodbye to Belal. There was this need to shed skin; that something had to die. The hair was the only primal sacrifice that came to my mind.

"It looks nice. Different." He turned his head toward me. "You could easily pass for a man. Did it have to be that short?"

Judging by Peyman's tone today, he was evading an unpleasant topic - but in contrast to my first day back in London, this time I intended to glean more information as to why he had lied to Shirin about us.

"Why is it that lately you only call me from hospital?" I asked. "There is nothing we have to be ashamed of. And don't come again with 'Shirin wouldn't understand'."

"It is more serious than you think." A heavy tone reverberated in that statement. "Solmaz *joon*, I am getting into serious trouble with not only Shirin but her family too. Everyone thinks it is not normal to be friends with your ex."

"We don't have anything to hide," I said. "It is your responsibility to make Shirin see the nature of our friendship." There was a buzz on my mobile indicating an incoming call. "I have to hang up. Rekha is on the other line."

I knew Rekha had been back for a couple of weeks and that sooner or later she would get in touch to invite me to a wedding party here. She said it would be a small gathering after their registry wedding.

"You sound off, sweetie. What is it?"

I told her I was going through a difficult time, but didn't want to talk about it. She didn't push.

Friday, September 22, 2006

When I went to see my old Czech lady, I noted she had pulled out her syringe driver. I gave her a long lecture summing up the host of reasons why morphine was good for her. She still declined.

224

"I know my own body better. I don't need it."

"Why is it that you want to die?

"There is nothing to look forward to apart from a dignified death." She was not in any way cold, though a bit cynical maybe. "What about you? Are you content, my dear?" she asked me.

"I don't feel happy at the moment."

"No, I said content, not happy."

"What is the difference?"

"Contentment is an inner peace, and happiness depends on outside conditions. It is a response to what's happening outside," she clarified.

"I am content here with you, which feels like a moment of happiness too."

"They do overlap. But happiness is not excitement." She exhaled. "Life has short moments of joy and sadness, we have to relish those transient moments and not wait for something long-lasting."

"What is that you need then, Eva?"

"What I need is to make arrangements to go to the Czech Republic before it is too late."

"Is this why you refuse morphine?"

"Yes, dear."

"Do you think that you won't be able to think and plan clearly?"

She blinked 'yes' with those ocean blue eyes.

I left her room pondering her wish. I thought if that was what she wanted, if that was what was needed to relieve her distress, maybe I should explore the options. I went to the consultant, who is a Catholic man, and when I told him that she wanted to go home he pointed to the heaven.

"That home?"

"No, Czech Republic home."

He said he would speak to the medical director and let me

know soon. Later I slipped into Ali's room. His eyes were half-open.

"Ali, you sleep with eyes open." I woke him up from his nap.

"Is it something bad, Doc?"

"No."

He raised his eyebrows and gave me a weary smile. I love his smile too.

"You need a rest, Doc."

"I am okay. Just got some bad news about a job interview." My eyes must have been still bloodshot and swollen from my nightly crying ritual.

The recent run of success with Eva and Eugene prompted me to take on Ali too. I attempted again to coax him to contact his family and fill them in on his condition.

"I am missing my prayer." He changed the topic.

"I could pray instead of you." I didn't know whether it was my imagination but I thought I remembered in Islam you could pray instead of someone else who was not able to. Besides, that could be of advantage in my negotiation with him.

"That is kind, Doc, but I'll try to pray later when the pain is better," he said. "You know how to pray? I thought you didn't."

He was referring to a conversation I had with a distant female acquaintance who was visiting him yesterday, a woman in her early twenties wearing a head scarf. She had asked me, while I was hanging up Ali's blood transfusion, whether I knew when Ramadan started.

"No. I don't fast."

"Aren't you Iranian?"

"Yes."

"You are Muslim?"

"I am not a good Muslim, but I do believe in God."

"You don't believe in Islam?"

"I don't need a religion."

226

"You read Quran? You have to read Quran, sweetheart."

"Okay, I'll do it at some point in my life."

"You might not be here tomorrow. There are laws and policies in life. Didn't you study hard to become a doctor? You also must work hard to go to heaven. Don't you think about the afterlife?"

"I worry more about this life, not thereafter."

"The Quran says God is kind, but He punishes too, though His mercy overrides His punishment."

Ali hadn't said anything all this time, but I am sure he had noticed the irritation in my face, because today he said, "My little friend upset you yesterday, didn't she?"

"She irritated me."

"There is nothing wrong with a little irritation, Doc, but you only need enough to get you moving and not to drive you insane."

"The morphine is kicking in, isn't it? Can you please give me the number for your family so that I can contact them? Do they speak English?"

"You can speak Farsi with them. My sister knows Farsi. She is married to an Iranian Kurd."

I took my notebook out to jot down the number.

"Solmaz," he called my name for the first time. "Just one thing if I may ask of you."

"Ali, you can ask me anything."

"Never say again you are not a good Muslim. You don't know how God decides on who is a Muslim and who is not. You are a good Muslim."

Tonight I feel blessed.

Saturday, September 23, 2006

Three months since returning from Bangladesh, and my first day without any anxiety. It was good timing because today was Rekha's registry ceremony, which I missed, but I arrived on time for the party in their friend's flat in central London.

Rekha and Manju, her husband, are soon moving to their own house in Edinburgh. He is a Scottish Indian - does such a thing exist? Manju looked youngish, dressed casually, and was humorous and attentive to guests - there were maybe twenty of us. Two tables had been joined together in a corner and bedecked with rice, chapati, chicken curry and vegetable samosas, drinks of various colours and much more. The flat overlooked the river Thames, set back from it by only a small sidewalk. It looked magnificent under the sunset under the sunset. When I found myself on the balcony with Shirin, I attempted small talk.

"I wonder what that funny egg-shaped structure over there is."

"That is the Gherkin."

"What is it?"

"An office building."

I was impressed. Apparently, she knew London much better than I did.

"This place is amazing. It must be expensive. How can two young people afford such a place?"

Shirin didn't say anything.

"Shirin, have something to drink. Come, try the chicken," Manju's mother called her.

Shirin strode across to her.

"It is not theirs. I suppose their parents are helping out with the rent," Peyman answered my question.

"Are you eavesdropping on us?" I said as a joke. "Have you met Manju's parents before? His mother seems to know

Shirin." What I really wanted to know was whether Shirin and Rekha had become good friends. How was it possible? Rekha had never liked Shirin much.

"Shirin invited them over for dinner a couple of weeks ago."

"Peyman," Shirin called and he was gone.

I felt awkward standing alone. I let my gaze wander, and discovered Rekha chatting to Shirin. Rekha was wearing a big smile and a red sari, displaying her *mangalsutra* - the heavy necklace of married Hindu women. She did look happy, or would Eva have said 'content'?

I went to get myself a drink, just to keep busy. Rekha came towards me for the first time alone.

"Sweetie, you look gloomy. Gosh, you've lost weight too. What are you living on? Water and air?" She hugged me. "Babe, you alright?"

"Yeah, I'm good..."

New friends arrived, and she turned to kiss them - another couple with twins, a girl and a boy. They looked like little angels.

"Look at this ring," the woman exclaimed. Manju's mother looked pleased. Shirin and another friend gathered around Rekha. I gave a smile and made an effort to feign interest.

"I chose this one because it passed the chapati test."

"Which is crucial," her friend said in agreement before explaining, "It's essential not to get any flour into the ring crevices when you knead the dough."

"I remember my aunt's engagement ring used always to have bits of white powder, but not this one." Rekha held her hand out to display her ring again.

I don't know why my gaze fell on Shirin's finger. Her ring was sparkling. I never had an engagement ring; I didn't want one. As a wedding ring, I had bought Peyman and myself a couple of silver rings from an Egyptian in Kaerntner Strasse in

Vienna and asked him to engrave the image of footprints on them as sign of '*yol-dash*', the Azari word for friend, or 'a brother for the road' in literal translation. I believed it romantic. My reminiscence was cut short by shouts from the children. There were five of them, who had all started out quite shy but within half an hour were making a noise like a bunch of football fans. They crawled under the table playing hide and seek.

I admit I felt like a thief; from the idyllic vantage point of those couples and children I must have been a homewrecker, a greedy and selfish woman who has set her eyes on something that was not hers. He doesn't belong to me; I don't have any right to him.

"A penny for your thoughts." A familiar whisper breathed down my neck.

I turned around to make sure it was who I thought it was.

"Did you think you could hide behind this tomboy haircut?"

"Oh, it is so good to see you," I said. "How are you?"

"Alive, as the English say, I can't complain." Fardin was in his signature black Calvin Klein jeans and a white Hugo Boss sweater. "I knew sooner or later we'd run into each other."

We had a cordial chat. He told me that he now owned a Victorian house in London, had passed his membership exams on the second attempt and was doing a rotation in cardiology. He asked me about my time in Bangladesh.

"So what do you say to that? Rekha is married now," I replied. I was not going to pour out my heart to him.

"See, how she's glowing now that she is married." Fardin said. "Getting married needs courage. I wish I were married with two children by now. I don't say that when one marries one's life becomes easier, but one becomes less stubborn."

"Rekha tells me you are seeing someone. Where is she?"

"She couldn't come. She had to be with her family."

"Iranian?"

"Always," he grinned. "She is feisty. In fact, she is much more man than you are. Thinking back, I don't remember what you moaned about, but you did moan a lot."

"Yes, I did. And still do."

"Are you with anyone?"

"Nope."

"What are you planning next?"

"I don't make plans anymore."

"I don't believe you. Losing control wouldn't become you."

"As Azaris say, '*You count and put aside, then wait for the final audit that the Safkeeper of all accounts performs.*'"

"Why did you come back early from Bangladesh?" He shook his head. "You are your own worst enemy. Your idealism holds you back from romance and your self-obsession from acting on your idealism."

"Charming." I gave him a peck on the cheek. "I gotta go."

"I take it we won't stay in touch. I am sure you have already deleted my number," he said. "I knew I had an expiration date, like a bottle of milk."

"You've got me there. Well, it seems a lifetime ago." I gave him a hug and left the party. No one noticed.

Thursday, September 28, 2006

The new dawn found us all gathered in Eugene's room: the nurse, a technician, me, and of course Eugene - the unconscious Eugene. His breathing had become shallow and irregular. Time was short, and we needed to deactivate his defibrillator so that it wouldn't start administering shocks to his body once he had gone.

"What about his son? I hope he manages to get here in time." I couldn't control my tears.

"Some wait for family to arrive, some for them to leave

231

before they go," the nurse explained, having seen it all before.

Not much later, the consultant called me into his room.

"You are taking the death of patients too much too heart. You need to set healthy boundaries."

"It is cultural, nothing else. Tears are not a big deal in my culture. We easily cry," I reassured him. This unfailing cultural argument never lets me down in the UK. It silences everyone and erases their common sense, suspending their judgment of right and wrong.

The only good news was that everything was ready for Eva's transfer to the Czech Republic. We were running out of time, and I knew she knew it. If she hadn't told me explicitly, her eyes would have given her away. She had vomited all last night and had severe back pain in the morning.

"Are you aware of the risk of driving 1000 miles in this serious condition?" I checked with her again.

She nodded a decisive yes.

"What if we waited a bit longer, until we have your symptoms better under control?"

"It might be too late by then," she said matter-of-factly.

"At 7:30 they are coming for me." Her blue eyes were brimming. Nurses had already washed and catheterised her. She was ready.

"Eva, are you content now?"

"No, dear. I am happy." She couldn't erase the smile off her sweet face. "Solmaz, dear. I am very grateful. Take good care of yourself, your loved ones and your patients."

At 14:30 we received a call from the ambulance crew. Eva had died outside Cologne about an hour ago.

At 19:59 I spoke to her nephew back home. He told me that Eva's body was in a German mortuary and will be transferred to the Czech Republic tomorrow.

At 21:21 the nurses bleeped me to certify Eugene's death. I went to his room and placed my stethoscope on his chest. *No air movement*, I wrote, then I placed it on his heart. *No heart sounds*, I wrote, then I opened his eyes, *pupils dilated and not reactive to light. May he rest in peace*, I wrote. I sat there on his chair, holding his Zimmer frame with one hand and with the other his warm hand that was not trembling anymore, and stared at the woman with the red curly hair in the picture on his table.

Monday, October 2, 2006

Ali's family arrived today. His two brothers and sister drove all the way from Frankfurt. They filled up the fridge, trying to feed him all the time, not realising he was dying. When I went in today, his sister asked me for the direction of Mecca so as to pray.

"My Doc doesn't pray," said Ali with a smile.

"I am fasting though." To please him, I am now fasting in Ramadan after ten years.

"Doc and I have reached a settlement. I pray. Doc fasts," he said

"How many years have you known each other?" his sister asked.

"Five weeks." I said.

Thursday, October 5, 2006

Yesterday was not a good day. Neither was the day before yesterday.

Sunday, October 8, 2006

"Can I call you Ali?" I asked when we first met.

"Call me whatever you like," you said.

They said you were dying on your feet.

Friday night, after finishing my shift, I quietly entered your room and sat by your bedside. You were sleeping with your eyes half-open once more. You turned your weary head and greeted me with a faint smile. Between us were the support rails of your bed. Lately, you had been weak and drowsy with morphine and had fallen out of bed a few times - the bruises on your legs and the graze on your nose bear witness to that. I watched you in your sleep, twisting and turning in bed. Every so often you would open your eyes and point to the glass of water. I would hold a straw for you to drink, and then you would drop off to sleep again.

"Go home, Doc." You said at 2 a.m. "You need to rest. Go home."

"Ali, do you remember that I told you I would be there for you when you got unwell. Your family is coming tomorrow. I don't think you need me anymore."

"You are already family, Doc".

That one word - family - was enough to make me dread saying goodbye to you.

"Ali, no matter what they say, I think you did well." This brought a smile to your face and your smile brought tears to my eyes.

This smile and these words were what I saw and heard as I kissed the soil and threw it on your coffin.

I love you.

I miss you.

I went to your funeral. There were suddenly so many men there. I don't know where they knew you from. Maybe they didn't know you and were only men from the mosque.

I know where you are. I will come back.

Saturday, October 21, 2006

"Why am I so little
That I get lost in the streets
Why does father, who is not so little
And is not lost in the streets not do something, so that the person
whom I have seen in my dreams
Brings forward the day of his coming."

Sunday, October 29, 2006

The little shred of ground I had found was pulled away from beneath my feet with his text: *I dreamt about you last night.*

My heart stopped when I saw Belal's name. I freaked out. Many times I tried to call Peyman. I couldn't get hold of him. He wasn't answering his mobile or his landline. So I rang Maman. Baba had left for Iran yesterday. She was alone. The second she answered the phone, I howled.

"I am not well. You can see it and you are only quiet. Why don't you say anything?"

"What should I say?"

"Just say something. You don't even ask what is going on with me."

"I don't know what to say. I am leaving you alone. I thought that is what you wanted."

"I am just trying to make right where you have gone wrong," I said.

I could hear she was upset. I needed her to mother me and say something, but she couldn't seem to find any words.

"Solmaz, I've never been asked to say anything. Your Baba never asks for my opinion. He has always decided for himself when to move house, buy something; he even used to buy furniture without consulting me. I was happy in Iran. Even

235

migrating to Austria was his decision." Her voice broke. "I am afraid of loud voices. As a girl I lived with my older brother and his family, and whenever your uncle shouted I worried that he'd blame me for something. Naneh wasn't living with us, she was staying with your aunt. I used to hide in a corner of the room behind the bed, making myself very small, and hope he wouldn't see me."

What she is saying is that she has heard Baba's voice so long that she can't hear her own anymore. She is just a scared little girl; I could see that for the first time. She is still hiding, hiding because she thinks she doesn't have any right to life. Being deficient is the message any girl gets, let alone a half-orphan one. She doesn't know anything, doesn't have anything but a mother's love to give, and I was sitting in judgment, accusing her of having failed even in that respect.

I feel sorry for her. I've seen her school yearbooks: they are full of poems, beautiful pictures, her dreams and hopes for a better future. We women don't make it easy on each other. We look at each other and despise our own weakness, passivity and helplessness, reflected in the other; we loathe the other's victim state. Men have an inborn right to exist, an authorisation to be, whereas we women have to legitimate our existence. I used to harbour resentment against my mother for her choices. I felt such a rage. Now, looking at her, I see that she is forcing herself to stay small; staying small, and staying invisible ward off predators. Staying small, in her mind, keeps her safe.

"I don't know how being loved by a man feels," she suddenly confessed. I had never said anything about Belal. Maman surely had a good gut feeling, or had she had a dream?

What are all the world's experiences good for when one is bereft of the mental and psychic structure to make sense of them? Life happens, and as it happens, the unknown sprouts up. When one doesn't know what to make of those happenings, when one feels more than one understands, chaos sets in. If we keep brushing off the unknown and uncertainties, a foul and explosive mess builds up.

God, end it! End this misery called life. Just end it. I hate You. You incapable, incompetent useless God. You have utterly failed Your creatures. You have created a mess, a pile of shit, and You have the audacity to call Yourself *God*?

Saturday, November 4, 2006

A new chapter. No grand things anymore, only the next step. Little by little, I can help myself. Little by little I can help life to come back to me, to take up residence in me.

What a good day to start a new life. I had a good belly laugh at work. I admitted a new patient and, while taking his social history, I asked what he did. He said something that sounded like *cook* but he said it in a whisper as if sharing a secret.

"Cook," I repeated.

"No, *cook*," he murmured, and checked out neighbouring beds.

"Cook? That is nothing to be ashamed of."

"No, criminal, you understand? Crook!"

"Oh." I finally got it. I didn't know the word, but it eventually sunk into my thick head what the poor chap was trying to hush up. "We don't judge here." I gave a big smile as proof.

Then there was this elderly matriarch of a large family who was slowly and peacefully dying. She had been unconscious for two days, and we expected her to die any moment. Today her large family got into an argument in her room, and the lady, who was more dead than alive, opened her eyes and sat erect.

"You all shut up. Behave yourselves," she screamed. "I am resting here."

With her comeback from death, she scared all of them into

237

silence and us the medical professionals into one of our many unexplainable puzzles. She died later the way she wanted: in a quiet room. When I went to certify it, I was anxious she might get up and yell at me. I am sure that until they cremate her, the family will expect her return.

I can breathe again. I can think about other things than Belal.

God, thank You.

Tuesday, November 7, 2006

The rain was falling. I settled on the couch in my room with a plate of omelette and pitta, watching the 10 p.m. news on the mini TV before me. That was when Omid's call came.

"Baba's plane arrived in Vienna before the scheduled time. When I got there, I found him outside the terminal. He was leaning on his luggage trolley, smoking." I picked up Omid's sigh on the last word. "He's okay, but he is somehow not himself anymore."

"What do you mean, *dash*?"

"He has lost lots of weight. His breathing is also much worse. Otherwise Baba is Baba. He talks about the politics of Iran, how much the exchange rate for the *toman* is, complains about Maman, that she doesn't respect him because he doesn't have money anymore," Omid said. "All back to normal."

"And he is still smoking?"

"He says he smokes 1-2 cigarettes per day. He has brought these cigarettes from Iran. I tell him they are no good, he shouldn't smoke them, but he says, 'Let me finish them first. It would be a waste.' He does what he likes. That's the way life is, you know. If you were only to do what people say that wouldn't be living." Omid paused. His voice changed. It had a tinge of secrecy to it. "Don't tell Maman. I didn't know it until today either. Baba was in hospital in Tehran for about two weeks."

"Did he have a heart attack?"

"I don't know. I will email you his documents. He has brought copies from Iran."

"Is he up? Can you put him on the phone please?"

"Oh, *gizi*, *salaam*. I am fine. It was nothing," I heard Baba's thin voice. "They make such a big fuss over nothing. I'm fine, thank God."

"You sound very weak."

"I don't have my dentures in. I don't know where your Maman puts them. She keeps fiddling with everything."

Suddenly I heard the anchor woman's voice on the news. We had hung up, but I was still sitting in the same position on the couch, staring into the air and biting my fingers. Then I looked around me, not sure what I was searching for.

Something I can't put my finger on is hovering over me.

Thursday, November 9, 2006

Rekha drew up a chair and sat next to me in our usual hangout, the Great Portland Street Starbucks. It was our own private leaving-do for her, since she is moving to Edinburgh next week.

"How are you, sweetheart? I am so sorry about your dad." She placed her hand on mine.

I pulled my hand back. "I am so weary of this family. They never plan anything; they never think anything through. I don't care what happens. I don't care whether he lives or dies."

"No. You only say this because you are upset."

"No, I mean it. I can't be bothered anymore." My voice broke. "I never told you why I came back early from Bangladesh." Her silence was an invitation to go on, so I confided in her the entire story with Belal: how we met, how our relationship deepened, and how I have suffered since it all ended. "In a strange way I feel in the right company only with my cancer patients."

"But they at least get sympathy from others, and you don't," said Rekha.

"Do you think it's childish to fall in love?"

"Oh no, I used to fall in love every day. But it *is* childish to take it seriously. I know that type - Mr Tragedy," she said with a sneer. "He acted according to a 'subcontinent script', especially when he told you he never gave you any hope." It was the first time I had seen her outraged. "Mind you, I regard you the more honourable one in this relationship." It was not love, in Rekha's view, but an exploitation of my 'gentle and pure feelings'. "He played this script with the wrong person. I wish you guys had a physical involvement instead. That would have been better than this emotional roller coaster with an honest and sensitive person like you. I believe if one hasn't had sex, long term attraction is increased." She went on, "I love you to bits, but you can be very naïve, sweetie. It was only a pastime for him, an adventure. He doesn't care about you. You will be a memory for his lonely nights. But what about you? Who looks after you?"

"It's over now," I said.

"I guarantee you he is blissfully unhappy."

By the time I reached home, my nagging unease had spiralled into rage. I rang him straightaway. It was the first time since my return to London.

"Rekha says you were playing games with me, that you were putting on an act according to 'the subcontinent script'. Were you?"

"I never played any games with you. I honestly don't know what to do." Belal's voice was shaky.

It was the early morning hours in Dhaka. In my mind's eye he was leaning against the wall in his living room, knees drawn up to his chest, with a laptop and the news running before him. We were mad at each other. Throughout the first half of our phone conversation, each of us blamed the other for letting them down. In the second half I played back the tale of my pain to him. There was a silence at first.

"I didn't realise you were doing that badly," he said finally. "I too feel lonely. It is difficult to think about the future."

"When are you going to Australia?"

"I am flying tomorrow."

"You alone?"

"I and the girls."

My bad! Once again I had forgotten that 'I' and 'we' were interchangeable.

"You were going to go without telling me?"

"It looks like it has already ended for you anyway. But I've written an email for you. I was going to send it tomorrow."

"I don't believe you."

"I'll send it now."

It read: *There are massive differences between your circumstances and mine. When I needed your support and advice, you turned your face away from me. You see everything in absolutes. Anyway I am leaving today with lots of pain from you. Be happy now and always.*

He won't come back. He is vanishing.

Friday, November 24, 2006

Baba had been to an appointment with the Iranian doctor on his own so that Omid wouldn't miss work.

"I got a call from his mobile number, but a stranger was talking. He told me Baba had fallen in the street. It looks like he hadn't seen the kerb and tripped," Omid told me on the phone.

Baba's left eye is completely blind. He relies on his right eye

Nowadays Baba spends most of the day in front of TV, watching the news and the many political debates on Iranian channels. He leaves it on until he falls asleep at about 2 or 3 a.m., much to Maman's annoyance as it's usually her who wakes up in the middle of the night and turns it off.

After I had hung up, I called Peyman. Still no reply. I spoke into his answerphone. Before long, my phone buzzed.

"Ms Hasti!" she said in a loud tone. "Ms Hasti?"

"Shirin, is that you?"

"Will you stop calling my husband?"

"What?"

"Stop calling my husband. Is that clear?"

"Shirin, Peyman and I are only friends."

"I don't care that you were brought up in the West. You know the Iranian culture very well. There is no such thing as a friendship between a married man and his ex-wife. It is simply unacceptable."

"Peyman is just a brother to me."

"Either you stop harassing us with your phone calls or I will start harassing your family."

"Sorry, I didn't know …"

"Go and get your own man."

Her voice was turning shriller by the moment. It was as though I had been thrown into a boxing ring - a left jab, a right cross, a left hook, and a final upper cut to my chin took me down. I was lying lifeless on the canvas floor, but she was still kicking my stomach, hitting me on the legs, arms and head with full power.

"Okay, I won't call him anymore." I couldn't think what else to say. My hands were shaky. "Goodbye."

I hung up and rang Peyman at his hospital. He was on duty.

"I had a call from Shirin."

"Solmaz *joon,* I am on my way to the theatre. I can't talk. I'll ring you back."

"No, no need. I just wanted to tell you that she talked to me like a dog protecting her precious, hard-won bone with all her might, barking and biting into my flesh. I didn't know she was that sick. You and I had promised each other to put the other's happiness first. I want you to be happy. So I will leave you alone. I only want you to know it isn't because I am afraid of her, but because I love you and genuinely care for you. Goodbye."

He responded in an email tonight. He expressed how very happy he was with Shirin, and that their only issue was me. He suggested I use his work email to stay in touch as Shirin had the passwords of all the others. What a cold slap!

There is nothing in my feelings for you to feel ashamed or guilty about. Therefore, no secrecy. If we can't be friends in the open, we are done. I emailed back.

Peyman wants conformity and I want change. He looks at social and cultural shopping lists for roles, relationships and values, and I want to run away from the shopping mall. He lets the doctrines and creeds tell him how, who and what to love, and who and what to call a loss, and how and when to grieve. His most intimate feelings are dictated, orchestrated by society. That is why he sacrifices me on the altar of marital harmony. To prove his loyalty to Shirin he betrays us, our friendship, our past. Our *we* feels threatening to Shirin. In Shirin's world there are *we's* that are respectable - the socially sanctioned and legal *we*'s. And there are *we's* that are degraded in that unspoken hierarchy of *we's*. That is not to say, I resent *we*. I don't. I long for a *we* like Baba and Belal. I too need a *we* for a sense of safety, as Shirin does. I also want to relate, to belong, but not on the current terms - not on men's terms. If I haven't attached my *I* to any *we*, it is because none has felt right, none has been inclusive. I've always sensed that Baba's and Belal's *we's* are just an extension of their *I's*. The current *we* is not a genuine *we*, but the inflated *I* of the man, the inflated masculine. In that *we* I don't play a role, I don't occupy any space. I need a *we* that doesn't crush me. What is more, as a woman I need the *I* before a *we*. Where has there ever been a female *I*?

Thursday, December 7, 2006

Another overcast London day, and a study day at the Royal College. Habitually I checked my mobile, which was on silent. There was a missed call from Vienna. I walked out to the corridor to ring back.

Maman was weeping over the phone. "When they were taking him, he said, 'Forgive me for all my mistakes, *khanom* - Mrs.'"

Omid and Maman had panicked when Baba had started to gasp for breath in the early hours of the morning. "He was on his bed." That is the couch in the living room. Omid sleeps on a mattress on the floor. "I heard loud noises. It was frightening. When I came out from the bedroom I found him sitting on the edge of the couch. He was leaning forward, resting on his elbows and his shoulders were raised. He looked chalky white and was making loud sounds as if choking. Poor Omid," she went on, "he was petrified too. I screamed, 'Someone help!' Omid called the ambulance."

I called Baba's hospital. Baba is having intravenous antibiotics and is on continuous oxygen. I didn't need to hear anymore. I packed my stuff and hailed a black cab.

"I need compassionate leave," I swallowed the tears back when my consultant's secretary answered the phone.

"Are you alright, Solmaz?"

"My father is critically ill." Suddenly it hit me. I started crying.

"I am so sorry."

"It is okay. Please let the team know." I hung up, sobbing and trembling.

"I am sorry," I said to the cab driver once I could recompose myself. "I am sorry."

"Don't be. It's alright."

Then he did what he could to help me - he sped up.

At home I booked a flight ticket online for 19:30, bundled some clothes and my palliative care book into a backpack and called another cab for Heathrow.

As I was waiting for my cab I emailed Belal: *Can you call me please? NOW!* Right away he rang.

"What happened?"

"Can you please hug me?"

"Is everything okay, Solmaz?"

"Don't ask any questions. Can we just for a minute stop everything and imagine ourselves back in your office in Dhaka? Can you hold me in your arms in silence?"

"Yes."

I closed my eyes. Belal and I were both quiet.

"Thank you. Goodbye, Belal."

"*Khoda hafez.*"

The minute the driver dropped me at terminal one, I hurried from one counter to the other in an attempt to plead for a seat on an earlier flight, but in vain. Flushed and sweaty, I gave up after one hour of trying.

Never before has Vienna felt so far away. Far is any place you can't go on foot to in a time of emergency.

I went to the airport pharmacy to get some diazepam.

"You know it is medico-legally not right for doctors to self-prescribe," the pharmacist warned me.

"It's an emergency. I'm sorry, but my father is…" and tears started gushing down my cheeks again as I finished my sentence and explained I needed something for anxiety while abroad.

"You are a doctor. You have to be strong," he advised.

It is 17:35, and in two hours my plane takes off to Vienna. Tears well up in my eyes at the sight of the elegant American gentleman at the next table in the restaurant. He doesn't look much older than Baba. I can't take my eyes off him as he is placing his order, his voice clear, strong and unworried. Why am I crying? Because I want to be there, at his table. Because I

245

want to be with him. I want him to be 'my people'. I want his life, not mine.

I dread this awful thing that lies before me.

VIENNA

Thursday, December 7, 2006

Coming back to a place full of memories is very different from going to a place without any memories. Coming back to familiarity isn't the same as going to unfamiliarity.

Once the plane prepared to descend towards Schwechat airport, my stomach churned. It was not the altitude, but a sense of dread and agitation at the looming prospect. At passport control, the line for EU citizens, though longer than that for Non-EU citizens, moved faster. The uniformed man behind the glass cubicle cast a quick glance at my Austrian passport.

"*Guten Abend*," he greeted with a smile.

I smiled back and handed him my passport.

"*Danke*," he said, and asked the next passenger to come forward.

That was it. Done. I detected a sense of pleasure and shame in me, stemming from the same place: the privilege of standing in that line, a line I occupied not for the merit of birth or marriage or my own effort, but because of the dreams, the wanderlust as much as the ignorance, of a stubborn boy from an Azerbaijani village in Iran; a man who now, fifty years on, was lying in a hospital bed in this strange land. He was not at the airport, still I felt his presence in the piece of paper I held in my hands, the piece that granted me the permission to move freely on Western soil - quite an achievement for those like us.

We wasted no time. Omid took me straight to Lainzer Krankenhaus. It was pitch-dark as we turned through an open gate that led into its spacious grounds. Omid drove up a meandering road, dimly illuminated by vintage streetlights, to the lung pavilion on the hilly side of the hundred-year-old hospital. We kept our conversation minimal and factual. I tightened my shawl around my neck and stepped out of the car. Omid grabbed a plastic bag from the boot and walked me through the back door that is used by the ambulance crew.

We were two flights of stairs away from Baba. The anticipation was sickening. I hadn't devised any concrete plans as to what to say or do. Omid told me Baba was in a temporary private room because of a bed shortage. Baba didn't like being alone, although Omid preferred that he was. The corridors were empty at that time of the night. I followed Omid to Baba's room.

"*Salam*, Baba."

"*Salam, gizi.*"

I stepped in and bent over him. He took off the oxygen mask and kissed me on the lips. His were dry and peeling.

"Why did you come? It wasn't necessary. I'm fine."

It was good he didn't show any sign of sentimentality.

"Yeah, right. You sure look fine." A joke was the easiest way to overcome the tragic nature of our coming together after five years.

It was only now, in the green hospital gown stained with phlegm and tea, drips running into his emaciated arms, the heart monitor above his head, the urine bottle attached to the bed, that I saw him aged, frail and powerless. There lay the stubborn boy with winter grey eyes, his face a cracked desert, thinned and lined by myriad caravans of a lifetime, his body weak, puffing for air, but not crushed yet. There was still the raw energy of an animal about him, at the end of his physical limits but not his will. Am I right or is it denial?

"You haven't touched your meal?" A tinge of irritation was noticeable in Omid's voice as he lifted the lid of the plate on his over-bed table. "You gotta eat something."

Omid took out two large juice bottles from the shopping bag and placed them on Baba's bedside table, turning them until the intense colours of the oranges and cherries were in Baba's view. Then he grabbed the remote control and pressed a button for the headend of the bed to lift. Hunching, he placed his hands on Baba's narrow shoulders and nudged him forward to adjust his pillows. With a gentle push he moved Baba's body back into the pillows. Next he swapped his oxygen mask for a nasal cannula so that Baba could eat.

I understood his need to do all these things. We are both keyed to act, he more than I.

"Rinse my dentures. They are there." Baba gestured with his head to the bedside table.

"Which one?" Omid asked. "You have two."

"The one that you always say looks better on me."

I never recall a time that Baba didn't have dentures. Allegedly, he had lost his teeth in a fight when I was a baby. Not often do I see him without them. I was glad he put them in. He looked less of a patient with them in.

"I can only eat the soft potatoes. Omid, son, cut them into small pieces please."

Omid did so.

"How was your flight?"

"It was alright." I pulled up the chair close to his bed.

"*Gizi* - my daughter, you have to speak into my left ear. Come over here. No one in this family has ever learned which ear it is that I can't hear with."

"Omid, son, make me a cup of tea." On our way to Baba's room I had noticed a table with silver flasks, teabags and sugar sachets in the corridor.

"Open the drawer, Solmaz, take my dosette box and give me my painkiller."

"Which one?" I scanned the loose tablets in the dosette box.

"The white one that is round and small."

"Baba, you are in the hospital. They give you the medicine here. You shouldn't help yourself to extras."

"I know what I'm doing, *gizi*. Just hand me that painkiller."

In much the same manner as Omid, I poured feelings into action. I had brought along some of my medical tools. I checked his oxygen saturation, blood pressure and pulse, listened to his heart and chest and looked at his observation chart which was hanging at the end of the bed.

"Should we bring you some teabags tomorrow?" I asked when we were leaving.

"No, I am fine with their black tea here. I need my magnifying glasses, a flask and some underpants."

When we finally arrived home, Maman came out of her bedroom. She was in her nightgown.

"You look pretty. You are just like myself. You look good with every haircut." We hugged and kissed. "Your Baba doesn't like short hair. But I do."

She hasn't changed a bit. She still wears her hair above shoulder length, carefully arranged to hide her grey roots. Her eyelids were drooping. It was way beyond her bedtime.

"Sorry I didn't come to the airport, but I thought you children would go directly to the hospital. I don't like hospitals." This aversion of hers towards hospitals or sickness hasn't changed either. "But I waited up for you. Look, I bought you your favourite flowers." Her gaze turned to the dinner table. A large bouquet of deep red tulips was displayed there.

Their one-bedroom flat is enough for two people, but becomes cramped and cluttered as soon as a third person intrudes. Maman unfolded the convertible sofa into a bed and covered it with clean white sheets for me. Omid slept on the floor. His soft snoring was already audible when I slipped under the blanket after a quick shower.

My mind shies away from imagining what I am up against.

My strength rests on my exhaustion, my medical skills, and not thinking far ahead.

I made a deliberate choice of my wardrobe for this trip before leaving London. First I went for a long skirt, but I felt vulnerable in that. Instead I picked my wide-leg trousers with a blouse - the Marlene Dietrich style confers boldness on me. I need to feel masculine.

Friday, December 8, 2006

I got up at first light.

"Where are you going? It is still dark," Maman called from her room.

"I'm going for a run. It isn't that dark. You go back to sleep."

When I came back, Omid had already left for work and Maman was in the kitchen, placing *aspand* - harmala seeds - on a round pot and heating it on the stove.

Each time I am in Vienna I study the pieces in the display cabinet next to the dinner table, shipped from Iran. Maman flaunts her keepsakes there, remnants from her life in Tehran: Chinese teapots, cups and saucers, a bronze Shiva sculpture, a Japanese fan, and amongst them childhood pictures of me and Omid. In a corner behind the memorials there's a black and white wedding picture of Baba and Maman.

Maman came to the living room, stood beside me. "That is against the evil eye," she said and wafted the pot with the rising smoke around my head, seven times for each day of the week. "You look worn out, Solmaz. Go take your shower. I'll make you breakfast."

"No, Maman." I was in a rush. I had to get to the hospital before the morning ward round. "Which tram do I need to take to Lainz? I forgot to ask Omid last night."

"Oh, I don't know. Omid or your Baba always take me around. I only know how to get to the city," she said.

Google came to my rescue and showed me the way to the hospital.

The ward round was a brief affair. A consultant, his assistant doctor and a couple of juniors attended to us with the ward nurse. Baba was sitting upright is his bed, one hand on his oxygen mask and the other smoothing his white blanket, and smiling all along.

"Tell him I can't eat. My mouth is dry."

I translated his words.

"The consultant says, the medicines and the oxygen unfortunately dry out your mouth."

"Ask him whether I will get better?"

"He wants to know the prognosis," I went on. "But I'm certain you can't say anything yet."

"He was very ill," the consultant said. "He's now on antibiotics. It will take some time before he responds to them. It hasn't even been forty-eight hours yet."

"They say …"

"What? Speak up," Baba asked of me.

"They say the antibiotics will help. You have just to be patient."

"*Gut, Doktor. Danke, Doktor.*" Baba gave a gratifying smile and lowered his head in respect.

Baba has always revelled in speaking the few German words he knows, unlike Maman, who lacks the confidence to talk in public even though she knows more words.

"Will you continue smoking?" I asked him after the doctors had left.

"Stop it, *gizi*! You don't tell a woman who's having labour pain that she shouldn't have conceived in the first place." He pinched my cheek in jest.

I stood at his window. It had a good view over the dejected

winter sky and the frozen hospital grounds. Lainzer Krankenhaus is near Wienerwald, and the air, the greenery, is all that a patient - especially a lung patient - requires. Still, its trees looked tired for not having been admired in a long time, rooted in the ground with other vegetation that has taken too much from them over the years.

"Do you think I'll come out of here this time?"

"You mean if you get better?" I turned back to Baba.

He nodded.

"Yes, you will come out of here." I paused. His eyes were examining me. "Are you afraid of dying?"

"No, I am not, *gizi*. Not a bit," he said, but I could see in his eyes a lust for life. His body might be perishing, but his soul is ever more burning.

"Are you sure?"

"As the Zoroastrians say in Iran, '*Good thoughts, good words and good deeds.*' Only a name remains. It's a journey. There will be another life. I'm curious. I'm not afraid. There is a God. One day we come, another day we go. What should I be afraid of?"

"Do you have a will?"

"Yes."

"Where do you want to be buried?"

"I don't care. It is just flesh. Take me to a forest and throw my body there."

"Yeah, sure. We'll dump you in the middle of Wienerwald." I smiled and he gave me a tired smile back.

We both went quiet until the junior doctor came back to take Baba's blood gas. She kept digging into Baba's wrist looking for an artery. Baba maintained a meek smile while the rest of his face recoiled in pain.

I stared at his arthritic fingers, the twisted roots of an old pine tree. His hands dissolved in front of my eyes and transformed into those deft hands of twenty years ago. I could recall that evening in Tehran when Baba had returned from work and found me sitting and crying in front of my homework. I had to make a cardboard farm for the next day's class. Baba changed into his pyjamas and knelt on the floor. With a cigarette in his mouth and a cup of tea in front of him, he made me a cardboard house, a cardboard cow and two cardboard trees.

Omid came later in the afternoon. He set about tidying and putting things in order, the way Baba likes it; throwing away the used tissues; taking the sugar sachets and stashing them away for later in the bedside drawer. Omid also brought him *ghand* - Iranian sugar cubes, which Baba likes dipping in his tea.

Omid goes to great lengths to adhere to a certain order, and is quite adept in arranging things so that Baba can navigate easily with his hands, despite his poor eyesight. Tissues for his phlegm and his dentures lay next to Baba's own teacup - he likes to see the colour of his tea - then his magnifying glasses, his small satellite radio to listen to Iranian news, and his mobile.

We sat there until his dinner arrived, at 4:30 p.m. He liked the banana yoghurt, but gave us the cake to take home. Maman binned it. She is afraid of his infection.

Wednesday, December 13, 2006

I chose to skip today's ward round; there is nothing new to discuss with Baba's doctors. So, I zipped my coat up and went for a jaunt in Kaertner Strasse, Vienna's most elegant shopping street.

Early mornings, those hours before the city comes to full bloom, have a magical air to them. In Vienna you sometimes get a sense that as time was marching through Europe, it bypassed Austria. I ambled up the street, weaving my way around delivery trucks, passing Café Heiner, Swarowski, Wolford and Palmers with their display of chic female underwear, and souvenir shops with images of Mozart with a white wig in a red jacket and white ruffle shirt, until I reached café Aida at Graben, opposite St. Stephen's Cathedral. The smell of freshly ground coffee, *Wiener Melange*, *Einspaenner*, espresso, and the sweet warm aromas of pastries, *Apfelstrudel*, *Topfenstrudel*, *Krapfen*, *Guglhupf* teased my nostrils. I got myself a takeaway coffee and *Krapfen* and turned into an empty alley to flirt on with memories.

"*Stinkende Auslaenderin*," - stinky foreigner - came a voice some way behind me, jolting me out of my fantasies.

"What did you say?" I wheeled round to see a little girl, probably nine or ten years of age, and a younger boy with a green truck in his hands. I must have spoken in English as the little girl came closer and thrust her chest out.

"*Ich spreche nicht English. Es ist Oesterreich hier, und in Oetsrerreich muss man Deutsch sprechen,*" she said with an air of reproach. 'I don't speak English. It is Austria here, and in Austria you must speak German.'

"*Ich spreche Deutsch nur wenn es mir past.*" - 'I speak German whenever it suits me.'

"*Stinkende Auslaenderin*," she echoed as I walked off.

Omid laughed when I told him how that little creature had made me, the adult woman, feel insecure and small all over again.

Sunday, December 17, 2006

"You know what he said when I visited him that day? He said, 'This time I think I will go. This time I shouldn't have come back from Iran.'" Maman said.

"What did you say?"

"What could I have said? I said, 'Only God knows our timing.'"

255

Baba has been moved into an isolation room since last week. His blood culture showed highly infectious antibiotic resistant bacteria. When I arrived, Baba was on the phone.

"*Abji* - sis - I can't breathe, but *merci* for your phone call." He hung up and turned to me, "They all call and ask me how I am, but I can't talk. My mouth is sore and I don't have the breath to talk. They mean it well though."

To me, these phone calls mean the world.

"Where is Omid? He wanted to give me a wash today."

"He is coming later."

"Is your Maman coming?"

"Later with Omid." I took the urine bottle from his bedside and emptied it down the toilet.

A nurse and the junior doctor came in.

"Here is his nebuliser," the nurse said, and she handed him a plastic container.

"Tell her to leave it there. I'll do it later." Baba left her hand hanging.

"He doesn't listen to anyone," the nurse complained.

I translated.

"I know what I'm doing," Baba said. "I like this blonde girl, she washed me last week. She's nice. I don't understand what she says, but she seems friendly." Baba smiled at her. "Tell doctor, I cough but not much phlegm comes out. Tell her, I am out of breath."

"He is very ill," the junior doctor broke her silence. "We discussed him in our multidisciplinary meeting today and the consensus is that if he gets worse, we won't instigate artificial breathing with him." She paused to check my expression. "You understand?"

"I do."

"They haven't changed my sheets. Get them to do that," Baba said. "They haven't emptied my urine bottle either." Baba kept grumbling long after they had closed the door behind themselves.

"Last night I rang the bell for the night nurse to give me water and a new urine bottle. That Filipino nurse came in, gave me a glass of water and left the urine bottle on the chair. I couldn't reach it. When she was leaving the room, I shouted 'oi, oi'. Then she came and put it into my hand."

"See, Baba. They are not donkeys in your village. You can't talk to them like that. They will be the same people looking after you when you come next time. Don't be rude to them."

"What did the doctor say?"

"Nothing. She says the medicines will take time."

"Thank God, I feel better today."

"Let me help you with the wash."

"Can you?"

"It isn't rocket science, is it?" I rolled up my sleeves.

Baba panted and tottered to the bathroom; clenching onto the Zimmer frame he pulled his weight forward while I tugged his oxygen cylinder behind us. He plopped down on the stool. I untied his hospital gown, slid it off him and opened the tap, testing the water temperature. He bowed his head for me to shampoo and rinse it. The reddening of his face and quickening of his breathing urged me to make it short, so I sped up my movements, scrubbed his back and legs and enveloped his stooped and weary trunk in a white towel. Then he asked me to wait behind the bathroom door as he changed into new pants.

Back on his bed there was a vibe of self-gratification and achievement in his demeanour, as after an intense workout.

"Has your mum sent me something to eat? They give me puree because of my mouth. It tastes awful."

I put the rice pudding Maman had made him into the microwave.

While he ate, I went to the bathroom to tidy up.

"Hey, *gizi*," he called to me. "I like your writing; you write large enough for me to read. Come and write me down some German words that I can say to these nurses. What is the word for 'later'? And how do I say, 'My mouth is sore'? They are stupid. They don't understand what I say."

"It's because you don't have your dentures in. It makes even your Farsi hard to understand, let alone German." Baba still has a very strong Azari accent, an accent that becomes more noticeable to me without his dentures; this and his mouth pain have altered his speech phonation. I need to listen very carefully to understand him.

I started writing in large capital letters the words he had asked for.

"That stupid chap," he suddenly said.

"Who?"

"Peyman." When I looked at him, his gaze was fixed on the swaying branches of an oak behind the window. "Leaving my gorgeous daughter for an internet girl."

I would have laughed had his face not been so earnest. Internet girl? He was serious. I shall never forget it. That was the best - and funniest - compliment ever, coming from someone who has an allergy to compliments; someone I have never heard saying anything positive about me, not my hair, my dress, my way of being or my choices - definitely worth the wait.

"It is good that Omid is trying. When I come out of here, I'll help him. He's a good boy. He's trying. He shouldn't be a receptionist for the rest of his life. I have plans. I'll speak to your uncle and we help him start up a business in Bratislava. I know people who can assist him."

"*Insha'Allah*," I said.

Shariati says, *Love is superior to being in love*. And Forough is waiting for the *one who is like no one*. I don't know what love is, but I know for sure that love entails courage. It needs courage to see when all you want is to turn away your gaze, to be present with the other when you don't have any words to say, to listen when there is silence, or worse, when, as now, there is the sound of death. To stay when all you want to do is to run away.

Friday, December 22, 2006

As long as I can remember I have been in a rush: in a rush to get somewhere, to prevent a disaster, to get somewhere before it is too late. I have been running for a happiness that is always on the verge of being snatched from me.

Growing through suffering? No. You do not suffer in order to grow. You suffer because something is growing in you. That something is either a messenger of new life, if you are lucky, or if not, another ending.

"My daughter, the nurse came and said something. I don't know what she wanted," Baba said a couple of days ago. I walked down to the nurses' station and talked to the consultant.

"I am afraid it doesn't seem he will improve any further than this. What he needs now is palliative care and the comfort of his home," the consultant said in a soft voice. His green eyes had the warmth of deep turquoise waters.

I nodded in agreement. Hearing him voice what I have known all along made my heart swell, and its lid, my chest, started shuddering. I steadied them by bringing my attention to the conversation rather than its meaning.

"He needs round-the-clock care. Shall we arrange it for him to be transferred into a nursing home?"

"No. We take him home. We can look after him there."

"You need equipment: oxygen, a hospital bed and more. I will send in the social worker to go through it with you."

"Of course. I just want to say thank you again. I know it hasn't been easy to look after my father. He doesn't speak German, and on of top of that he's not the easiest man. He's rather stubborn."

"It has been our pleasure. We liked him here." He looked at the Filipino nurse and added, "Most of us did."

Since then Omid and I have been on the go.

At home I rustled up a to-do list for my remaining time here before turning in. Omid was sitting on the opposite couch with the TV on, the volume very low. I was tossing and turning.

"You wanna play *takhteh* - backgammon?" Omid called to me.

"I don't know how to play. Never learnt it."

"I thought Peyman taught you."

"Nope. I was not interested."

"I used to play with Baba a lot. He taught me."

"Who used to win?"

"He did, of course."

"You let him, or did he really win?

"I let him."

"Seriously?"

"Yes. It gave him pleasure. He got upset if he lost. He would say, 'Don't move my pieces' or 'You cheat. You set the dice.'" Omid was looking at the TV, but his voice changed. "When he won, he would say, 'I told you, you can't beat your Baba. True I taught you, but you still have lots to learn from me.'"

"Why is it that they are so alone?"

"Just part of ageing, not being in the mood, not having money, I assume. You need money to socialise. Let's face it, you don't make friends in casinos. Casinos are very addictive. Instead of burning crack, you burn money. One gives you a rush and the other one makes you high. It isn't a sociable place."

Omid changed the channel to MTV.

Dear God, I need You, and I need myself.

I feel sad. Not so sad that it turns into tears, but also not so little that I can gloss over it. It is a sadness that has made itself at home inside my heart and is now accompanying me everywhere.

Sunday, December 24, 2006

Baba's gums are still too sore and dry for his dentures, but he has regained enough strength to be unpleasant and bossy when we, Maman, Omid and I, rallied around his hospital bed this evening. He had asked Omid to bring him the bag of his medicines from home. He raised himself up on the bed, hunched over his magnifying glass that he held a few inches away from the medicine boxes, and picked pills to put into the slots of the two dosette boxes.

"Baba, I told you they are giving you your meds here. You are just mixing everything up."

Only today it dawned on me that what he called painkillers were what he was taking to control his craving for opium. He has been doing it for years, getting it from that Iranian doctor, but this was the first time I was really hearing about it. Omid knew, Maman did too, but not me.

"You can't have it. It is buprenorphine. It is an opioid and you are already getting strong morphines. They interact," I said.

"I know what I am doing." Baba's breathing was better.

"Listen to Solmaz," Maman reasoned with him.

"You always take the side of your stupid daughter," Baba yelled.

"I won't stay here if I am called stupid."

"God should either kill you all or me so that I am free," I heard Baba's voice as I slammed the door behind me.

Maman came after me. We went downstairs to get coffee from the vending machine; it's exactly the same one we used to have in medical college. That instant coffee with the foam in the brown plastic cup has always soothed me, probably for its sugary taste. Two patients were sitting on the plastic chairs opposite the vending machine. One was silently sipping at his drink, while the other was staring into blank space.

"He loves you a lot. He has never been a good husband to me. He is short-tempered just like yourself, but - don't say this to Omid - he loves you a lot. One night he took your picture, the one on the TV stand, and he touched it as though he were pinching your cheeks and then kissed his fingers. 'Solmaz is something else,' he said."

Back in Baba's room, I saw a happier Baba bent over the dosette box. To appease Baba, Omid was bowing to his demands.

"Help me sit up. My tea is going cold." Omid stooped down. Baba linked his arms around his neck and straightened up on the bed. "Put the two pillows behind my back and the other one on my left, so that I can prop myself up. How much oxygen am I getting today?"

Omid checked his oxygen cylinder.

"You know, my son, I need to know everything," Baba said.

Tuesday, December 26, 2006

Dear Solmaz,

I have already sent both Kurt and Annette an email (and a copy to you per CC) - with your phone number - and asked them to kindly ring or email you.

I send you my warm thoughts and wish you all the best for everything that is touching your heart, especially in these challenging hours.

I had to shove Bernhard's letter into my diary. It is a stroke of luck that I have managed to trace this acquaintance from almost a decade ago. The family never knows what they are taking on, so I googled a doctor from an internship in my student time. Bernhard is a consultant in palliative care now. I rang him. How lucky that he still remembers me.

"My father is terminally ill. We want him to die at home, but I don't know the palliative care services in Vienna. Can you help?"

He was in the middle of his ward round and said he would get back to me.

I also rang Amme - Aunt Sara in Canada. She will book the first flight to Vienna.

Friday, December 29, 2006

On the way to Baba's hospital yesterday afternoon, a young mother and her son hopped on the tram. I overheard the boy reading loud from a book.

"I walked down the stairs, and blum blum I fell, then I went to the pavement, and blum blum I fell. Then I realised what was wrong. Do you know what? I had my shoes the wrong way round."

I got up to offer them my seat.

"See, the nice lady is giving you her seat." His mother accepted.

"Today, I was a wolf in kindergarten."

"And what was the new girl?"

"Tatjana?"

"Yes."

"She was a dog."

"Oh, you all became animals when you went to the kindergarten."

"And when it was time to go home, we weren't animals anymore."

Tuesday, January 2, 2007

Baba is home. His rectangular space is comprised of him, machines and medicines; at the foot is a stand with various drugs, and before him another table with his Nokia mobile, magnifying glasses, the dosette box for the pills, a mound of paper tissues, a plastic water mug and his Persian teacup with saucer, all arranged in one straight line; in the second line are his inhalers, mouth sprays, and tubes of cream.

"He is not a real doctor. He's a social worker," Baba said about Kurt, his palliative care physician. Still, he asked Maman to give Kurt pistachio nuts and some *ghorme sabzi* with rice to take home.

"He looks like a nice doctor," observed Maman.

"A friendly guy," said Omid. "He spent an hour with Baba. Let's see what he can do."

They all appeared hopeful after Kurt's visit, and Baba had a good day. He walked up to the window and stood there for a while, then he said, "If Dr Kurt fixes my mouth, I can fix my lungs myself."

Baba loves life. I have never done so. Life is a game I am trying very hard to take seriously.

In me there is a vast sadness, a continent of grief near a continent of chaotic thoughts, next to a continent of shy dreams: dreams in the shape of captured animals, whining for release; refugees from the continent of disappointments, betrayals and promises never kept, which adjoins the continent of anger, where my heart is cold, my blood boiling and my words are inflamed. But then comes the infinite continent of 'all is well'; the continent of stillness, no longing, no pain; the continent whose waters catch every tear, whose air accommodates every hope in its breezes, and whose earth recognises yet another gem in every brokenness.

Friday, January 5, 2007

When Amme Sara arrived, she and Baba hugged each other and cried.

She brought just one small piece of luggage. Amme has that simplicity about her, the stereotypical village simplicity; a kind heart, a big and kind heart. The poor thing must have been shocked to see her brother like this, reduced to skin and bones.

Sitting upright on the edge of his adjustable bed and with his bare feet dangling down, Baba was slouched over the plate of rice and yoghurt in front of him. He had just woken up and was hungry. Amme Sara managed to feed him tiny chunks; even eating made him gasp for air.

Amme hasn't changed at all. Like Baba she is slim built, lean-faced, and exudes warmth and an effortless kindness.

"Baba, there is juice in the fridge, also the astronaut's chocolate drink you like so much," Omid said.

"Omid has hoarded juices and fruits in the fridge and on the balcony," Maman whispered into aunt's ear. "There's no empty space left."

Once Baba fell back to sleep, I went and sat next to Amme Sara. It felt as though we had never been out of each other's sight. Old familiarity came back, and from the way we talked, you would think I had just come back home from school and found my aunt visiting.

"You don't look good, Solmaz."

"Sorry, Amme. I can't beam. My Baba is dying a little." I smiled over our mutual grief.

"No, I wanted to say, you look old."

"Last time you saw me I was fifteen, so I bet I do." I sat cross-legged on the chair. "So, how are you?"

"What should I say? It isn't easy to see *dash* Yousef like this." Amme's eyes misted over. "When I saw him in Iran he was red in the face, and whenever he coughed or couldn't breathe, he would go redder. Now he looks jaundiced."

"Thank you for coming."

"Why are you thanking me? He is my brother. It's my duty. It's not easy here. In Iran you have family and friends. You can tell them the tales of your heart. Here one is alone. Loneliness is only meant for God," she said.

I haven't thought of my relatives in, say, a decade or so, but now that Amme is here, at a time that it matters most, I feel our closeness hasn't diminished with the years - not one bit. I realise how present our past is. Memories are *real*, they are not just reminders of our past; they show how meshed people, places and events are. Our past *Is*.

...So relieved Amme is with us. I am at my wits' end.

Wednesday, January 10, 2007

Last night I stayed with Baba in the living room, Omid went to spend the night at his girlfriend's place, and Maman and Aunt Sara shared the tiny bedroom. Baba's coughing didn't stop until 4 a.m. I suppose what worked the ultimate magic was the accumulation of morphine that sedated him enough for the cough to pause.

Maybe I managed to get a couple of hours sleep too. At about 6 a.m. I swayed to the breakfast table to sit with Maman and Amme.

"He sleeps most of the day, Solmaz," Amme said. "How long do you think he has?"

"I really don't know, but it's probably a matter of days."

"He does worry about you, you know? In Iran he used to say that you always get migraines, and if you were married you wouldn't have so much pressure."

"What else did you guys talk about?"

"Here I spoke to him only once properly. I asked him, 'Do my sons owe you any money?' He said, 'I don't care.' I told him,

'You've grown a white beard, let me shave it.' He said, 'Omid will do it when he gets time.' He told me he was mad at your uncle as he had told everyone in Tehran to hide his cigarettes after his discharge from the hospital. He said, 'Now everyone thinks he has become somebody and can boss me around. It's too late now anyway.'"

The phone rang.

"Sara, you answer the phone," said Maman. "It will be from Tehran, and they like speaking to you anyway."

"*Salam.*" Amme grabbed the receiver. "He's sleeping. He's fine," she went on. "No, he is fine."

After that another call came in, which proceeded in much the same fashion. Amme Sara resembled a Scottish widow - not that I have a clue about Scottish stereotypes, but she simply reminded me of the ad for Scottish Widows in the UK: the entirely stoic and composed woman.

"Amme, what are you waiting for? Why don't you tell them?"

"Tell them what?"

"That Baba's condition is critical."

"Why should I upset them? Let's wait."

"Wait for what? Baba doesn't get any more dying than this."

"You think so, Solmaz?"

"Yes, worse than this is death."

Baba got up late afternoon. He was more lucid than in the night.

"Mrs, make me an egg omelette."

Maman saw to it that he got what he craved for, and Amme Sara fetched him a cup of tea with the sugar cubes he likes so much.

"Mrs, make me some salmon and rice."

"Baba, it is not a restaurant here. We don't have salmon. You just asked for omelette."

We sat in front of him while his sister helped him to eat.

"Mrs, we should go visiting Akbar this evening."

We all looked at each other. Akbar, Maman's brother and Baba's friend, has been dead for over a decade.

"We'll do it. Eat now," Maman replied.

Then he looked at me and mumbled something in Azari. Usually I understand Azari but I couldn't really figure out what Baba was saying.

"What did he say?" I turned to Amme for help. She shrugged her shoulders and pressed her lips together to express that she didn't have a clue either. Baba repeated it. I went and sat next to him on the bed.

"You are speaking Azari, Baba. And I can't understand you without the dentures. Isn't it funny?" I said. "See where we have ended up! Daughter and father don't understand each other's tongues."

He smiled.

"Now let me give you your injections. I have to go to see Dr Kurt." I needed to stock up on Baba's end-of-life medication. I drew up his morphine and midazolam and attached the syringe to the butterfly needle in his arm.

"I want to go," Baba stared at me.

"I am not ending it, Baba. Just to be clear. This is only an injection to ease your pain and breathing. The rest is between you and your God."

"I spoke to Him."

"You did? What did God say?"

"He said, 'Your wish is my command, my son.'"

"Sure, She did." I emptied the syringe.

"Now you are the boss in the family, Solmaz," Baba said in an amused voice and poked my waist. "*Gizi* is the boss."

When I returned, he was asleep. Maman and Amme went for a walk around the block to get some fresh air, while Omid and I changed Baba's soaked pyjamas and bed pad.

"I can't stay here. I will be with my colleague who is covering my shift at the reception at the student hostel tonight. Give me a shout if you need me."

I knew he was going to have some beer. He couldn't drink at home in front of Maman's scrutinising gaze.

As I am writing these words, Maman and Amme have retired to the bedroom and it is again Baba and I cloaked by darkness and silence in the living room. That is not entirely true. The darkness is illuminated by the moonlight and the flickering of the candle I lit earlier, and the silence is suffused with the hissing noises from the oxygen cylinder and Baba's gurgling breathing. Every time he moves or has a bout of coughing, I look for signs of pain or discomfort on his face. Up until now I have rung Dr Kurt twice.

Baba's intermittent tossing in bed and the rapid movements of the chest wall unsettle me, but his death rattle - the coarse sound of bubbling phlegm - is far more dreadful. I used to tell the relatives of my patients that the death rattle was just the sound of the phlegm and that it didn't imply the patient was choking. I didn't know then how distressing it really is when you are the relative. I puzzle whether or not to give him more injections as he is rubbing his hand on his abdomen and shoving away the blanket. I can't. I have to adhere to the minimum intervals between the doses. I don't like the creeping fear and the thoughts swirling in my head. Just earlier, in order to bridge the hiatus between the injections, I lowered the rails of his bed and sat at his side. He is naked to the waist, so I started rubbing a cream on his chest and humming a half-memorised song. I don't know any proper Farsi songs. I sang the first that came to my mind: *One lonely night, moon will come to our dreams, it will take us from road to road…*

All of a sudden, even in the dimmed light, I could see bruises appearing on his torso. That rang an alarm for me. What if these bruises spread to his face too? It would kill Omid to see him all blue.

"Baba, if you want to go," I said, "It is okay. I am here. You don't need to wait for anything. But if you want to stay longer, it is also okay."

Sitting here with Baba I don't feel desperation; I only hope we get through this night gracefully.

And I feel like 'enough'. Enough of all this anger, fear and sadness. Enough of fixing others. Maybe, even enough of fixing myself. Enough of running away and running fast. Enough of waiting, waiting for tomorrow, waiting for the right time, the right place, the right other, waiting to be seen, to be heard, to be loved. Enough.

I was living my life as though my today was only a trouble to overcome so that I could attend to my *real* life, a life that always lay in some distant day, a life that was constantly deferred. And while I was busy getting the work done, to tidy up the mess before stepping into my life, my father decided to die. Baba is dying. I haven't even arrived in my life and he is already going.

If Baba could hear me, I would ask whether he liked his life, because then I could let him be and live mine, start mine. As long as he was well, all I was concerned about was what he was to *me*, why he wasn't the father *I* wanted him to be, *I* needed him to be; why he was such a chauvinistic, manipulative and selfish man; an addict, a gambler. But none of it matters anymore. Now that I have time to think harder, to look for him in the dusted photo albums of the past - far back in a time when ice cream and kebab were only eaten on Fridays, the neighbours spoke his language and our phone rang off the hook in the evenings - I find that kind and caring man at the beginning of his journey. Remembering him, I remember myself.

Death, my good old friend, death. I am at home with death. Death doesn't answer any questions. Death doesn't solve anything, it dissolves everything. It makes my mind, my desires,

270

my pain, my anger and my never-ending search weightless, like a body in an ocean.

Looking at Baba's ebbing breath, I recall when the wind blew off Belal's cap on our first and only bike ride. That was when the man became a boy, when the Charming Prince that was born the minute I was named a girl, turned into just another human.

Watching the receding colours of life on Baba's face, all I can recognise is not my father, but another fellow human. I am sitting with him without knowing anything, without being the slightest bit wiser. I haven't figured out anything, but I know one thing: I love him. I don't know him and I love him. Death and Love sit comfortably with what we call paradox.

I miss You, God. I miss myself with You. There is no replacement for You. You give me a home and safety that no one else does.

Oh, was I mad at You, God. I thought You had let me down, but you hadn't. I thought you had disappeared, but you hadn't. I thought You didn't care, but You did. You have always been available for me. You have always come to my rescue, only not in the forms and shapes I was expecting. I thought I had lost trust in You. Now I see I had lost trust in forms, in concepts, in ideas, in belief systems, in words, in men and in Gods, but not in You. They separate me, they fragment me, and in You I find continuity. In You I find my *Mokhatab*.

As a woman I used to think that man is the other. The poor man, he is only a fellow traveller. You are my other. And as my 'other' changes, I change. I am not the same anymore. I am not the same anymore because I see You see me.

Only Thee do I worship, and only Thee do I speak to.

At 3:45 a.m. I rang Kurt for the third time. This time around I didn't ask him for reassurance about the drugs I was pouring into Baba's failing body, instead I begged him, "Come here please. He is restless, keeps twisting in bed and his breathing is harsher. It sounds as if his chest is full of fluids."

Within twenty minutes he was at our doorway. Maman and Amme Sara didn't hear him coming in. I stood beside the foot of Baba's bed, and Kurt took over. In a flash he administered a diuretic and inserted a urinary catheter. Seeing the enormous amount of urine that came out, it made sense why he had been waggling his legs the entire time. Urinary retention as a possible cause had skipped my attention. Moreover, upon the injection the loud gurgling breath sounds and the moist cough disappeared. Then Kurt, still bent over Baba, tilted his head and fixed my eyes.

"Solmaz, it is the end."

"Can you please help me to wash him?" was my immediate response. "I know it isn't your job, but he is drenched in sweat. I'd like him to look better before waking up my mum and aunt."

I sneaked into the bedroom - both women were still fast asleep - and opened the wardrobe and picked his shorts and the blue shirt, Baba's and my favourite colour. I grabbed Maman's large rice bowl in the kitchen, filled it with lukewarm water at the sink and plunged a towel in it, rushing back to the living room. Without saying anything, Kurt cleansed Baba's body, wiped it dry, changed the dirty sheets and put the shorts on him. His breathing was now shallow and delayed, his face pale. I rubbed cream on his cheeks, forehead and chest, cut the back of his shirt and slid his arms into the sleeves. After I had tucked in the torn ends of the shirt at the back, it looked properly arranged. I lifted Baba's head, smoothed his pillow and dropped his head back onto it, running my fingers through his white beard and grey hair.

"Let me bin the rubbish, then we'll wake them." I assembled everything in a heap and carried it to the kitchen.

"Solmaz," Kurt called. "He's gone."

I ran back to Baba. Kurt stood behind me. Baba breathed out once. I bent over. "I love you." He breathed out once more. "You have been such a pain." I gave him a soft punch on the cheek. I brought my lips close to his and caught the next breath with a kiss. "I'll see you." I waited for another breath. There were no more.

I threw myself in Kurt's arms, fastened my hands around his neck and sobbed. Then I released myself from his embrace.

"Thank you."

"He was an extraordinary man." Kurt bowed to free his nostrils from the oxygen tubes.

"Thank you."

I dried the tears on my face and walked to the bedroom.

"Maman! Amme! Wake up. Baba is gone." They both jolted.

Maman rushed to the living room, behind her Amme Sara, and then the wailing began.

"*Dash* Yousef." Amme Sara cupped Baba's face and kissed him. Maman rambled along the edges of Baba's bed like a lost child on the streets - looking at him, turning her gaze away, and then looking back at him again.

"It is okay. It was fast and he was comfortable." I gave both of them a hug and then left them wailing in each other's arms. I dialled Omid's number from the bathroom so that he couldn't hear the howling. "Baba is dying. Come home."

Kurt said he would inform the coroner. Before he left, he signed the death certificate I have so often signed for my patients. Time of death: 4:34 on Thursday, January 11, 2007.

The minute Kurt was gone, I seized a handful of old

grocery bags and chucked whatever held the slightest hint of Baba into them. First I went for all the juices on the balcony, the astronaut's drinks and yoghurts Omid had bought for him. Then I targeted the three tables around his bed and wiped them clean of all the pills, creams, sprays, tubes, tissues, the nebuliser machine; even his teacup and saucer, dentures, magnifying glasses and hearing aids were submerged into the bags. I managed to lug them out and dispose of them in the refuse chutes before Omid got home.

"Baba is dead." I met him in the corridor. His expression didn't alter. It didn't need to. There was already a rock-solid sadness in it when he met my eyes. He stepped in, lingered at the door and looked at Baba's motionless face. Then without a word, but also without taking his gaze off Baba, in a similar vein to Maman he crawled back, keeping a safe distance from the wall enclosing his bed, and sat on the chair at the opposite wall.

"Oh, Omid!" Maman threw herself at him. "Cry, cry," she screamed.

Omid didn't move.

"Maman, let him be," I said.

"He must cry. Don't hold it back." Maman sobbed. "He's bottling it up."

Omid didn't bat an eyelid. He sat there and stared.

"Did he call for me?"

"No, he didn't wake up again after you left. And he was comfortable," I said. "It went fast."

As for me, the worst part was the waiting. I didn't know any Islamic rituals, nor could any of us say any prayers. At least Amme Sara knew the *ayatul korsi* by heart. She and I stood at Baba's bed and I reiterated after her the short Quranic verses to bless the dead. When we finished, she slid her hands under Baba's blue shirt on his upper chest.

"His body is still warm."

The coroner arrived at 8:45 a.m., a female coroner with a

male assistant. He gave his condolences, but the coroner just sat down at the dinner table, looked at Kurt's records and then signed off a paper and left. With that we had achieved something that was important to Omid. Baba wouldn't have a postmortem.

Next was some more waiting for the undertakers. Two sleepless nights had left me completely depleted and exhausted. I laid down in the bedroom, but each time I was about to drift off I would jolt awake at a cough or a noise from the living room. Oh, Baba needs his cough medicine, I would think - then it would dawn on me that Baba was dead. The dead don't cough, therefore it couldn't be Baba who was coughing. Baba was dead. The oxygen cylinder was off, therefore the noise was not that either. I literally needed to take my fatigued mind step by step through the obvious logic in order to comprehend the reality - the new reality.

At 11:11 they came for Baba's body. They buzzed and I peeked out into the hallway: three tall men in black outfits, and between them a silver casket on wheels.

"Maman, Omid, Amme, you all go to the bedroom and come out only when I tell you." They obliged in an instant. Only Baba and I dealt with the undertakers. They put the casket next to his bed on the floor. I went to the window and turned my back to them.

"Is there anything else you want us to take? Any suits for him?" one of them asked in a neutral tone.

"No, he will have an Islamic burial, no suits." I threw a quick glance at them out of politeness. From the corner of my eyes I could see my father in the cold casket.

"Then we'll close the coffin?"

"Wait," I walked to Baba's stand, took the Quran and crouched down. "I'll see you soon." I fitted the Quran between his head and the metal, kissed his forehead and walked back to the window, my back to them.

"Should we take him now?"

"Yes, please. Take him."

Friday, January 12, 2007

A bleak, frosty, and snowless winter morning. We have a fierce-looking Egyptian as cemetery manager, a warm Turk as Imam, alongside two Afghan men who wash Baba's body and a couple of Austrians with a small bulldozer to close up the grave. Omid, his colleague, the Afghani men, the Imam and I carry Baba's coffin, followed by Amme Sara, Maman and Omid's girlfriend. It is only when they are lowering the coffin into the hole that Omid bursts into tears.

"Whom do I make tea for now?" He conceals his face in both hands.

I put my arm around him and squeezed him tight.

"Don't believe what you see," I say. "This is not the end."

Thursday, January 18, 2007

Dear Solmaz,

Your letter which arrived here today touched me deeply - thank you - thank you for taking time to write a letter.

I'm grateful for being able to count people like Kurt amongst my friends, people who simply act upon an email of mine, act without asking much - and that was exactly the crucial point.

Our encounter many years ago was just the same too, an open and honest one; that is how it has become a treasured memory in my heart, it has become part of it, so that it resonated when I heard your call for help.

Maybe one day soon you will be in Austria, maybe it is time to talk

276

about this and that...you can tell me a bit about what you are up to in England, what your realities are.

With heartfelt solidarity and best wishes for all that may and must find a place in your life just now.

Bernhard from Linz

DREAM FOUR

I am inside a bell tower, running up the winding stairs to take flight from a flood. I run and run while the water level is rising. I keep looking back and checking on the water. Fear and panic take hold of me. I speed up. After what seems an eternity I manage to get to the top. When I finally come to a stop, I press myself against the railings and glance around. I realise that apart from myself I've saved many others including my own family. An old man in colourful clothes approaches me and mocks my grey hair. I look straight into his eyes, cut a lock and give it to him. He gently grabs the strand of hair and walks away. Shortly afterwards he returns. That grey piece of my hair has turned golden. He extends his hand, the golden hair is in his palm and he offers it to Maman as a gift.

Acknowledgements

Our book has been blessed with many good-hearted and attentive midwives on its seven-year journey. It is one of life's many gifts that nothing is ever created or grows in isolation. In chronological order, from our manuscript's foetal days to its delivery, we wish to thank:

Katherine Gogarty, a beautiful and generous soul, who was the first person to read our raw draft in 2010. We couldn't have found anyone better to entrust the fragile beginnings of our endeavour to.

Ursula Owen, the kind stranger who welcomed us into her home and imparted her decades of experience and professional expertise with respect and kindness.

Tariq Ali and Tahir Shah, two other kind strangers and established writers, who demonstrated wonderful humility by answering our emails.

Eva-Maria Kargl, Reza Jafari, Hamed Etesam, Mauro Scagnol, Gillian Miller, Serena Pongratz, Nicolas Brown and Delyth Hughes, friends who supported us either with their art or through their feedback and faith in us. In times when writing feels rather a test of stamina and self-doubt kicks in, friends who are simply sweet, warm and loving are priceless.

Professor Istvan Pogany, a sharp and curious mind with an unbeatable sense of humour and an infectious passion, who helped us to simplify what seemed overwhelming and to explore what appeared simple on the surface.

Juliette Ikss, our **photographer**, whose easy-going nature and radiant smile made the photo shoots fun.

Zipfish, our **website designer,** for their efficiency and reliability.

AND **OUR EDITORS**

Sarah Willans, who we consulted three times over the last seven years. The first two times, she sent us back to the drawing board with some well-intentioned criticism. And each time, after overcoming our initial defensiveness, we realised she was right. All the more reason for being so pleased when, at long last in February 2016, she felt that our manuscript had matured and agreed to edit it. Sarah engaged with us and our book with an 'old fashioned' work ethics that combines dedication, and professionalism with common sense and warmth. She goes beyond her job description in order to deliver the best for her client.

Simenon Honore. We met Simenon in 2015 for the first time, just in time. He 'unstuck' us. Before meeting him, we didn't know how to end our book, but with his encouragement and methodical as well as intuitive approach, he set us off in the right direction. We wrote the final chapter within three months - after years of agonising about it. He is your 'tough love' kind of editor. And, like Sarah, he has always been there for us, mentoring and sharing his views and suggestions with integrity and dedication whenever we reached out to him.

AND **PETER GOLDMAN** for being who he is, for being the one who restores our faith in humanity, each time, without fail. We love you.

In addition, we would like to extend our gratitude to the following websites and books for the English translation of the poems quoted in our book:

Poems of Khayyam taken from:

http://www.poetsgraves.co.uk/Classic%20Poems/
FitzGerald/rubaiyat_of_omar_khayyam.htm (July 2016)

Poems of Hafiz taken from:

http://www.sattor.com/english/ghazaliatofhafiz.htm (July 2016)

Javadi, H. and Sallee, S. (2010). Forugh Farrokhzad: Another Birth and Other Poems. Washington.

Homa Katouzian, Sirous shamisa and Dominic Parviz Brookshaw In *Forugh Farrokhzad, Poet of Modern Iran: Iconic Woman and Feminine Pioneer of New Persian Poetry*, edited by D. P. Brookshaw and N. Rahimieh. London and New York: I.B. Tauris & Co Ltd in association with Iranian Heritage.

Printed in Great Britain
by Amazon